In the Midst of Darkness

In the Midst of Darkness

Kelly Aul

Printed in the United States of America

ISBN   978-0615931623

Dress made by Matti's Millinery & Costumes

Making Your Costume Dreams Come True!

www.mattionline.com

BOOKS *by* KELLY AUL

NEVER FORSAKEN

Special thanks to:

- ❖ My family, who again helped me so much and put up with living this book from the very start.

- ❖ To my mom, Maggie Aul, and sister, Natalie Aul, thank you so much for all your eager help with editing.

- ❖ To Hannah Burkhardsmeier and Matti Wangerin, thank you for graciously allowing me to use another beautiful dress for the cover. This book wouldn't be the same without Matti's Millinery & Costumes.

Most importantly, I give all the glory to my Heavenly Father, my Lord and Savior, Jesus Christ, and the precious leading of the Holy Spirit.

**I dedicate this book
to anyone who has ever been
in a dark place with seemingly no hope.**

I've been there, but thank God, I found hope! Jesus Christ has already conquered the darkness and has made a way of escape for you! You can be free. Jesus said, "Come unto me, all ye that labour and are heavy laden, and I will give you rest. Take my yoke upon you, and learn of me; for I am meek and lowly in heart: and ye shall find rest unto your souls. For my yoke is easy, and my burden is light."

For those who have gone through some things, you know it feels anything but burden free and restful. He has come to set you free. All you must do is turn to Him.

He's waiting for you!

(Please see page 255 ... for more details)

"He bowed the heavens also, and came down: and darkness was under his feet."

Psalm 18:9

PART I

CHAPTER ONE

Langdon, Massachusetts   *August 1821*

As the carriage slowly drove through Langdon, Frederick Dorcet couldn't believe he was actually having second thoughts.

Should I go through with this? William will hate me, Frederick then pushed aside his guilty conscience. *I will not be weak! William's my son. He will have to abide by my wishes. Surely he'll see things my way…eventually. Besides, he's brought this on himself. Going behind my back all these months! Well, no more!* Right when he felt his anger beginning to rise, the carriage came to a halt. The driver jumped down and slowly opened the door.

"Here we are, sir." But Frederick didn't answer for he was completely dumb founded as he gazed outside.

"How could William do this to me…to his family?" he muttered.

"What was that, sir?"

"Oh, nothing," Frederick finally made himself step out. He'd heard of the meager living conditions of the Irish community, but he'd never witnessed it before now. Thankfully, he wouldn't have to stay long, that is, if he could find her.

"You there," he called to some children, who were playing on the street.

"Aye sir, we're sorry for gettin' too close to yar gran' buggy. We won't do it again," one of the boys meekly stepped forward.

"Never mind that," Frederick couldn't help but glare at the dirty child that smelt of human waste. He needed to leave this place as soon as he possibly could! "I need to find Kylene Brodie, do you know where she might be?"

"Well nigh, yar standin' in front av her house." With that, the children ran off.

Frederick turned to the sad excuse of a building. The sign that hung over the door appeared to be a butcher's craft.

Well, let's get this complete waste of time over with.

Frederick entered the shoddy store and was greeted by a stale smell of meat, followed by a short man, who wore a bloody apron.

"May I help ya?" Once he glanced up, he was taken aback by the rich looking man. However, he immediately thought he looked just like another wealthy man he knew.

"Kylene Brodie...does she live here?"

"Aye, she's me sister. What might you be needin' to see her aboyt?"

"Well, that would be between her and I," Frederick sighed with irritation. Right at that moment, a woman came down the very narrow stairs. She had been humming until she saw Frederick.

"Kylene, this man needs to spake with ya."

"Alone," Frederick cut in.

"A...alright," the young woman came forward and silently followed him outside. Frederick couldn't believe how young this girl was. Sure, she was quite attractive, but he guessed that she was no more than a mere thirteen years of age!

William, you're a bloody fool, he thought.

A knot slowly formed in Kylene's stomach as Frederick turned to face her. There was something in his eyes that frightened her, yet at the same time, he swiftly reminded her of—

"Now, I'll just get right to it then." After he cleared his throat, Frederick began to set his cruel plan into motion. "I'm sure you're wondering who I am, and why I'm here. I've come to offer you some money, or at least clarify an amount that will silence you."

Unfortunately, Kylene was beginning to understand what was happening all too quickly. However, before she could say anything, Frederick continued.

"So, what will it take to cut off your relationship with my son?"

"William...." Kylene whispered under her breath. When William Dorcet told her what his father was like, she hadn't believed how ruthless he'd made him out to be. *Perhaps it's all true.*

"Well?" Frederick asked again.

"Sir, I don't mean to be disrespectful, but I cannot be paid aff an' jist stop the feelings that William an' I have for each other." Frederick couldn't believe how insolent this Irish nobody was being. He thought Kylene would jump at his generous offer without question. It was then that Frederick realized he would have to revert his plan to a more desperate nature.

"Perhaps you wouldn't decline my offer if you knew what I am capable of," a wicked grin slowly formed on his face.

"What do you mean?" Kylene dared to ask.

"I'm surprised William hasn't said anything, but I'm a man of great means. For example, if I wanted to, I could put you and your family out on the street. Then I could make sure you never—"

"No, please," Kylene stuttered.

"If you really cared for my son, you would leave him alone."

"But I do love him!" she couldn't help the tears that came to her eyes.

"I don't believe you," Frederick simply replied then congratulated himself for how calm he kept his voice. "How could you possibly expect society to accept you? There's no place for the likes of you in William's world. The only reason I came all the way here, was to make you see this…to let him go so he can be free to marry someone who could make him truly happy," Frederick kept lying.

"Ya mean there's someone else?"

"Yes, just as soon as this hindrance is taken care of."

"I'm not a hindrance!" Kylene backed away. She'd had enough of this rude man. Nothing he could say would change her feelings for William.

Frederick was shocked when Kylene suddenly turned her back to him and was about to go inside.

"But what about your family?" She still wouldn't stop. "Accidents can happen you know." It was only then that she finally came to a halt. Frederick couldn't help but smile to himself, "They happen all the time." As soon as he said it, he knew that she understood his implications. With that, he set down an envelope on the bench just outside of the shop, climbed into his carriage, and left.

CHAPTER TWO

Kenwood ~ Boston, Massachusetts

 as father left yet?" William bounded down the stairs and into the dining room, where his mother and sister were just finishing up breakfast.

"Yes dear. Aren't you going to eat something?" Sarah called after him as he began to walk to the front entrance.

"No, I've got some business to attend to. I'll return later," William then left without another word.

At least once every week, William waited until Frederick had left before making his way to Langdon. And that's what he'd done for nearly a year. Ever since he met Kyleen Brodie, she was all he could think about. He was even beginning to consider asking for her hand, although, his family hadn't the slightest idea. Elizabeth was the only one who was starting to ask questions.

But what could a girl of ten and three know anyway? William thought as he mounted his steed and was off.

"Well, Mr. Dorcet, what a gran' surprise this is," Colm Brodie greeted as William entered the butcher shop. "I believe Kylene is already outside....probably awaitin' yar arrival."

"Alright. Thank you, Colm," William quickly made his way outside and down the trail that led to their favorite spot by the spring. Every time he visited, they would take long walks along it.

"Kylene," he called, once the beautiful woman came into view. Every time he saw her, William immediately fell in love with her raven black curls and large hazel eyes all over again. Somehow he knew that he would ask her to marry him that very day.

"Hello William," Kylene quietly replied, but she didn't turn to face him, for she didn't want him to see her tears.

Ever since Frederick's visit just a week prior, Kylene hadn't been the same. Her heart was breaking, but she knew it wasn't over yet. As if it wasn't horrible enough, Kylene was the one who had to end their relationship! She tried to think of another way, but it was no use.

The more quickly I tell him, the easier it will be, she kept telling herself, but deep down she knew it wouldn't be easy at all. Just the thought made her heart break all the more.

William slowly approached and gently touched Kylene's shoulder, but she quickly pulled away.

"What's wrong?" he asked when he caught a glimpse of her tears. *Why would she be crying?* William fearfully thought. Kylene knew she had to say something. If only she could make herself calm down enough to speak!

"Is it something I said or did?" he asked again.

"No...it's nothin' like that," she choked. William finally stepped in front of her and grasped both her hands.

She is crying! And quite upset about something. "Then what is it, Kylene? You can tell me." The emotion she heard in his voice was her undoing. She hated to face him.

"It's just...that...I can't see ye anymore." There, she said it. *If only it were that simple,* Kylene thought.

"What do you mean? Why not?" William felt as if he'd just been punched in the stomach.

"I can't tell ya," Kylene buried her face in her hands after pulling free.

"What? This isn't like you. What's wrong?" William warmly embraced her as if that would make her think more clearly.

"Ya must let me go. Please," Kylene cried, although she could remain wrapped in his arms forever.

"No, I won't...not until you tell me what's truly going on." Then, without warning, William leaned down and kissed her, longer than he'd ever done before. She had to see how much he loved her. But it didn't last. Once he loosened his hold, Kylene wedged her arms against his chest.

"Ya must let me go!" After what seemed like an eternity to Kylene, he slowly let her go. "Nigh leave me!" she now shouted.

"I don't understand."

"You don't 'av to…just leave!" William's shoulders slumped in defeat as he slowly made his way back to his horse.

William had never been so confused. He thought long and hard as he slowly rode back to Boston. Kylene had never acted that way before.

I don't understand what's happening. I thought everything was alright. Another thought crossed his mind. *Why didn't I think of this sooner? She wants to marry!* William quickly pulled the reins and turned the steed around. *She'll see things my way, I just know it. As soon as I declare my love, Kylene will surely come to her senses!* William told himself time after time as he rode back to town.

As if on cue, Kylene was just returning to the store. William didn't say a word as he nearly jumped off his horse, rushed over and took her hand. He silently pulled her back to their special spot in the woods.

"What are ye doin'? I said I didn't want to see ya anymore," Kylene shouted until he came to an abrupt stop.

"I've come back to ask you…to marry me." She slowly gazed up at the hopeful yet at the same time stubborn man.

Why is he doing this? He's making it so much more difficult.

"Why are you crying now? I thought you would be happy," Fear and panic washed over him as he reached out to wipe yet another tear on her face.

"It's too late," Kylene hung her head for she couldn't speak any longer. Suddenly she got an idea. Although it would be a lie, Kylene didn't know what else to do anymore. "There's someone else…." Even through her tears, Kylene could see anger and despair in his eyes.

"What?" It was now William's turn to choke, though he tried

to hide the emotion in his voice. "How can this be? I thought we…you love me! Forget this other—"

"William, stop," Kylene stopped him before he said something vile about another man who didn't even exist.

Unbeknown to the sorrowful couple, was that someone else had just come upon the scene. Colm couldn't believe what he found as he strolled down the path to fetch Kylene for lunch. Although he couldn't hear their soft conversation, Colm knew it wasn't going well. Both young people were crying, nearly sobbing as they held hands. They looked so young to be having such a troubling relationship. But Kylene was only fifteen years of age, with William only four years her senior.

Hopefully, they'll be able to work things out, he thought, before he quietly snuck back to town.

"I'm so sorry," Kylene whispered as the man she dearly loved finally released her and slowly backed away. She'd never seen a man look so hurt and hopeless.

"I'm sorry as well," William knew he would never love another. He could never love again.

William stomped up the steps that led to the front entrance. While he knew he must appear normal to continue to fool his family, he wasn't sure how he would go about it.

How am I to go on without her? William asked himself after he shut the door behind him. He heard voices coming from the drawing room, one of which was his fathers.

Why is he home already? William anxiously thought. Needless to say, Frederick Dorcet was a workaholic. Ever since he'd started the Dorcet Bank, that's all he truly cared about. He would usually remain there until late into the evening.

Sometimes not until ten at night. Surely something's wrong. It's only nearing tea time. Perhaps he isn't feeling well. William wasn't sure if he should enter the room or not. His father might suspect something amiss. *But he'll definitely think it strange if I simply walk pass without greeting them.*

"Hello Father, Mother. Is everything alright?" he finally stepped in the room. He couldn't help but notice that Sarah looked as if something wasn't right. It wasn't like his mother to be so quiet.

"Everything is fine. Quite good, in fact," Frederick stood and patted William on the back when he approached.

He suspects something. William barely breathed while his father's gaze was fixed on him. Unbeknownst to him, Frederick was wondering the same thing. He was certain if William had met with his secret Irish friend since his own visit to the horrible place.

Did that naive girl tell him of our meeting? Did she heed my orders?

"I've come home earlier than usual to share some wonderful news. That is, I hope it will be good news," Frederick finally moved away and sat down across from Sarah.

"Have a seat, Son."

"I'd rather remain standing," William solemnly stated. He couldn't let himself get too close. If Frederick missed the sorrow in his eyes, surely his mother would see it.

"Terrence Edith came into the bank today and we talked over some business for quite some time. Anyway, we spoke of other things as well. He has a great desire for his daughter, Harriet, to find a suitable husband. But he has yet to find one."

Here we go again, William couldn't help but sigh as he sauntered over to the window and peered out. His father never let him forget that he had an obligation to marry well and to eventually take over the bank.

I wonder what he would say if he would've found out about Kylene and I...her being Irish and all. Suddenly Frederick startled William by getting to his feet and touching his shoulder.

"I know you don't like being talked into this sort of thing."

"Forced or tricked, you mean," William cut in, but immediately knew it was a mistake, when his father quickly took a step back.

He does know what I've done! Frederick thought. He was able to hide emotion from his features quite easily. *I'll just play along.* "William, what do you think? Do you actually presume that I would trick you into something? Never! I only want you to be happy."

I think not, William quickly thought, but this time he didn't voice it. Frederick began talking again, but William wasn't listening any longer. *There has to be some way I can talk Kylene into marrying me instead. If I only knew who it was. Who would steal her from me? Perhaps I could find him and...wait...I could never forgive myself for stepping in the way of her happiness. I will not become my father! There's no hope for me then, Kylene is gone.*

"William, are you listening?"

"Yes Father," he lied.

"In other words, I've made a smart match for you, Son. And, it would be wise to consider it carefully." For a moment, William thought his father's suggestion sounded more like a threat.

If I actually do what my father wishes, I could finally have peace from him. And since there's no hope with Kylene, I might as well. "Alright, I'll do it, if it will finally make you happy." Frederick easily ignored William's disrespectful reply and glanced over at Sarah. She appeared to be upset. But if truth be told, he didn't care. His plan had worked. This arrangement would make Frederick and his whole family very rich indeed.

October 1821

"What a pleasant event it turned out to be. Everyone seemed to enjoy themselves," Frederick sighed after he and Sarah climbed into the carriage.

"Are you quite serious?" Sarah spoke up for the first time in a long while.

"What do you mean?"

"Everyone enjoyed themselves, except for the bride and

groom. If I didn't know any better, Harriet seemed just as unhappy about this arrangement as William."

"Dear, William agreed to all this," Frederick argued.

"Don't dear me. Everything you've done and said has been a lie." Frederick was completely taken back. He'd never heard Sarah speak like this before, especially to him.

"You forget your place, Sarah. Besides, how could I expect you to understand? A woman doesn't have a mind for business. Both Harriet's father and I know this is for the best. It will make a very pleasurable life for all of us. And it will ensure William and his new wife's future." Unfortunately, Sarah did understand, quite well in fact. The truth of the matter was, the Edith's now held many stocks with Frederick's bank. This new arrangement would indeed make them wealthy.

But most likely, miserable in the process, Sarah thought, but she remained silent for the rest of the evening.

CHAPTER THREE

Kenwood ~ Boston, Massachusetts   *May 1826*

William had just gotten home from the bank, where he spent most of his time of late. As much as he hated to admit or tried to stop it, William was slowly becoming his father. It seemed that it couldn't be helped. Ever since he'd married Harriet and slowly started to take over Frederick's duties, William had tried to keep from getting pulled into that life, but it was consuming! The bank, or money rather, had a controlling affect that wrapped its way around men's necks. However, it crept in slowly enough that it wasn't noticed until it was too late.

The remaining light beckoned William to stay outside. Besides, he needed a moment to think a bit. Earlier that day, Frederick left right after lunch, complaining of a headache, for it had been a stressful day. William knew it had to have been pretty severe to cause his father to slow down.

Well, I'd better go say goodnight to Harriet. It wasn't as if William was avoiding his duties as a husband. It was just that Harriet was still bedridden after having given birth to their second son. It had been nearly two weeks ago, but she was very small and fragile, easily becoming ill. She had always been that way. When their first son Theodore was born, Harriet had been very weak for at least three weeks.

William was about to get up from his place on the front stairs when his thoughts suddenly moved to Kylene Brodie once again. Every time it happened, William scolded himself.

I've got to stop this foolishness! I have a wife and two sons to care for now. The thought actually made him cringe a bit. With that, William took one last breath of fresh air then went inside.

"How are you feeling?" William greeted Harriet after dutifully kissing her cheek. *I can't believe it's still happening!* It seemed that William was being haunted by his former Irish lass yet again. Nearly every time he kissed or so much as approached Harriet, William could almost see Kylene's face. They didn't even look anything alike. Kylene's black curls and dark eyes were nothing like Harriet's features, which were much fairer.

"William?" Harriet broke into his troubling thoughts. "You were a million miles away, weren't you?" Her tone wasn't condemning. And that's what hit him the hardest. It was the fact that she knew William didn't love her that made him feel so guilty. He might have been able to fool his father, maybe even his mother, but Harriet knew.

Although I will never be truly happy, I don't want to ruin Harriet's life as well. "I'm sorry. Work has been troubling of late. Are you feeling any stronger?" William tried his hardest to appear interested.

"Yes, but very slowly. It seems worse than when Theodore was born. I hope I'm not coming down with anything."

"I surely hope not," William replied, although he'd witnessed how easily Harriet could become ill.

"Ma'am, the wee babe is hungry," the nursemaid, who held Edwin, came forward and gently placed him in the crook of Harriet's arm.

"Well, you rest now. I'll say goodnight," William then nervously left. Never did he think he'd be comfortable with his wife, or ever truly be himself in his own home.

The next morning William decided to briefly play with his two year old son before he left for the bank. He was playing horsey when someone knocked on the door of the nursery.

"Come in."

"Common!" Theodore mimicked his father in his little voice. William couldn't help but chuckle, that is until the door opened and he caught a glimpse of the maid's solemn expression.

"A messenger brought this," she held out a note. Once

William read it, he ran out of the room without another word. Before going downstairs, he stopped at Harriet's bedroom that was on the way.

"Harriet, my father has had an attack. I'm going over there straight away."

"Oh, no….I hope he'll be alright," she replied from her place on the bed.

"I'll be home later."

"William, Thank goodness you're here!" Sarah sighed when he finally arrived and they quickly embraced.

"When did it happen?" William spoke as they made their way to the master bedroom.

"Very early this morning. It's such a shock. He merely came home early from the bank with a headache. It wasn't until he went right to bed when I began to worry. Then this morning, I woke up because I heard a strange noise. It was your father. The pain was so horrible that he held his chest and said it was his heart." By the time they reached the bedroom door, Sarah was in tears. As much as she despised the things Frederick had done, Sarah loved the man dearly.

"You're not going to accompany me?" William asked when his mother backed away.

"He wants to see you so badly. He just kept saying something about having to tell you before it was too late," Elizabeth spoke for their mother. With that, she opened the door and motioned William to go inside the dark room. If William had been a bit anxious before, he now was having second thoughts about entering. What was so important that his father wanted to see him so desperately?

Frederick knew he didn't have much time left. He had to tell William the truth and ask for forgiveness. Somehow he knew in order to obtain God's forgiveness, he had to ask for his son's first, for the horrible things he had done.

"Father, I'm here," William quietly called. He was relieved that the heavy drapes were drawn shut so he couldn't see Frederick's face. It was easier to speak to his father this way.

"Mother said you needed to tell me something."

"I do….I do, Son. I'm afraid you're not going to like it," Frederick began. "You mustn't say anything until I'm finished for I don't have much time left." By the desperate tone in his voice, William sensed that he would indeed pass quickly.

"Alright," he replied.

"I've done so many things…things I regret," William didn't want to hear this…the ramblings of a dying man. But he couldn't just leave.

"I don't really know where to begin," Frederick coughed dryly, "After I had spoken to Harriet's father, I found out about you….and Kylene Brodie." At this, William nearly fell off of the chair he previously sat down on.

All this time, and he knew? He tried to regain his composure, but it was no use. Thankfully Frederick continued with hardly any hesitation, but William's discomfort was about to become much, much worse.

"I perceived you would never consider marrying Harriet Edith until your other relationship was ended." Suddenly Frederick stopped. He couldn't catch his breath. It wouldn't be long now.

"Father?" William knelt down beside the bed to make sure he was alright.

"I just….have to catch my breath," he tried to smile so as to relieve his son. He met William's gaze for the first time. It made his guilt wash over him all over again.

How many years I've wasted…and for what? My bank? Now my son can't stand me. He'll think me even more despicable after today, Frederick thought before being able to talk again. "I took matters into my own hands and traveled to Langdon myself. It was there I spoke to Kylene and forced her stop seeing you."

"What? How?" William now backed up a bit. He couldn't keep silent anymore.

"I told her….you were going to marry another and that it

would be beneficial for her and her family if she just let you go."

"What did you do?" William swiftly got to his feet. He was so angry he could hardly speak. *Kylene didn't love anyone else. She lied to me because of my father?* "You mean you tricked me? You tricked Kylene?" William touched his forehead, which was perspiring and paced the room, trying to calm himself.

"Yes," was all Frederick could say.

"For what reason? For money? For some preposterous holdings for the bank?" William knew he shouldn't talk to his father this way, but he couldn't believe what he'd done. His life was ruined. The thought that angered him above all others was that he couldn't do anything to change it.

Without another word, William stormed out of the room and nearly slammed the door behind him. He rushed downstairs and passed the drawing room.

"William, where are you going?" He heard Sarah call after him, but he didn't care. He had to get out of there and breathe some fresh air. He had to think and get himself back together.

Frederick must have told him everything, Sarah thought and could only watch him leave in sadness.

William quickly decided against returning home. Instead he mounted his horse to go for a long ride. He didn't care where he went either.

How could he do this to me? My own father. Why didn't I see it? He was behind everything. What am I to do now?

After what seemed like only minutes, William's horse stopped. When he glanced up, he found the reason. A spring was directly in front of them.

What? It can't be. After looking around a bit, it finally dawned on him. He had absently ridden all the way to Langdon!

Am I ever going to be able to forget her? "Oh Kylene," he muttered as he rubbed his jaw in frustration. It was then that a single thought crossed his mind. More of a temptation really.

However, it was swiftly followed by justification.

I'm in Langdon....practically in the same place where we came all those times together. Perhaps I could see if she's married or not, William pulled the reins and directed his horse along the brook that led further into town.

He'd just approached the Irish part of town when it hit him. *What am I doing? What can I gain by coming here?* "Whoa," William called and stopped the steed, "I can't be here."

"Go home and be with your own wife." Something came up inside of him so strongly that he turned around and started for home. It was indeed the hardest thing he'd ever done.

CHAPTER FOUR

July 1826

 arriet slowly awoke to the sound of Edwin's cry, demanding his breakfast. She lifted the covers and slipped out of bed. When Harriet approached the crib, she hesitated because she usually didn't have enough strength to lift her son.

Will I ever regain my strength? Two full months had gone by since she'd given birth, but her health hadn't returned. It actually seemed to deteriorate since. But today was different somehow. Harriet slowly reached down and managed to lift Edwin out.

"Perhaps it has returned," she nuzzled her son. After feeding Edwin, Harriet planned to finally leave her stuffy room and go downstairs. Although her private quarters were quite large, the long months seemed to shrink them.

Just a half an hour later, she slowly made her way down the hall to the grand staircase. Harriet felt so strange. She wasn't weak, yet she felt as if she was in a warm daze. She had ascended just two steps when her legs suddenly gave way.

"Mama," William turned and found that Theodore was gone. He hadn't gone far, for he could hear him in the other room. William got up from his desk to see where the energetic toddler had run off to.

"Mama," the small boy stated again.

How strange. Why would Theodore be saying that if Harriet is in her bedroom. When he found his son, William froze in his steps. Harriet was laying at the bottom of the stairs, unconscious, Theodore standing beside her.

"Mama seeping," the boy turned and met his father's gaze.

"Harriet!" William rushed to her side and fixed his gaze on

her to see if she was breathing. "Help, Martha! Someone," he yelled to the maid, but he wasn't about to wait for them. "Someone send for the doctor!" William easily picked up his fragile wife and brought her back to her bed.

Why would she try to come downstairs? Why didn't she ask for assistance at least? William tried to figure out what had happened as he sat outside her quarters, while the doctor examined her.

"You can see her now," was all the doctor said when he emerged.

"How is she? Will she be alright?" William stood.

"Your wife is very ill."

"What do you mean? Harriet has had a difficult time recovering from child birth, but we presumed that was all," the man moved closer to William and placed his hand on his shoulder.

"She is suffering from meningitis. While giving birth has weakened her, the fall she endured is the worst of it. From a broken rib and a hit to the back of her head, it's a wonder she lived through it."

"But?" William knew there was more by the serious tone in his voice.

"She won't live through the night. I suggest you stay with her now, but don't let your children near her so they're not exposed to the illness. I'm sorry, William, there's nothing more I can do for her," with that, the doctor took his leave, for there was nothing more to be done.

First my father, now Harriet. Although Frederick was alive, despite everyone's expectations, he was still bedridden. Thankfully, William had one of his servants fetch Sarah right after coming back with the doctor. In the meantime, William would heed the doctor's orders.

As he entered the room and approached Harriet, he was completely at a loss for words.

What should I say? What could he say? Even though they'd been married for several years, William hardly knew anything about her. He'd only thought about himself and what he was going through.

"I feel so foolish," Harriet whispered when she saw him.

"Why?" William pulled a chair up to the side of the bed and sat down.

"I shouldn't have tried going downstairs without help. Did the doctor tell you?" she asked, and he only nodded in return.

"I'm sorry that I'm leaving you alone with the boys." It was now that the tears came. Harriet couldn't leave them, not now. Her boys were so young.

"Don't worry about the children. They'll be well taken care of. Though, they'll miss their mother," he couldn't stand seeing the tears that now streamed down her face. How could he have been so heartless towards her, as if it was all her fault. Even if he didn't love Harriet as he did Kylene, it didn't give him a right to be distant and depressed all the time.

Harriet deserved so much better. Suddenly William knew what he had to do. "Harriet, I want you to know how sorry I am," he began.

"For what?"

"For only thinking of myself all these years....and for being a terrible husband....for not caring," William choked on the lump that had formed in his throat. Perhaps he did love her.

"I know it's been hard for you, William. I haven't been the easiest wife to you either. My heart was with someone else as well," Harriet admitted for the first time. It left William in shock. "You weren't the only one who didn't want this," she quietly continued. It finally dawned on William, which made him feel more guilty and horrible.

I've been so stupid....thinking how this marriage was so unfair to me and only me, while all this time, Harriet was in love with someone else!

"I did grow to love you," Harriet spoke up again. At this, tears welled up in William's eyes. Harriet had been far more faithful than he.

"Oh Harriet…." Right at that moment, they were interrupted by the door that opened.

Sarah rushed over and embraced Harriet. William backed away in the process.

"The driver who came for me told me everything. I'm so sorry," she comforted, which made Harriet cry all the more.

"Sarah, thank you for coming. I'm so frightened."

"Oh, dear…there's nothing to be scared of. Heaven is a glorious place, where there isn't any pain or sorrow." William moved and let his mother take his seat. It was as if he wasn't even in the room anymore.

"I…I haven't served God as I should have…and now it's too late," Harriet admitted again and began to sob.

"Harriet, it's never too late for the Lord. All He's waiting for is you. You can make Him your Savior right now." William marveled at Sarah's words. Giving comfort was so natural for her.

"Will you…will you help me, Sarah?"

"All you have to do is ask Him. Ask Him to forgive you and save you," Sarah admonished. After praying, a peace washed over Harriet and her face radiated it.

Several hours had passed and William stayed by his wife's side all through the night. When the time came for Harriet to go home, she was at peace. She was no longer afraid to stand before her heavenly Father. Just before dawn, Harriet grasped William's hand, simply smiled, then breathed her last. William actually wept. He would never forget that night. After seeing the joy on his wife's face, he knew that he needed God's forgiveness as well. And after doing so, he realized that he must also make peace with Frederick, before it was too late.

"Then shall thy light break forth
as the morning, and thine health
shall spring forth speedily:
and thy righteousness shall go
before thee; the glory of the
LORD shall be thy reward."

Isaiah 58:8

CHAPTER FIVE

May 1827

"I'm so sorry for your loss."

"Thank you," Sarah replied to several family friends as they slowly left the cemetery. Finally William approached his mother and sister.

"Shall we go now?" After they both agreed, he offered his arm to Sarah and began walking back to the carriages which were lined up on the street.

"The things you said during the service were very nice. Your father would have like it."

"Thank you. Shall I take you home straight away or would you like to come over for a while?" William asked once they were about to climb into their carriage.

"Elizabeth, is it alright with you if we don't return home just yet?" Sarah turned to her daughter.

"That is fine."

As they started for Kenwood, William knew the matter must be brought up sometime.

Why not the present? "Mother, how are you and Elizabeth going to live in that big house all alone?"

"We'll be alright," Sarah quietly replied. "It will just take a little getting used to."

"Well, I think you should both move to Kenwood. You're there nearly every day anyway, and the boys need you," William persisted. Sarah was about to speak, but when she glanced up, she found his gaze fixed on something outside the window.

"What is it?" she finally asked.

"Driver, stop the carriage!" He quickly stuck his head out and shouted.

"William, what has gotten into you?" Elizabeth's question was completely ignored as they swiftly came to a halt and

William jumped out. Both women watched as he ran toward the busy docks of Boston.

It can't be. It can't be her! The crowded harbor was like a maze to get through all the people, but William hardly noticed. All he knew was that it was her! He was fully convinced that Kylene Brodie was about to board a ship.

It has to be her! No one else has the same long ebony curls. "Kylene…Kylene Brodie!" he shouted like a mad man.

"Someone's callin' for ya," Colm nudged his sister. When she turned and saw William, she didn't recognize him at first. His brown hair was graying at the temples. He looked much older than she's remembered him even though it had only been six years. He'd been through so much for his twenty and five years of age.

When he finally got her attention, William realized he hadn't the slightest idea what he was going to say once he arrived.

"Kylene, please don't get on that ship," he blurted. Kylene didn't know what to say, and she didn't speak until moments later.

"William, what are you doing here?" He said nothing at this.

"We're returnin' to our homeland," Colm stated as he approached.

"Where's yar wife?" Kylene meekly asked after several minutes of awkward silence had passed.

"She…passed away almost a year ago."

"Oh, I'm so sorry."

"But I can't bear to see you leave. Can't you stay awhile?" Tears stung William's eyes, but he tried to hide it as best he could. He was bound and determined that he was not going to lose the Irish lass again.

"We can't…we've sold our shop. Colm 'ill be takin' over the shop back home for our uncle. There's nowha else for us ter go," Kylene replied quietly. *I can't believe I still have feelings for him…after all these years!*

"You can come to Kenwood. There's plenty of room," William hastily suggested. When the Brodie's said nothing, he continued to try and convince them.

"You can always board another ship. Please…please consider it." That was all Kylene needed to hear. However, she didn't say anything without seeing what her brother thought about the idea.

"Well, I suppose it wouldn't hurt. At least for a short while." William could have jumped for joy when Colm finally agreed. Although he wouldn't argue with them now, William had no intention of letting Kylene get anywhere near another ship, unless he accompanied her, that is.

PART
II

CHAPTER SIX

Ireland   *March 1835*

olm jumped off of the wagon and frantically ran to the house. It was engulfed in flames.

"Laura, where are ya?" *Surely they can't be inside!* He dearly hoped as he scanned the nearby trees to see if his wife and her mother were safely away.

"Lord, please help!" He didn't know what to do.

His gaze was instantly brought back to the house when he thought he heard a muffled voice. It was coming from inside! Colm's heart raced as he realized it to be true and not merely hearing things.

"'elp! Help us!" a woman screamed and pounded her fists on the inside of the door. Something was keeping them inside. But what? Colm shielded his face as best he could with his arm and neared the door. The flames were so hot he could barely breathe, but he didn't care. To his horror, he found the door padlocked!

Who has done this? He thought yet he had no time to reason further.

"Help!" the screams were getting louder.

"I'm comin'," Colm tried to kick the door in, but it was too solid. He finally turned from the house to find something to get it open. Thankfully he quickly spotted a shovel sitting against a shed. Once he fetched it, Colm struck it against the lock several times before it broke.

"Got it," he blurted. When he finally swung it open, he found Maureen deep inside the flame and smoke ridden house. She was holding onto Laura's arms, trying to drag her towards the door.

"Laura!" Colm cried.

"The house is fallin' in raun us an' hit her," Maureen choked and coughed. Colm rushed to his wife, picked her up and followed Maureen out.

The moment the clean fresh air hit their lungs, their coughing worsened and left them gasping for breath. They had made it out just in time for half of the small house caved in suddenly. Now that they were safely away from danger and he could breathe again, he went over to get a better look at Laura. She was unconscious and there were burns on the side of her face and neck.

"Oh Laura," Maureen fell to her daughter's side and wept, for her wounds looks severe.

"Lord, what shud I do? She needs help!" Colm cried out. Suddenly it came to him, "Follow me, we nade to git her help," he told Maureen, who was beside herself. He picked Laura up into his arms again.

By the time they neared the house, the sun was just going down. Colm thanked the Lord when he saw it come into view. He got down from the wagon seat and went to the back where he'd carefully laid his wife.

"What is this place?"

"Lord Kerrich…me landlord." Maureen looked at him as though he'd lost his mind so Colm went on as he hurridly picked up Laura.

"I nu they'll help us. They treat Irish kindly."

The door opened before he neared it by a footman.

"What's happened?" he asked in concern at the woman's nasty wounds.

"Someone started a house on fire with the lass locked inside. Please, she nades 'elp."

"Hurry, bring her inside."

"Unto the upright there ariseth light in the darkness: he is gracious, and full of compassion, and righteous."

Psalm 112:4

CHAPTER SEVEN

Kenwood ~ Boston, Massachusetts   *November 1838*

When another round of thunder sounded, William glanced up and looked out the window. It was pouring now. It was strange weather for the beginning of November, but a rain storm wasn't unheard of. It was then that the door opened and a maid emerged.

"Is everything alright?" he quickly stood. She couldn't help but chuckle at her employer's nervousness.

"Yes sir, everything is just fine. It's just begun. It all takes time, you know." She went about her duties and walked down the hall to retrieve more linen, leaving William alone with his uneasiness. He plopped back down on the small mahogany settee, directly across from Kylene's bedroom door. Several years ago, he'd sat in the very same spot. It was the day Harriet died. Despite the love that he never had for his former wife, William's admiration grew for Harriet that day, more than he had realized at first.

"Sir, the doctor you sent for is here," the maid interrupted William's musings.

Thank goodness, he sighed. He was greatly relieved that he was here. And after telling him so, William watched them both go inside. To settle his anxiety, he decided to walk down the long hall. When he neared the end, Kylene's beautiful portrait came into view. He truly believed finding Kylene that day on the docks was the Lord's doing. After both Harriet and Frederick's passing, within several months of each other, William became quite discouraged. It was Kylene that had saved him, or so he thought. Regardless of all the talk and gossip, he and Kylene married only three months later. William could still remember the stares and remarks that had gone on at the wedding, but he could have cared less. It was the happiest day of his life. However, the day their daughter was born, William quickly realized his mistake, for that was indeed the greatest. The ten years that followed were wonderful, yet there were a few sorrowful times that poisoned their happiness.

It was Kylene's faith that helped us endure them. William recalled as he slowly returned to the settee. After having Brenna, Kyleen had two miscarriages. So when she was finally with child again, they took all the precautions to ensure the health of the baby, as well as Kylene. That was the main reason for the doctor's arrival. Otherwise a midwife would've been more than suitable.

"Papa!" Brenna came running up the stairs and threw herself into her father's arms.

"Hello dear," William kissed her forehead.

"Why, Papa, how come you look so sad? I'm going to have a baby brother or sister tonight!"

"Yes you are. I'm just feeling a bit tired," he replied and tried to lighten his features. *What a dear girl...always worrying about me,* he thought. Brenna was joyful all the time and she was practically perfect in her parent's eyes.

"Papa, you're staring at me," Brenna stated as she waved her little hand back and forth in front of William's face. The act made him laugh.

"You look so much like your mother."

"You're silly."

"Why?" he asked.

"Because you say that all the time."

"Do I?"

"Yes. Then you always say that you love my name because Mama picked it, and it's Irish." After William sat down, Brenna got on his lap, leaned her head against his chest, and sighed.

"You know me well, Brenna Rose."

"When will the baby come?"

"Soon, dear," William replied.

"Please tell me a story."

"What kind of story?"

"How you met Mama and when you asked her to marry you," Brenna pushed back the dark strands of hair from her face and gazed up at William. Although he'd told her the story many times, at least it would take his mind off his worries.

"Well, the very first time I met Kylene was in Langdon. Some business things I was doing for my father required me to ride through the small town. Suddenly the carriage jolted and I heard a girl scream! Once the carriage came to a stop, I jumped out and looked around. I feared that we had run someone over. Thankfully, we narrowly missed a girl, who had fallen to the side of the road. When I approached her, I found that she had dropped several packages. I also saw that she was very beautiful. She looked just like you," William momentarily stopped, glanced down at Brenna, and touched her dark hair. "After I helped her up and made sure that she was alright, I left."

"But you couldn't stop thinking about her," Brenna finished.

"You're right. I couldn't get her out of my mind. So, nearly a month later, I went to Langdon again, this time to find Kylene. After that I kept going out there…and we fell in love."

"How come you didn't get married then?" Brenna asked.

"Well, it's complicated," he sighed in return. "It wasn't until seven years later that she finally became my wife," William wasn't about to burden his daughter with the truth. Although he forgave his father before he died, the thought that so many lives had been ruined for the sake of Frederick's bank and his love for money was still considerably painful.

"I don't understand one thing."

"Yes, what is it?" William wanted so badly to tell Brenna everything. Some things he knew he wouldn't be able to bring himself to tell her. Not just yet, anyway.

"Theodore and Edwin say things…like…." Brenna hesitated. She couldn't think of the right words.

"What? What do they say?"

"Well," Brenna could tell that William was beginning to get angry, not at her of course, but at Theodore and Edwin. They seemed to never tire of being mean to Brenna and making her upset. The ten year old might have been a bit high strung for her age, and a little spoiled at times.

But that doesn't give the boys a right! Before William got too angry, Brenna finally knew what to say.

"They say that Mama isn't their mother, so they don't have to listen to her. How come I only have a mother but they don't?" There, she said it. Brenna wanted to ask him about it for a while, but she could never gain enough courage to. Although it was silly, for she could talk about anything with her doting father, who seemed to love her more than the boys.

"Oh, I see," the vein suddenly disappeared in William's neck as he slowly calmed down. "Well, before I married Kylene, I was married to Harriet." Brenna was so surprised. She no longer leaned against William, but sat up and gazed at him in confusion. William hoped she would just hear him out and fortunately, she did. "That's when Theodore and Edwin were born. A few months after she had Edwin, Harriet became very sick and died. So they're correct, my dear. Harriet was they're mother, and Kylene is yours." Thankfully, they were interrupted right then, so William wouldn't have to explain further.

"Sir, Mr. and Mrs. Davis are here. Shall I send them up?" the butler asked.

"Oh yes," William lifted Brenna off his lap and stood to greet his sister and her husband, who was also William's dear friend he'd known since childhood.

"Thank you both for coming," he greeted by embracing them.

"Mother would have liked to come as well, but she hasn't been going out very much lately. She says she's not feeling well," Elizabeth informed.

"I'm sure Kylene would enjoy having your help and encouragement," William then suggested, for it had been his wife's wish.

"Oh, I was hoping you might say that," With that Elizabeth excitedly entered the labor room.

"And you'd better start getting ready for bed," William met Brenna's gaze.

"May I stay up until my baby brother or sister arrives?" she hopefully asked and put on her sweetest face.

"Very, well," he couldn't help but give in and say yes.

"How are you fairing through all this?" Loren asked as William led him further down the hall. He desperately needed to voice his fears to someone.

"I can't say that I'm only a little anxious," he replied.

"I'm sure it's only normal," Loren was always the practical one.

"Yes, but it's taking far too long. All the other children would have come hours ago," William nervously rubbed his jaw as it had become a habit.

"You worry too much, old friend," Loren playfully pushed William's hand away from his face.

"You forget Kylene has had two miscarriages. Perhaps she's beyond the years of child birth."

"Obviously not," Loren cut in.

"She is a bit over thirty years of age, Loren. Isn't that considered too old?"

"Don't be so worrisome. Kylene is strong," he tried to comfort William, but nothing he said seemed to help.

Theodore was just coming up the stairs to say goodnight to William, when a baby's cry was heard.

"It's here! The baby's here!" Brenna jumped up and down excitedly.

"See? Everything is fine," Loren shook William's hand before he rushed up to the door just as it opened.

"How is she?"

"William…." Elizabeth placed her hand on his chest, but apparently he didn't notice the seriousness in her voice. He started to move by her to see Kylene and his new child.

"Let me pass."

"There's something you need to know," she stated again, but William wouldn't listen. He nearly pushed passed his sister.

"I want to see my mother," Brenna marched up to Elizabeth and demanded.

"Not yet, dear."

"I want to see the baby." Thankfully, the girl wasn't as

strong as William, so Elizabeth was able to shut the door when the doctor and maid also emerged.

As soon as William entered the room, he wished he would have stopped long enough to hear what Elizabeth and the doctor wanted to tell him so badly. In truth, he was too frightened to hear it. Somehow, if nothing was said, it wasn't true. There was something definitely wrong though. Kylene's face was gravely pale.

"William," her voice quivered. It was no more than a whisper. William immediately felt sick.

"There's not much time, William," Kylene desperately said his name again. He couldn't do this again. His worst fear seemed to be coming upon him.

"No," William cried and quickly knelt by her side. Through his tears, he saw the small baby in her limp arms, but he didn't care. The only thing he could think of was Kylene. "You can pull through this. Please…I can't live without you."

"Ye shouldn't say that. You can live withoyt me. Ya must…for the children's sake. And…God is still with ya." It took all of her strength to speak. She had to make sure her family would be alright without her.

"I don't care about God. Only you," William persisted in between sobs.

"Don't say that," Kylene scolded. Suddenly the door burst opened. Brenna ran into the room and crawled onto the bed, to her mother's side.

"Mama, what's wrong?" When Brenna saw how upset William was, she also couldn't help but begin to cry as well. Kylene didn't seem to notice. She was going to stay strong so she could tell them everything she could before she left.

"Brenna, this is your baby brother. His name in Benjamin. You need to take care of him because I won't be here, alright?"

"No! Where are you going?" Brenna quickly moved her gaze from the babe, to Kylene.

"You mustn't be sad. I'm going to heaven, where Jesus an' al' the angels are. An' I'm gonna wait for ye there. It won't be long 'til we're al' together again," Kylene managed to speak over

43

William's cries that now became louder.

"You need to teach Benjamin about God… just like I taught you. William," Kylene took her husband's hand away from his flushed face.

"I'll always love you. You'll only find true comfort and happiness in the Lord. Remember that."

"Mama!" Brenna screamed when Kylene shut her eyes and was gone. Now Benjamin began to cry from all the noise.

CHAPTER EIGHT

April 1839

hat are you looking at?" Edwin sauntered into Theodore's spacious bedroom. Once he approached his brother, who sat at his desk, Edwin saw that he was staring at a calendar.

"It's April ninth today," Theodore stated as if Edwin knew what that day represented above others.

"I can see that…what does it matter?" Theodore turned to look at his brother.

"It's been four months since Kylene's death and Father still hasn't come out of his room. How long is he going to go on like this?"

"I don't know," Edwin sighed as he sat down upon the edge of the bed. "He's got to come out sometime. Why does he only let Brenna come to him?"

"You don't know anything, Edwin," Theodore snapped, although he didn't mean to. The boys usually got along fairly well. They had small squabbles from time to time, but in the end, Theodore and Edwin had always felt as if they only had each other.

"Don't you notice anything that goes on around here?" the older of the two continued.

"What do you mean?" Edwin, who admired and looked up to Theodore more than he cared to admit, was desperately trying to understand, but he only ended up even more confused.

"Father prefers Brenna above anyone else in this house…even before his first born son," Theodore muttered the last part through clenched teeth. How he hated his younger sister.

"Why?" Edwin asked yet again. This time Theodore showed his frustration by sighing heavily.

"Because, Father loved Kylene more than our mother," Edwin obviously wasn't noticing something else. His brother's growing aggravation, for he asked another question.

"Then how do you explain why Father won't go anywhere near Benjamin?"

"Edwin! Must I explain everything? My guess is that having Benjamin was what killed Kylene, but Brenna on the other hand, looked exactly like her."

"How could you know that he loved Kylene more than mother? I thought you were only three years of age when she died." Now Edwin was indeed trying his brother's patience for mere pleasure.

William finally decided that he would leave his room today. As much as he wanted to hide away, he had four children to raise by himself now. He couldn't stay locked in his room forever. At least that's what he told himself every morning when he rose out of bed. However, for the past few months, he seemed to be a prisoner in his quarters, no matter how foolish he thought it to be. Every time William remembered anything about Kylene, tears would instantly come to his eyes in torrents and he would end up weeping. He couldn't bear the thought of his household seeing him that way. Brenna was the only one who was able to comfort him now.

After he dressed, William opened his bedroom door and peered down the hall.

Just take the first step! he told himself, over and over. Sure enough, William began to make his way to the stairs. In the process however, something made him stop just outside of Theodore's room. Since the door was open a bit, he couldn't help but slowly approach.

"How could you know that Father loved Kylene more than mother? I thought you were only three years of age."

"I know plenty. Even though I can't remember much, I've heard people talk. I overheard Cook in the kitchen. She said Father wasn't half as sad when our mother died…and I fully believe it. He sure didn't mourn for four months," Theodore finished and tried to hide how upset it really made him. He hated William and intensely wished it would have been him that had dies instead of Harriet.

Edwin didn't have time to think of a reply, for right at that moment, William burst into the room. He marched up to Theodore and struck the side of his face with such force that he fell right out of his chair and to the floor. Theodore didn't know what happened!

"How dare you speak of such things. You don't understand anything!" William shouted. When Theodore tried to stand, William shoved him to the floor again. He was completely outraged and had to fight the urge to do much worse. Instead, he rushed out of the room and back to his room.

The boys had never seen their father like this! For a moment, Edwin thought William could have killed someone with the anger he'd witnessed in his eyes. Theodore must have been fairly shaken himself, although he would never admit it. When he slowly got to his feet, he raised his hand to where William hit him. It was already beginning to swell and bruise.

"What are you doing?" Edwin broke the silence when Theodore moved to his dresser and opened the top drawer.

"What does it look like? I'm getting out of here. Father doesn't care about us," he pulled out a small wooden box and opened it. There, he had saved money for just a time as this.

"Well I'm going with you. I hate Father just as you do," Edwin spoke up.

"Get your things then," Theodore replied but didn't look up from his packing. He was actually glad that Edwin planned to accompany him.

CHAPTER NINE

*W*here are those two going? Brenna thought as she spied her brothers walking down the road. Her bedroom, which was larger than Theodore and Edwin's put together, overlooked the servant's entrance into the back of the house. The fact that they used this very entrance was the first thing to arouse Brenna's suspicion. *They would never go that way.* "Please hurry, Lucy…I must go!" Brenna let her ladies maid finish quickly arranging her hair before sneaking out to find out where her brothers were off to.

They weren't walking very fast so she quickly caught up to them, yet staying far enough behind to remain hidden from sight. One of her favorite things to do was pestering Theodore and Edwin. Although Brenna disliked when they were mean to her, she always knew she had the upper hand in the end. Strangely enough, the boys were nearing the busiest part of the city. The harbor was only two hours in walking distance from Kenwood, but it seemed much longer to Brenna.

If Papa ever found out that we went to town on our own, he would be very angry, she thought, though she knew well that William would swiftly punish Theodore and Edwin before ever scolding her. In fact, Brenna had never experienced being punished, and it showed.

We'll show him. Father will be sorry when he finds out we're gone, Theodore just wished he could witness William's expression when he realized they'd run away. *If he even missed us at all.* The longer they walked, the more Theodore began to doubt their rash actions. *He's never struck me before. Perhaps his grief caused him to overreact. What I said was disrespectful.* "Edwin, do you think we're doing the right thing?" he stopped when they reached the edge of the harbor.

"What are you talking about? You want to walk all the back

48

home?" Edwin snorted. Theodore was surprised that his brother hadn't even thought about what they were doing.

Edwin never does look back or think about his actions.

"Doesn't your face hurt anymore? You should see it. It's starting to turn black and blue," Edwin taunted and sat down on one of the hundred trunks and crates that lined the docks, waiting to be loaded.

"I know…I know. But perhaps we should go back," Theodore sighed. *Why should I try and talk him into going back? He would follow me anywhere.*

Brenna was able to hide behind some trees and was also close enough to hear what they were planning. However, when she leaned further out from behind a tree, she somehow lost her footing and went flying right out into the open, giving a quick shriek in the process. That was all it took to gain her brothers attention, along with some other people who were nearby.

"What is *she* doing here?" Edwin quickly stood.

"Brenna!" Theodore shouted as she slowly got up and wiped off the front of her cranberry colored dress.

"She's probably spying on us for Father," Edwin stated. He was always one for egging things on. Especially when someone was in trouble and a possible fight was most likely to follow.

"I was not spying," Brenna protested.

"Then what were you doing?"

"I wanted to see…where you were going," she finally admitted.

"See? I told you, Theodore," Edwin put in smugly.

"Brenna, go home," Theodore pointed toward the road that led to Kenwood.

"No. I want to stay with you."

"You can't…we don't want you here," Edwin moved closer and pushed her.

"You better stop being mean to me. I'll tell Papa!"

"I'll tell Papa," Edwin mimicked.

"Stop it!" the oldest of the three finally cut in, "Brenna, I told you to go home."

"And I told you that I don't want to," Brenna bravely stood

her ground. They couldn't do anything to her, or so she thought.

"You're a spoiled brat, just like Kylene." Angry tears immediately stung Brenna's eyes.

"Take that back, Theodore!" she screamed, but he ignored her request.

"Come on Edwin. Let's go." With that, the boys started walking back home, but Brenna didn't follow. Instead she marched over to a trunk and plopped down on it.

"I'm not moving. They can't leave me," she whispered to herself.

"We better stop and wait for her." As much as he hated to give in, Theodore knew that they couldn't very well leave her on the busy streets of Boston. Edwin obviously didn't think as clearly, for he kept moving.

I wish we could get rid of Brenna...for good, Edwin was so angry, that he didn't notice the sailor he was about to run right into.

"Watch it boy," the man growled. As Edwin backed away, he quickly found out why the man wasn't in a very friendly mood.

"We're supposed to set sail for London in only two hours' time...Captain's orders."

"Well the Captain can—" the aggravated sailor began, but the other man cut him off.

"Hey...hey now. Keep quiet. Do you want to continue workin' for Weston? Is this how you act, right when I got you this job? Now see here, Captain Weston is a forgivin' man, so you'd better help me get the ship loaded. All the cargo on the first dock must go." Edwin nonchalantly watched the calmer of the two sailor's point to the very cargo that Brenna now stubbornly sat upon.

"Alright...alright," he finally agreed.

"Good, but first I came to fetch ya cause Weston wants to speak to you."

What a brilliant idea! Edwin quietly watched them leave and smiled wickedly to himself. He was about to run back to Theodore and tell him of his plan, when another thought crossed his mind. *Theodore will never go along with me. He thinks too much.* He had never been more proud of himself!

<hr/>

"Brenna, come on," Theodore shouted again.

"Wait, Theodore, I've got a better idea. Let's put her in one of the trunks for a while. That will teach her to be so high and mighty."

"Well, uh," Theodore looked as if he was about to protest, so Edwin quickly thought of a way to talk him into it.

"Just for a while. We can go into town for a bit, then come back in a few hours. Then she'll surely come with us." After several minutes, Theodore finally agreed.

Brenna didn't have the slightest inkling of what was coming, as her brother's slowly approached her.

"Have you come to apologize?"

"No," Edwin smiled, "something much better." Theodore grabbed her arms as Edwin swiftly went for her legs.

"Let me go!" she screamed. Unfortunately, when they opened the trunk, it was full of wool. Now Theodore had to manage Brenna alone, along with covering her mouth while Edwin quickly emptied it. When that was done and they'd nearly flung their sister inside, they finished the job by setting a heavy crate on top of the trunk.

As they began to walk away, Theodore's enjoyment was beginning to wane. Brenna's poor cries seemed to ring in his ears. She was afraid of the dark after all, but Edwin managed to talk him out of turning back several times. They had to stay in town for at least two hours, for only Edwin knew that if they did, they would never see Brenna again.

"Wherefore he saith,
Awake thou that sleepest,
and arise from the dead,
and Christ shall give thee light."

Ephesians 5:14

CHAPTER TEN

renna hysterically kicked and screamed for help after
being locked inside the musty trunk, but no one
came. This went on for almost an hour. However,
when her voice was too hoarse to shout any longer,
she began to cry for fear of being left there for good.

*Why did they do this? If only Papa knew I went after
Theodore and Edwin. He would save me.* "Papa!" she sobbed as
the darkness began to close in. It seemed to choke her. Suddenly
she felt something move against her, although, she couldn't tell if
it was only her imagination. The only thing she could think of
was the not so small rodents that roamed all over the harbor.

What if there's one in here with me? a shiver went through
her at the thought. "Papa, help me!" she cried out. When it was
clear that no one could hear her pleadings, Brenna curled up as
tight as she could and eventually fell into a fitful sleep.

"Come along, Edwin. It's been quite long enough,"
Theodore couldn't bear the guilt he felt any longer. He had told
himself that she deserved it many times, yet he couldn't rid his
mind of how defenseless and scared Brenna had been when
they'd left her nearly two hours ago. If truth be told, he had
wanted to return much earlier, but Edwin had done an excellent
job of distracting him. And he was still trying to detain their
return to the docks.

"Edwin, hurry up!" Theodore once again turned around and
waited for his brother to slowly catch up. As they came around
the corner that faced the harbor, Theodore's nightmare had just
begun. The trunk, along with all the cargo around it was gone.
Completely gone! For a moment, he thought he was looking at
the wrong dock. He had to be! The docks that lined the shore did

all look alike.

The trunk was the very first dock of the harbor, Theodore thought as he slowly moved his gaze back to it, hoping against hope that he was just seeing things or that he was merely looking in the wrong place. Fear, along with a cold sweat, washed over him when he followed the dock out to the end. The ship that was once there had also disappeared. He silently turned to Edwin, who was trying his very hardest to appear as shocked as his brother, but he didn't succeed. Theodore quickly saw the wicked smirk on his face.

"What did you do?"

"What do you mean? We're finally rid of her," Edwin was completely oblivious of his older brother's rage. Theodore suddenly grabbed Edwin by his collar.

"Are you saying you knew the ship was leaving?"

"I thought you'd be happy," Edwin tried to pull away, but it only made Theodore pull tighter.

"Happy? Are you daft? As much as I dislike Brenna, she's our sister."

"Half-sister!" Edwin was finally able to shove him away.

"Don't you see? Now we can never return home. Father will never forgive us," Theodore rubbed his face with his hands, much like his father did when he was upset.

"Well, let's don't return then. Let's run away like you wanted to," Edwin simply stated. It did nothing to lift his brother's spirits.

"What have we done?" Right at that moment, a carriage drove down the street. It could have kept going, but instead it came to a halt directly in front of them. When Theodore glanced up, he immediately recognized it as one of the many Kenwood carriages.

Oh no! What should we do? he started to panic. Thankfully, it was only the butler who climbed out.

"Sedrick, what are you doing here?" Edwin calmly asked as if nothing was out of the ordinary. Theodore couldn't help but stare at him and marvel at his heartlessness.

"I could ask you the same, Master Edwin. Your father has

been looking everywhere for you two."

I doubt he's looking for us. It's Brenna he's most worried about, Theodore thought. Then, as if on cue, Sedrick asked that very thing.

"Where is your sister?" Theodore's heart nearly stopped as he tried to come up with an answer.

"We don't know...haven't seen her all day," Edwin answered for him without the slightest hesitation whatsoever.

"Well, get in then. I'm to bring you home." Sedrick moved aside and stood to the right of the carriage door.

"If you ever say anything to Father, I'll tell him that Brenna's disappearance was you're doing," Edwin managed to whisper the threat to his brother before they both climbed inside. As they started for home, Sedrick told them all that had happened since they'd left. Just as Theodore presumed, William didn't notice anything amiss until he realized that Brenna was gone. Then he quickly went into action. All the authorities were now out looking for them, along with nearly everyone who worked at Kenwood.

Theodore almost had the carriage stop several times on the way home because he thought he was going to be sick. However, it only grew worse when they finally arrived home and he saw William standing at the entrance, waiting for them.

"Did you find her? Where is she?" William ran down the steps to the carriage.

"I only found the boys, sir."

"Well, keep looking for her. The sun will only be up for a few more hours," William ordered.

"Yes, sir," When Theodore and Edwin stepped out, William never asked where they had been or why.

"Did Brenna go with you? Have you seen her at all?" Thankfully Edwin did all the talking once again, for all Theodore could do was nod. All he wanted to do was go to his room to be alone.

As he finally climbed the stairs to the second story of the house, Theodore suddenly felt years older and what had only been several hours, seemed like several days. His guilt would only get worse.

"For thou wilt light my candle:
the LORD my God will
enlighten my darkness."

Psalm 18:28

CHAPTER ELEVEN

It had been a little more than four hours since the Hester set sail. Now the vessel was rolling heavily. Weston moved his gaze from the horizon to his crew.

"You there," Weston gained the attention of one of his new sailors.

"Aye, sir?"

"What was your name again?"

"Rob, sir. Rob Sullivan."

"Oh yes. I'm sorry, but we've got several new sailors on board and I've yet ter memorize aw their names. Anyway, would you and Samuel go down and check the cargo and make sure it's secure?"

"Aye, aye, Captain."

"Looks secure over here," Samuel shouted from the other end of the hull. He had to holler for the ship was creaking more with the larger waves. *I hope there's not a storm comin',* he thought as he made his way to where Rob was. When the other sailor came into view, he appeared to be quite pale. It was like he'd seen a ghost!

"What's the matter?"

"I…I hear something," Rob stuttered.

"Aw, it's probably just a rat," Samuel replied and couldn't help but chuckle.

"No, it's something bigger," Rob began to lift different boxes and things, trying to find where the strange noise was coming from.

"Bigger than a rat? What could that be…a stowaway?" Samuel joked for he thought Rob was only kidding, but he didn't laugh or so much as smile. He just kept searching for whatever it was. Suddenly he stopped.

"See? I told you I heard something," Rob turned to Samuel and saw the color drain from his face as well, for something or someone inside the trunk before them was pounding against the sides.

"It must be a stowaway!" was all Samuel could say as they both lifted a heavy box that was on top of the trunk.

"Surely a daft stowaway."

When Brenna awoke and found that she was still in darkness, she panicked and began to kick the walls that surrounded her. She knew she had to get out soon because she could hardly breathe anymore! She was indeed about to pass out for lack of air when the lid swung open without warning!

"It's a bloody lass!" Rob jumped back as Brenna slowly sat up and gasped.

"Where am I? Who are you?" she cried as Rob lifted her into the plank floor.

"Who are we? Who are you and why are you stuffed inside this trunk?" Rob asked. Brenna was about to reply when Samuel beat her to it.

"We have to bring her to Weston straight away."

"Wait, where am I? Where are you taking me?" Brenna was completely ignored as she was led to the deck. She continued to ask, getting more upset as every second passed. Especially when she realized that she was aboard a ship!

By the time they brought her into the quarter deck where the captain was, Brenna was in quite a state.

"Stop squirming, lass," Rob tried to hold the girl's arm, but it was becoming an impossible task for she was now trying to bite his hand.

"Captain, look what we found," Samuel stated as Weston slowly turned around to face them. "She was inside a trunk."

"Well, wot do we 'ave here?" Weston gazed down at Brenna and smiled. The girl surprised him by boldly looking him right in the eye.

"I demand that you take me back home, this instant!" After a few moments of silence, all three men began to laugh, along with other sailors nearby. This was not the reaction Brenna had anticipated. She actually thought they would take her seriously.

"Well, men...let's turn this whole vessel 'round for this little lady," Weston continued to chuckle. "How did ya get inside a trunk?" Brenna was about to reply when Samuel stepped forward and beat her once again.

"Captain, what if she's a stowaway?"

"I am not!" Brenna quickly protested. If truth be told, she had no idea what a stowaway was. It didn't sound good, whatever it was. When it was apparent that they had no intention of bringing her home, Brenna knew she would have to take matters into her own hands and somehow make then listen to her.

"Well now, I don't think this little lass snuck on aw by 'erself. She was trapped in the trunk after all." Right at that moment, Weston was interrupted by a yelp that escaped Rob's lips. When he moved his gaze to the sailor, he saw that Brenna had prevailed in biting the tip of Rob's thumb and was now running straight for the helm. Once there, she tried to pull the wheel out of the first mate's grasp.

"Hey, what do ya think yar doin'?" he glanced down at Brenna. When she continued to try and pull it, he began to smile, for she couldn't make any progress whatsoever.

"You have to take me home!" she shouted. Brenna suddenly became so panic stricken, she almost looked as if she'd gone mad. The girl darted down the quarter deck steps and to the side of the ship.

"Stop 'er!" Brenna heard the captain's orders.

If I jump overboard, they'll have to turn the ship around for me. While it would be frightening, she was a good swimmer. All those times Theodore and Edwin snuck to the small lake near their home for a swim, she would tag along. She was convinced her plan would work as she neared the rail. That is, until someone grabbed her.

"You can't be doing that," the sailor who now held the thrashing girl tried to contain her. He was surprised at how strong she was.

"Let me go. You're hurting me," Brenna screamed as she was carried back to Weston.

"Someone go and get Hephzibah. She'll kna wha ter do."

"Yes, Captain," Rob went to do his bidding once again.

"And wot is this?" A woman appeared on deck minutes later, with Rob following close behind. Once Brenna saw her, she immediately thought she looked familiar, but then again, Brenna couldn't recall who. When the woman slowly climbed the steps to the quarter deck, Brenna saw that she was probably in her early sixties and sort of waddled when she walked, for her middle was a bit plump.

"We found 'er inside a trunk," Weston quickly informed.

"I can clock why she's quite upset, but why is our Nathaniel havin' to contain 'a?" Hephzibah asked.

"She's trying ter jump overboard so we'll turn the vessel 'round and take 'er home."

"Well now…isn't that daffy dahn dilly," Hephzibah approached Brenna. Instead of speaking to her, she caught the sailor's gaze. "Nate, can't you see you're hurtin' t' poor dear and prolly scarin' her art of her wits."

"You can release 'er now," the captain agreed when Nate glanced at him in question. He slowly loosened his hold and backed away.

"Are you alwigh', honey?" Hephzibah lowered herself to Brenna's height, but she didn't reply. The woman's kindness confused her. "You must be starved. Just come wif me," she gently reached out to dry a tear on the girl's face, wrapped her arm around her, and brought her to the hull.

CHAPTER TWELVE

"*T*ake me home! You can't keep me here," Brenna protested all the way to the kitchen that was located in the hull. But she didn't try to pull away from the older woman's gentle grasp. Something about her had some sort of calming effect on her. Once Hephzibah sat Brenna down at a long, narrow table, she scurried into the kitchen part of the strange looking dining room.

"Can't you hear me? I must go home," she continued, but Hephzibah just kept ignoring her. She soon reappeared and set a large serving of oatmeal down in front of Brenna.

"Theear now...you just eat that, and then you'll feel as good as new," she finally spoke.

"I don't want to eat..."

"I'll onny be talkin' to thee when you've finished."

"But—" Brenna tried to say something, but Hephzibah only raised her hand and walked back into the kitchen. The last thing Brenna wanted to do was eat. However, her stomach immediately rumbled by the smell of the food that was before her. She slowly sat down and ate the strange warm pudding with dried fruit.

"That's betta," Hephzibah smiled when Brenna was finished with the meal that had been more than generous. "A full stomach nivva fails to make a person feel loike new and think more clearly," she took the girl's plate into the kitchen.

"Now then," she came and sat down across from Brenna, "How is it that ya became locked inside a trunk? Wor it a game of hidin' that went 'orribly wrong?" Brenna met her gaze at the question. She was about to reply when suddenly she looked past the woman. Hephzibah then turned to see what had caught the girl's attention. It was Captain Weston that had entered

"How is she fairin'?" he quietly asked Hephzibah.

"I was just abaht ta ask her how she got 'e. She's mighty

stubborn." When they both took a seat, Hephzibah noticed that Brenna immediately stiffened at the captain's presence. "It's quite alright, love. The mighty Hester's captain is right kind." Brenna silently watched as they exchanged glances. They seemed to know exactly what the other was thinking. Hephzibah was the one who began to gently question the girl.

"Like I was sayin', how did ya get into the trunk?" After several moments, Brenna finally spoke, but it was no more than a whisper now.

"My...my brothers."

She's a completely different person now, Weston mused, *Hephzibah sure has a way with people.*

"Was it onny an accident?"

"No...well, I don't know."

"And you live in Boston. Wheear are thy parents, child?" Hephzibah slowly continued, and Brenna eventually began to regain her spunk after she forgot the captain was in the room.

"My father doesn't know what's happened to me. If he did, I know he'd be furious," she stood, "He's very wealthy and he'll pay anything you like. Just please take me home." When Hephzibah glanced at Weston, his presence was made known to Brenna once again.

"I'm so sorry. Ya see, we're a long ways out and if The Hester dunt dock in London village on time, Captain Weston 'ere would be in a horrible situation. There's nothin' we can do right naw, but...." Hephzibah felt absolutely wretched as she watched Brenna raise her hand to her quivering mouth.

"London? I can't go there...my father will...." as tears began to stream down her face, Weston nervously moved behind Hephzibah.

"I wish there was somethin' I could do," he began, but Hephzibah unintentionally cut in.

"Why don't we mek a place for you to bo-peep for tonight," as she kindly wrapped her arms around Brenna, and was about to lead her to another room, Hephzibah quickly turned to Weston and bid him to leave. "We'll get all of this sorted out on the morrow. Don't ya worry na." It was still fairly early but Brenna was exhausted and she was beginning to think this was all a horrible nightmare.

Maybe if I fall asleep, I'll eventually awake out of all this, she thought as she followed Hephzibah behind the kitchen to a very small room. She began to gather some blankets and things to make a bed on the floor. Once she was done, Brenna didn't think it looked like much, at least nothing like she was used to. Fortunately, she was much too tired to complain.

"There ya are," Hephzibah sighed and motioned for her to sit, "I sleep right yonda," she then pointed around the corner, which Brenna could see by just leaning to the side, for it was only a few feet away.

"And don't you worry one bit, for none of the bloody sailors are anywhere near this room. Bein' the onny woman with all these men is jannock hard sometimes, but you get used to it afta awhile," Hephzibah continued to talk as she fluffed a pillow for the girl, "Sorry if they scared you earlier. They didn't mean to. If ya ask me, you prolly surprised them much more than you kna." Brenna could only stare. Never had she met anyone who talked nearly as much. The older woman barely hesitated long enough to take a breath! But at the same time, she was very kind. It was almost as if she'd known Hephzibah all of her life.

"Now, seein' that you're not used ter being on the sea, the waves might make your orange peel feel a bit squeamish so there's a bowl right at the foot of your bed…just in case," Hephzibah was about to leave when she heard Brenna sigh heavily, "Oh child…you need not fret the night away. Just nip on to sleep as if you 'aven't a care in the world, for tomorra will cum soon enough. Would you loike me to say your prayers wif ya?" Brenna slowly shook her head. "Goodnoight, golden dove." With that, the lady left and Brenna laid there for a minute before she fell asleep. Her last thought, before the waves actually seemed to lull her to sleep, was that she would soon be home in her own bed and finally be free from this queer dream.

As Brenna awoke, she looked about without getting up. Dread slowly came over her when she realized where she was.

"Oh, no! Papa...I want my papa!" Brenna turned against her pillow and sobbed into it. This was the scene that Hephzibah came upon.

Poor girl, she thought as she listened to Brenna's cries. *Lord, please give me the words to say.* "Don't cry, love," Hephzibah quickly covered the distance between them and stiffly knelt down beside her.

"I want to go home," Brenna continued to weep. She had been so sure it had all been a dream.

"And ya will, dear. Just as soon as we unload the bleedin' Hester's cargo."

"When will that be?" she slowly sat up.

"Well, we'll be 'rrivin' in London village prolly the beginnin' of June," Hephzibah pushed a few strands of her graying nut brown hair that had fallen from the simple bun out of her face.

"But that's two months from now!" Brenna shouted, which made the older lady flinch in surprise. The almost silent girl from the night before had obviously disappeared.

"Aye," Hephzibah then took both of her hands in her own, "But I promise ya this, when we do arrive, I will personally clock thee home safely. No matter what it takes, you have my word." Even though she knew nothing of this peculiar woman, Brenna was fully convinced she spoke the truth.

"While we wait, we moight as well make the best of the situation we're faced wif. A person can make the best of anything, you kna," Hephzibah simply stated in her queer way as she stood up, but not without a grunt. She was about to make her way to the kitchen when she realized Brenna still sat upon her bed solemnly. She turned and put her hands on her ample waste.

"There's always plenty of fettle ta be done on The mighty Hester...and you can help me wif sum of it if ya loike."

"No thank you," Brenna finally replied. Hephzibah was so surprised at her response that she was actually left speechless, which in her case, didn't happen very often.

Well then, isn't she an interesting sort. Does she expect to just sit there and sulk for two months? She thought as she went on her way to begin breakfast. *She probably just needs a bit of time.*

However, four days wasn't exactly what Hephzibah had in mind. Sure, the girl came out to eat and ventured out on deck for a little fresh air, however that was the extent of it.

"Lord, I kna she's prolly scared and homesick, but it's beginning to seem as if she expects to be treated like a queen for the entire voyage," Hephzibah sat at her very small writing desk that doubled as a nightstand. Every morning, before the first light, she would read her Bible and pray quietly before beginning the breakfast preparations.

"Well, if I were her, I'd be bored out of my mind just mopin' abaht!" she continued. Right at that moment, Hephzibah heard Brenna stir. She was shocked when the girl got up and actually approached.

"Miss…Miss Hephzibah?"

"Good mornin' love. You can just call me by my given name. I know it's a strange wahn, but I think it fits me…the bloomin' strange sort that I am," she chuckled.

"You read from that same book day and night?" Brenna asked in a raspy voice, still groggy from sleep.

"That I do."

"What is it?"

"It's me Holy Bible…been in me family for ages," Hephzibah shut the book and sighed, "Well, that's enough lollygaggin' for one morning. It's nickel and dime to start breakfast." She decided it was high time for Brenna to start some sort of job that day. But first Hephzibah had to see what the girl could do. "Would ya like to help me today?" she asked the same question three times a day for four days now. Brenna's reply was the very same.

"No thank you."

"Beggin' thy pardon, but a person could go mad just sittin' theear day afta day on a journey like this…think of it as earnin' yar keep if it suites ya." Brenna was completely taken aback. No one had ever spoken to her that way, much less a common cook. Hephzibah was just surprised when she heard a stubborn snort come out of the girl! Now she was very glad she was forcing Brenna to help.

Perhaps this voyage will be good for her yet. Hephzibah began humming a cheerful tune to lighten the mood while she retrieved the ingredients.

After breakfast was served and everyone was taken care of, Hephzibah finally sat down and sighed heavily. Today she realized how much work these next two months would be. Teaching Brenna anything would indeed be far worse than she first thought. First Hephzibah gave the girl the job of cracking the eggs into a pan, but after she dropped two and Hephzibah found more than five shells in the food, she moved her to the counter to stir the biscuit dough.

What a mess, Hephzibah recalled the morning. *It's apparent that the girl has never worked a day in her life.* Thankfully, she was patient and she had yet to fail in teaching practically anyone how to cook. *And I don't plan on Brenna being an exception. It will just take time...a lot of time!* she sighed once more as she took a bite of her egg, which crunched in her mouth.

CHAPTER THIRTEEN

ight days had passed and Brenna eventually learned how to accomplish some basics in the kitchen. *She seems to be enjoying it now. At least I don't have to force her to help anymore.* Hephzibah awoke and began to get ready for the day. Now something else was causing her to wonder about the girl. She thought it very strange that Brenna never talked about her family, other than how wealthy they were or what her father had to say about certain matters. Even when Hephzibah questioned her about things, Brenna would close up and stop talking.

I've never seen a child like this, Lord. Very strange indeed.

"Good morning," Brenna greeted when they both entered the kitchen.

"Mornin' child. I thought today would be t'day I start teachin' theur how ta chuffin' cook and not just prepare for the meal."

When all the men had been served, Hephzibah and Brenna finally sat down themselves, as they did at every meal. Before taking a bite of oatmeal, Brenna hesitated because Hephzibah usually prayed over the food in her queer sort of way. Instead, she met Brenna's gaze and smiled.

"Would ya loike to say the prayer, golden dove?" The question barely escaped the older woman's lips when Brenna quickly replied.

"No."

"Why, don't you kna any?"

"Yes, but I just don't care to." Hephzibah couldn't miss the sadness that washed over the Brenna's face. There always seemed to be an almost melancholy sorrow that came from the child, but this was different. There was something else that accompanied her sadness. Hephzibah couldn't put her finger on it, but it was some sort of anger that burned in her.

"Well na, it isn't hard. Aw prayin' is, is talkin' to thy Heavenly Father. Don't ya eva do that?"

"No," Brenna replied with a huff as her gazed lowered. While Hephzibah knew she should stop pressing the girl, something inside her made her continue. It was partly because of her shock.

Surely everyone has prayed sometime or another in their life, her mind reeled. "Wot? Do ya mean to say that you've neva said a prayer?" Then, without warning, Brenna slammed her fork on her untouched plate and quickly stood.

"Blast your persistence! I used to say them, but now I don't…and I never will again." With that, she rushed out of the kitchen, leaving Hephzibah to her confused and guilty thoughts.

Rob spied Brenna leaning against the rail of the bow. The sailor noticed that she'd been up on deck a lot more lately. All she ever did was merely stare out over the waves. Sometimes she cried, but not today.

"Don't worry, the voyage might seem like an eternity now, but if you don't dwell on it, we'll arrive soon enough," Rob tried to comfort, but she wouldn't reply. In fact, the girl never really did interact with any of the sailors. When Rob felt Nate's eyes on him, along with several other men, he quickly went about his duties.

Brenna sighed heavily as she scanned the horizon as if land would suddenly appear if she longed for it hard enough. Instead of catching sight of the shores of England, Brenna saw the cook coming from the hull.

Oh no…not her again, she sighed again. While Hephzibah was kind, and meant well, Brenna wasn't used to having someone on her all the time. She was always telling her something that she hadn't the slightest wish to hear about, or trying to get her to talk of family. At Kenwood, everything and everyone were on her terms, where and when she wanted.

"Hello, dear." Brenna didn't answer, as if it would make Hephzibah leave. However, she knew fully well that it wouldn't work.

What is she going to nag me about now? Brenna thought.

"I came up here first of aw, to apologize for me rash behavior the other day…askin' you all sorts of questions. You must think I'm an awful nosey. Can ya eva forgive this old maid?" Brenna didn't know what to say. No one had ever asked her that before.

"Uh…yes," she finally said in a whisper.

"I guess my curiosity just got the betta of me. I don't get to meet roight many new people…bein' around this hoppin' lot all the time. To tell ya the truf, I was pretty exasperated when I saw that you were a lass! And such a pretty lass at that," Hephzibah put her arm around Brenna's shoulders and squeezed her against herself. "Now, before I go, moight I just ask wahn question of ya? But you don't have ta answer if ya don't want too…"

"Alright, what it is?" Although she thought Hephzibah was quite the chatter box, she always managed to make her smile. She never met anyone like her, that much was true. Hephzibah had such a sweet nature and all she ever wanted to do was take care and serve everyone around her. So much so, that she made it hard to resist in liking her.

"How is it that ya said you'd neva pray to God agin?" Hephzibah hoped against hope that Brenna would confide in her and not shut her out again. While she waited for the girl's reply, Hephzibah silently prayed for the right words.

"I just don't care to…that's all."

"Why is that?"

"I don't care about God." Hephzibah was completely shocked. Never did she expect this!

"I used to," Brenna continued, "But that was until…until," she suddenly choked.

"Until what, dear?"

"Until He took my mother."

"Wot?"

"God took my mother away from me. So now I never want

to talk or think about Him again."

"Oh, I'm so sorry." Hephzibah tried to hide the tears that began to well up, "How do ya kna it was God that did this horrible thing?"

"He just did. Everyone said so."

"I see," she didn't know what to say after that. There were so many things she could have said, but something kept her from doing so, at least for the time being. Brenna was finally opening up. Now, more than ever, Hephzibah had to watch over her words, for it was a delicate matter.

"For God, who commanded the light to shine out of darkness, hath shined in our hearts, to give the light of the knowledge of the glory of God in the face of Jesus Christ."

2 Corinthians 4:6~7

CHAPTER FOURTEEN

ephzibah awoke with a start. It took her a few moments to realize that the horrible cries were coming from the other room. Although most of it was incoherent, the only thing she could make out was Brenna desperately calling for her mother. Hephzibah nearly jumped out of her cot then rushed to the girl, but not before fumbling to light a lamp.

"Brenna honey, you're dreamin'! Wake up…wake up na," Hephzibah's hushed tones immediately seemed to comfort her as she slowly escaped the nightmare.

"There now… don't cry, love. Hephzibah is here," the older woman gently lifted Brenna's head on her lap and began to caress the hair that was wet from her fatigue, pushing it away from her face.

After crying for several minutes, the trembling girl was finally able to speak.

"She was walking down the hall. I called after her so many times, but she just kept walking," Brenna's tears started again.

"Thy muther?"

"Yes. When I tried going after her, someone grabbed a hold of me and wouldn't let me go. No matter how much I struggled. Then Mama was swallowed by the darkness," she now sobbed, "Why did God take her away from me? Doesn't He know that I need her?" All the while Hephzibah sought wisdom from the very person Brenna loathed. Then, as if on cue, Hephzibah understood what she must do.

"Can I tell ya a story?" she glanced down and met Brenna's tearful gaze.

"My papa always told me stories…I would beg him to every night," Once Brenna blew her nose with the handkerchief that was given to her, Hephzibah began.

"Long ago, in a faraway land, there was a great King. In fact, he was the greatest King that evva lived. Wahn day, he bought sum men...men 'oo' ad been caught for steelin' or otha horrible things and were then sold as servants. One of which was a young lad by the name of Breckin. Afta several months had passed, Breckin couldn't believe the kindness that the King and his Son had shown him. The servant had never met anyone loike them. They didn't treat him as their slave, more like a bonnie friend that they'd knahn forever. In fact, Breckin and the King's Son were alike in years so they becem much loike brothers. Anyway, sum more time had gone by when—" At that moment, the bells were heard, announcing that it was a mere four o'clock in the morning.

"Oh, dear me. I must start breakfast," Hephzibah grunted to her feet.

"But what about the rest of the story?"

"Perhaps I'll be able ta finish it lata this afternoon," she stopped and turned to face Brenna, "I'd finish quite a bit sooner if...." To her surprise, the girl quickly stood also and began to ready for the day.

"There now...I think this is the last of it," Hephzibah set the tall stack of tin plates on the wooden counter beside the sink. Brenna surprised her further by helping with everything she could get her hands on and with every bit of determination she could muster.

"After this is done, can you tell me the rest of the story?" Brenna glanced up at her in question.

"Of course, dear," Hephzibah smiled to herself as she set about washing the narrow table in the cramped dining area. It never seized to surprise her how messy the crew left the place after each meal. *If I would have known how much Brenna liked stories and what she would do to hear one, I would've told her a hundred by now!*

Brenna finished quickly and dried her hands. She hurried over to one of the stools by the table to wait for Hephzibah to waddle over.

"Na then, where was it that I left off?" Hephzibah nearly jumped at how quickly Brenna spoke up.

"You were just at the part where Breckin and the King's Son became good friends...even closer than brothers."

"Why yes. Aye, I remember naw. A little more than a year had gone by, Breckin, the King's servant, was going abaht his duties, mindin' his own business. As he made his way dahn the long hall, he suddenly passed the door that lead to where all the kingdom's jewels and riches wor kept, locked up deep inside the gran' castle. The onny reason Breckin knew where it was, was because he'd gained everyone's trust and was allowed to nip on nearly everywhere because of it. Something inside of the servant made him stop in front of the door. Strangely enough, the door was unlocked!"

"What did he do?" Brenna asked when Hephzibah stopped to take a breath. She placed her elbows on the table and rested her head on her hands in suspense.

"Sadly, Breckin's greed was too much for him."

"Oh no," Brenna sighed.

"He went in and began pickin' some of the chuffin' most valuable things, for he swiftly planned to take them and run away. However, as he dashed out of the room, he was in such a hurry he didn't watch where he was going and ran reet into anotha trusted servant. Well, as ya might suspect, they got into a quarrel when the otha geeza realized wot Breckin had done. In the end, Breckin shoved him against the stone wall and knocked him out cold, for he wouldn't let him leave. He then snuck out of the castle. Wot he didn't nu was, his hasty act killed the other poor bloke."

"How could he do such a thing? What happened next?"

"He managed ta get away and there was nah sign of the bloomin' servant for several months, nor any clue as to where he'd gone. That is, until one day, an angry mob burst into the court where the King was. Nah wahn knew wot the commotion was all abaht, until they dragged one man forward."

"Breckin!" Brenna blurted in concern.

"Aye, the men who caught him were actually related to the poor geeza that Breckin accidentally killed. Needless to say, when they found him, they didn't treat him roight well. They were goin' to hang him, but asteead they decided to seek justice from the King. He would kna what had to be done. The men holding the servant reminded the King of all he had done, although the King knew fully well. When they'd finished, the King solemnly asked Breckin if all they had said was indeed true. And after some moments, he admitted everythin'. All except purposely committin' murder. Although the King loved him like a son, the law was clear. Breckin would be given the death penalty. Everyone in the angry crowd cheered, however, they all suddenly became silent as anotha bloke stepped forward. The King's onny Son stepped down from his place of honor and stood beside Breckin. Breckin couldn't believe what happened next, for the King's Son boldly declared that he would take his place. He would receive all the punishment and the servant would be set free. Because he was well loved by all in the kingdom, everyone begged him to reconsida. But nothing moved the King's Son. He loved Breckin and knew this was what he was meant to do. The law was carried out the next mornin'. When three days had passed since the fateful day and the days of mournin' were over, Breckin went to the King. He knelt down before him and wept as he begged the King for forgiveness. To his surprise, the King took his hand and pulled Breckin to his feet. He then made Breckin the heir to his throne and made him a true son." When Hephzibah finished, Brenna was completely speechless. She knew she couldn't just leave the story at that and went on, "But does thee know what happened, love?" "A miraculous thin' happened. A wonderful and strange power was in the land, many folk called it magic, but others were afraid of it, because they didn't chuffin' kna wot it was. The King's Son rose from the dead just three days lata. For many months everyone thought he was a ghost, but soon the whole kingdom celebrated loike they'd nivva done before." Hephzibah looked at Brenna, who remained silent. Hephzibah had made the decision earlier, to no longer nag or push the girl into anything. So instead of saying anything more, she simply stood and made her way to the kitchen. However, Brenna caused her to halt.

"Was that a true story?" she quietly asked as if to test her.

"Aye, and I'm also a daughta of that great King. He's the one that I serve."

CHAPTER FIFTEEN

"Why Captain Weston...what are ya doing here sa early? I didn't think thee could smell me cookin' already, seein' that I've just set some water ta boil," Hephzibah chuckled softly. As soon as Weston joined in with his loud, boisterous laugh, she quickly shushed him.

"Shhh...Brenna is still sleepin'."

"Oh, my mistake. The lass is actually why I came down here. How is she faring?" Weston carefully peaked his head around the corner and sure enough, Brenna was still sound asleep on the small pile of blankets that laid on the plank flooring.

"She's doing alright. At least she's helpin' me on a regular basis now. I quite loike her company. The onny thin is, she is a strange one. Nivva met anotha one like her," Hephzibah continued to stir a large bowl of batter.

"What do ya mean?"

"It appears that the girl comes from a wealthy family and has nivva worked a day in her short life. But yet, wif all of her fancy upbringin' and speech, she hasn't any idea of most things...things that really matta in this life."

"Aw, I see. I dare say she's met the right person to show her," Weston met Hephzibah's gaze and winked.

"Well, I don't kna about that," she smiled in return.

"You don't know about what?" The very person who consumed their conversation, stepped into the room and began to wash her hands. However, when Brenna realized the captain was there, she stopped and quickly glanced over at Hephzibah.

"It's quite alroight, dear," Hephzibah quickly reassured her, "Captain Weston came ta see how you're doin', but does thee want ta know wot I think? I think he chuffin' came daahhn 'ere to see if he could snitch sum breakfast before the others."

"That I did...that I did," Weston's cheerful laugh seemed to relax Brenna a bit. "Well, as long as everythin' is in order down here, I'll let you two get back to work. Brenna couldn't help but notice the way Hephzibah and Weston looked at each other.

They aren't smitten with each other, are they? The minute the thought crossed Brenna's mind, she quickly pushed it aside, for Hephzibah appeared to be years older than the captain.

"Oh, before I go," Weston interrupted her musings, "I thought the little miss would like to know we're more than 'alf way ta London." Weston left after giving a quick wink in Hephzibah's direction. The act confused Brenna even more.

Nearly an hour had gone by, and Brenna hardly said two words the entire time they'd been cooking. Hephzibah tried to figure out why, but she was at a loss.

"Is there somethin' on thy mind, love?" she finally decided to ask.

"Well," Brenna did indeed have several things on her mind, one of which was the possibility of something going on between the captain and Hephzibah. Since she wasn't bold enough to ask her first question, she went on to the second.

"How come bad things happen?"

"Wot do ya mean?"

"Why do bad things happen to people…who have never done anything wrong?"

"Child, everyone does wrong every once in a while." Hephzibah replied.

"How come God does bad things then?" Brenna asked yet again, beginning to get frustrated.

"Well now…how can I explain it," Hephzibah glanced around the room until her gaze finally stopped on the stove top right in front of her.

"Ah, take this for example. Let's say you're cooking and I warn you ta be careful 'cos the bleedin' stove is hot. But what if you don't listen or believe me, and touch it onnyway? Whose fault is it that you wor burned?" she asked, all the while preparing the meal.

"I suppose I'm at fault."

"Aye…I didn't come over, grab thy hand and put in on the

stove. But you can be bobby sure that even though I told you not ta, I would rush over to see if you wor alroight and ease your pain. It's the same way wif God. He warns us, but sometimes we do it onnyway, but He'll allwus be there ta bring us comfort and pick us up. 'He'll be with us in trouble,'" Hephzibah quoted. "Does that make sense?" Brenna's back was turned toward her, so the only reply Hephzibah was given, was a quick nod. But all of a sudden, the girl sniffed as if she was trying to hold in a cry. Once she heard yet another sniffle, Hephzibah moved to look at the girl and found that she was trembling. She then dropped what she was doing and quickly stepped across the small space between them.

"It's just loike the tale I told you. God, me great King, gave His onny Son for us…ta die for us and ta be our sacrifice. He did it just for you, love," Hephzibah slowly reached out and wiped away a single tear on Brenna's face, "Because He loves ya. He could nivva, and would nivva bring you harm." Brenna tried to speak, but she only choked on a sob.

"What is it?" Hephzibah embraced her gently.

"I…I want to be a daughter of the King too."

"Oh honey, I thowt you'd nivva say it." Now tears blurred Hephzibah's vision.

"Amen," Brenna finished repeating Hephzibah's prayer then glanced up at her. Although she said nothing, Hephzibah immediately caught a glimpse of change in the girl's blue eyes. A peace, that was swiftly swallowed by doubt.

"What's the matta, child?"

"Well…I don't feel any different," Brenna was surprised when a short chuckle escaped Hephzibah before she could stop it.

"For some the change isn't straeight away. It's a gradual process. But thee can be bobby sure that the Christ has come ta live inside ya, even if you can't feel anything. Don't let thy feelings guide you…onny believe." Hephzibah continued to hold Brenna, until she suddenly realized they were in the kitchen. "Oh dear me! It's nearly time for the seven bells and I hardly have breakfast ready," she scurried back to the bowl and began to stir vigorously

"I'll help," Brenna finally spoke.

"Alroight, why don't ya stir this, and I'll start the oatmeal," a smile slowly formed on Hephzibah's face, "there's no tellin' wot the captain moight do if he dun't start his day wif a hardy breakfast this fine day. He's liable to maroon us on an island," she chuckled

"Speaking of Captain Weston," Brenna brought up timidly, for she wasn't sure what to say, "I saw him…well…I couldn't help but notice how he acts around you."

"What are ya talking abaht?" Thankfully Brenna knew she could just ask because Hephzibah's smile never wavered.

"Well, he winked at you earlier…and…."

"Ya think he's sweet on little old me?" Now she really laughed. It quickly made Brenna join in.

"So, is he'?"

"Well now, isn't that the silliest thing ya ivva heard? Captain Weston, sweet on 'is own sister!" the older woman roared with delight.

"Wait…what?" Brenna stopped laughing once the news sunk in. When Hephzibah finished wiping her joyful tears, she continued.

"I should say, his much older sista. I came ta fettle on me brother's ship when my Mr. Melling passed on in the bloomin' war years agoa. I've been 'ere ivva since. But because we're pallies and all, I suppose I can let ya in on a wee secret. But you have ta promise to keep it to yourself. Can't av Weston's men losin' their respect for their fine captain. So would you loike to hear it?"

"Yes please!"

"As you prolly realize by now, I'm not like many folks."

That's for certain! Brenna instantly thought.

"Me mother was much more so…a strange and queer sort indeed! This ship is actually names afta her…Hester. Let's just say, she had a knack for pickin' names…Hephzibah Eloisa for example. But my wee brother had it much worse and he was horribly made fun of. That's why he onny goes by Weston," Hephzibah sighed.

"What is his name?"

"Allard Lynnwood Wensil Weston. The chuffin' reason for his menny names wor 'cos he was the only bloke bairn in three generations of Mother's family. And now ya know why he onny goes by Weston," Hephzibah chuckled, "So wot does thee think?"

"Oh dear," Brenna met her gaze and smiled.

"Well, enough of this gabbing, we've got a meal ta serve. And adam 'n eve, believe me child, when I say that it's a roight scary thin' to face a crew of 'ungry sailors, empty handed."

"This then is the message which we have heard of him, and declare unto you, that God is light, and in him is no darkness at all.

If we say that we have fellowship with him, and walk in darkness, we lie, and do not the truth:

But if we walk in the light, as he is in the light, we have fellowship one with another, and the blood of Jesus Christ his Son cleanseth us from all sin."

1 John 1:5-7

CHAPTER SIXTEEN

June 1839

O
h buggar...her again, Nate sighed heavily as he coiled up some rigging and watched Brenna slowly walk across the deck to her usual spot. Ever since the uppity girl had been found in the hold, it irritated Nate to no end with her presence.

What kind of captain is Weston that he would allow a stowaway to stay on board without so much as a word...then to treat her better than the crew, the thought itself made Nathaniel's temper stir. *If I were the captain, I would have taken advantage of her obvious wealth and held the brat for ransom. Otherwise throw her overboard and be done with it. Well, everyone else can play the fool in believing the girl's pathetic lies, but I won't. If she gets in my way, she'll be sorry.*

As if on cue, Brenna unintentionally began to approach. Nate gritted his teeth in frustration.

"Lay, heave to take in sail," the first mate called over the deck, "Haul up the jip on the main and trysail." Unfortunately, Brenna continued to walk right when Nate moved to heed the order. It caused him to trip over her. Nate swiftly got to his feet then turned his furious gaze to the girl.

"Move out of my way!" he grabbed Brenna by the arms and shook her. He didn't really know what had come over him, but the sailor's hold began to tighten. It was as if he took all of his frustration in life, out on her.

"Unhand me! You're hurting me," Brenna screamed.

Rob, who stood nearby, heard the almost blood curdling cry. He immediately dropped what he was doing and rushed over to see what all the commotion was about. He couldn't believe what he found.

"Hush you worthless stowaway!"

"Nate, what do ya think you're doin'? Stop!" Rob had to

shout over Brenna's cries, but Nate wouldn't cease. Rob had to rush up to him, catch both his arms, and pull until Brenna could get away.

"I won't play the fool any longer!" Nathaniel growled when he watched Rob approach the trembling and terrified girl.

"Have you gone mad?" Rob asked as he gently took Brenna by the hand and led her to Weston's cabin.

"What was all that about?" Samuel asked Nate as soon as they'd gone.

"Nothing."

"Well, I hope you didn't just ruin your chances of working for Captain Weston. Like I told you at the beginning of the voyage, Weston is a good captain to be workin' for."

"Leave me alone, Sam!" Nate shouted and finally returned to his intended duty, "It's none of your business anyway. Weston is a complete imbecile," the sailor said the last part under his breath.

Thankfully, when Rob was called to enter the captain's quarters, the sailor found Hephzibah already present.

"Hephzibah!" Brenna rushed over to her open arms.

"Gran' heavens child, what's happened?" Hephzibah 's gaze quickly shot from the upset young lady to Rob, and then to Weston in concern.

"What happened, Rob?"

"It's Nate…he hurt the lass."

"What? Why?" Hephzibah gasped as she hugged Brenna closer as if to protect her.

"Why did he do this?" Weston then asked.

"Dunno, Captain. I just heard the commotion and found him hurting her," the sailor solemnly replied. Silence filled the room, until Weston spoke.

"Please tell Nate I need ta speak to him."

As soon as Rob left, Hephzibah quickly lowered herself to Brenna's level.

"You poor thin'! Are ya quite alroight now?"

"I think so," Brenna sniffed.

"Don't worry lass. He won't hurt you ever again. I'll see ta it myself," Weston promised.

"Aye, you don't have to—" Hephzibah was swiftly cut off when a knock sounded at the door.

"Come in." Nate slowly entered and by the captain's tone, he knew whose side held Weston's favor.

"You wanted to see me?"

As if he didn't know, Hephzibah thought. She was taken aback by his obstinate attitude in his words and the way the sailor defiantly glared at Brenna. It caused the girl to cling onto Hephzibah even tighter.

"It's been told ta me that you av treated this young lady in disrespect." Hephzibah couldn't help but smile for she never tired of witnessing her brother turn from a kind and gentle man, to a successful captain who held authority.

"As you well know, I will not allow that kind of behavior from the crew, nor a bad tempered bloke employed on The Hester." Weston was fairly certain Nate would apologize at this, but he didn't. Instead the stubborn sailor starred at him, clenching his jaw tightly. There was something in his gaze that troubled Weston.

"What say you?" he finally asked.

"Well…if you're going to believe Rob and this lying stowaway—"

"I'm not a stowaway!" Brenna shouted, but was ignored.

"As I said, a worthless stowaway, then I don't want to work on this bloody ship anyway."

"It's a shame you feel that way," Weston replied and did an excellent job of hiding his amazement. No one talked to him that way, let alone a mere crewman. "You could av been a gran' sailor. Unfortunately you and you alone ruined it by abusing an innocent child and now you'll have ta face the consequences.

"What will it be, twenty lashes or the brig?" Nate sighed, his scathing tone never left.

"Impudent man…indeed, that's wot you are!" Hephzibah

couldn't take it any longer. Before she could finish speaking her mind, Weston calmly raised his hand to stop her.

"Nate, you are dismissed as of today."

"What? You can't do that…we're almost to London and I've already worked most of the voyage…you owe me!" Nate nearly shouted.

"Since *I* am the captain, I'll do as I think best. I could av you thrown over for such insolence. Instead, you will work for the remaining of the journey, for that's what you agreed ta. Once we dock in England, I'll only pay what you've earned until now. However," Weston's voice lowered, "If you continue ta cause trouble or refuse to follow orders, you won't get any pay whatsoever. Am I clear?"

"Fine," Nate said with a huff.

"Yes, sir," the captain quickly corrected him.

"Yes, sir," the sailor obstinately heeded Weston and left without another word, leaving Hephzibah prouder than ever.

CHAPTER SEVENTEEN

"*H*ephzibah , please wake up!" Brenna gently nudged her until she finally began to stir. Ever since The Hester docked in the London Harbor nearly a week earlier, Brenna never ~~seized~~ *ceased* in asking when they would begin the promised journey back to America. If the girl thought the voyage seemed to drag on, just sitting in the harbor, motionless, loading and reloading cargo, was endless. The day finally arrived as she gleefully found out on deck that very morning.

"Dear me...wot is it?" Hephzibah yawned.

"The ship! The ship is all unloaded. So now all they have to do is load it back up with cargo, then I can go home!" Brenna jumped up and down with excitement.

"Well, don't ya sound loike a regular sailor. You soun' as salt as Neptune himself, they say. Now all we've ta do is nip on the market and replenish our scran supplies," Hephzibah got up and poured water in the small basin to wash her face.

"I'll help."

How much she's changed. Hephzibah smiled to herself.

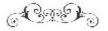

The city of London was nothing like Brenna thought it would be. All the beautiful sights and buildings were tainted by what surrounded them. The mere smell from the piles of trash and both animal and human waste was almost unbearable.

Inland must be better and cleaner than this, Brenna thought as her and Hephzibah made their way down the gangplank. *At least that's what it's like in Boston.* "Won't we need help carrying all the food once we buy it?" Another thought then crossed her mind.

"No, all I do when I go to the market, is orda all the supplies we need for the voyage, then me brother will send some of the crew ta fetch it. That way the store has time ta put the supplies in crates."

"Goodness…me legs aren't wot they used ta be," Hephzibah panted after some time had gone by.

"Will you be alright?" Brenna asked in concern, "How much further?"

"Not too much…if we tek a shortcut," Hephzibah stopped in front of a long alleyway. "The market is just through here," the minute she said it, a strange feeling crept up in her. But it disappeared as the pain in Hephzibah's knees reminded her of how tired she was.

"Through here?" Brenna hesitated.

"It will be jannock alroight," Hephzibah reassured as they slowly walked down the dingy street. They were about halfway down when she began to realize this wasn't a very safe decision on her part. This section of London could be less than honorable, especially when the contents of her money purse was considerably large. Right at that moment, Hephzibah's worst fear came to pass when she heard a low, strangely familiar voice.

"Well, well…what do we have here?" Both ladies quickly turned to where two men sauntered out of the shadows. One man reached down and slowly picked up a piece of wood that had fallen from the side of a rundown building. He pounded it in his hand, all the while wearing a wicked grin.

"Nathan, wot do you think your doin'?" Hephzibah breathlessly asked the other horrid man. After Weston fired the sailor and had him escorted off the ship once they docked, she thought she'd seen the last of him. She'd never seen the other bloke.

Probably just a hungry street urchin.

"I couldn't help but notice how heavy your money purse is. I could carry it for ya." As Nate spoke, Hephzibah silently pushed the trembling Brenna behind her.

"Now Nathan, you know thee shouldn't be doin' this. Just

nip on and leave us be." Brenna couldn't believe how calm
Hephzibah sounded. Her voice never wavered.

"The way I see it, your fool of a captain still owes me. But
instead, he chooses to give that brat his favor," Nate growled and
continued to approach, never letting his gaze stray from the
purse, "So hand over the money and we'll leave," the sailor
demanded, but Hephzibah didn't move.

"Oi…you 'eard 'im. 'and over the bloody purse!" the
stranger suddenly took action by rushing up and grabbing the
purse. What the two men didn't take into consideration was
Brenna's high pitched scream.

"Belt up, you!"

"Stay there, Harvey…I'll shush her," Nate also ran up and
immediately covered the girl's mouth. He was so rough that
Brenna thought her nose had broken from the force of his large
hand.

"Tek thy hands off her!" Something rose up in Hephzibah
that actually surprised her a bit. As a motherly instinct rose up in
her, how tired she was didn't matter anymore, nor her age. All
that was important was Hephzibah loved Brenna much more than
she thought.

With a force that came from something outside of herself,
Hephzibah grabbed a hold of Nate's hands that held Brenna and
sunk her nails into his flesh, all the while frantically searching for
something to defend herself with. Then she saw it. A rod from a
chair leg came into view, just a foot from her. Thankfully Brenna
chose that time to lash out, biting, scratching, and kicking the
unsuspecting sailor. It gave the older woman time to reach for the
item.

"Harvey, don't just stand there, get them off me," Nate
yelped as Hephzibah hit his head several times. Harvey, or so he
was called, was oblivious to his plead for he'd just grasped the
money purse. Once he realized what was happening, he dropped
the purse and tightened his hold on his own jagged piece of wood
in his other hand.

For a moment, Brenna thought Nate was about to give up, but then a loud thud was heard. She caught Hephzibah's gaze for just a second as time seemed to slow. It was as if Hephzibah was trying to tell her to get away from there by the frantic look in her eyes. Blood began to trickle down her face and her eyes rolled back as the older woman fell to the ground.

"Hephzibah!" Brenna cried and struggled to free herself from Nate. As soon as he caught sight of the unguarded money purse, he quickly released her. By the time Brenna knelt down beside the still figure, lying on her back, the blood that came from her forehead was transuding at a fierce rate. *?not according to my dictionary*

"Wake up! Please...come back to me," Brenna wept. With trembling hands, she quickly tore the hem from her dress to hold *clothing* over the awful wound. She was vaguely aware of the two men digging through the bag behind her, as if searching for treasure. They hastily let a few items fall until Nate found it. He slowly pulled out the money and then they were off. However, when they were about halfway down the alley, Nate abruptly came to a halt and turned to look at the pitiful scene.

"Why are ya stoppin'?" Harvey asked. Nate didn't answer as he slowly began to go back.

"We already av the bloomin' money...let's just go." But Nate continued. Harvey had little choice but to follow, since the sailor held the money.

Brenna didn't hear anything over her sobs, so she was completely taken back when Nate grabbed her hair and roughly pulled her to her feet.

"I say, let's just go," Harvey tried again.

"Be quiet and just hold her," Nate shoved the girl to his accomplice.

"Leave us alone!" Brenna screamed hoarsely, but it was no use. It was hopeless to try and get away. Nate turned from her and slowly walked over to Hephzibah. He glanced back at Brenna for just a moment to make sure she was watching, then violently kicked the lifeless body. No matter how much she struggled or shouted for help, she knew it was hopeless to get away. Nothing stopped the sailor from kicking Hephzibah twice more.

"And now to deal with you," Nate finally seized and turned his attention to Brenna, who quickly shut her eyes and waited for the inevitable blow. Then without warning, a large rock came flying out of nowhere and hit Nate directly on the head.

"Leave her be!" A strapping young man, no more than a couple years older than Brenna, stepped out of the shadows, holding another fist sized rock.

"This ain't none of your business," Harvey shouted in his direction. Brenna's eyes shot open and she watched in wonder as the boy threw the other rock at Harvey as he ran up to them. Harvey released her just as he shielded his head from yet another blow. All Brenna cared about was Hephzibah, so she darted over to her. She ignored the men struggling in the background as soon as she saw the older woman move ever so slightly.

"Oh Hephzibah, get up…don't leave me," Brenna fell to her side and begged.

"Everythin'…." Hephzibah began to whisper, but it was barely audible. Brenna had to lean in closer to hear and tried to calm her incontrollable sobbing. "Everything is goin' to be alroight," she tried her very best to sound reassuring, for she felt herself quickly fading. She blinked several times as if she could will herself to stay with the frightened girl.

"Please don't die and leave me alone! Please,"

"Dear…death is noffin' ta be afraid of," At this, Brenna began to weep again, fear was evidently all over her as she grasped Hephzibah's hand tightly. "If thee serve the King, then all it is, is simply fallin' asleep then when you wake up…you find yourself at home. It's just going home, golden love."

"I don't want to stay here. I want to go with you."

"God will always be wif ya," Hephzibah raised her hand, with Brenna's hand still clinging to it, and placed it on the girl's heart, "Right here."

"No! I want you," By now, the commotion behind them had all but stopped. The strange rescuer had managed to scare them off for the time being. Before Nate left he threatened that they would be sorry.

The young man raised his hand to his jaw where he'd been hit as he turned to look at the hysterical girl.

"I love you, Brenna," Hephzibah slowly shut her eyes and Brenna felt her hand go limp in her own. The girl was left, beside herself as she embraced Hephzibah with everything in her.

"God, don't let her die! Bring her back to me." At first the quiet stranger didn't know what to say. The sight cut him to the heart. He presumed them to be closely related and very dear to one another.

Why would someone want to harm this defenseless woman? He asked himself since he hadn't seen the much longed for money purse they'd gotten away with. All he knew was they had to get out of there as soon as they could.

"I'm sorry but we need to leave, now. They're going to come back." Brenna glanced up at him as if it was the first time she was aware of his presence.

"I won't leave her," Brenna stated and turned back to her lifeless friend. He momentarily moved his gaze to Hephzibah and knew there was no point in staying. She had passed.

Can't blame her…if it was someone I loved, no one would be able to persuade me to leave. No, he would have to go about it in an entirely different way. "We'll get help, I promise."

"You go get help and I'll wait here." Without moving, Brenna quickly replied,

"You don't understand. You have to come with me right away!" Whoever this child was, she was obviously used to getting her way. In a desperate act to save her life, the young man moved closer and took hold of her arm.

"Let go of me!" Brenna cried as she was pulled toward the main street. "I have to stay with her…Hephzibah!" By the time they emerged from the alley, Brenna was completely inconsolable. He tried to tell her to be quiet, but it was no use.

Someone is bound to think I'm abducting her! He thought. Once they were about two blocks away from the alley, the man finally stopped and turned Brenna to face him. All the while, holding her shoulders.

"Where are your parents?" he solemnly asked. The girl only sobbed in return.

"Do you have family close by? Why won't you tell me who you are so I can help you?" he finally sighed with frustration. *This is getting us nowhere.* Suddenly he caught sight of a constable walking down the road a ways.

"Take me back to Hephzibah," the girl choked.

"Come on," he ignored her yet again and led her down the street.

"Officer, someone has been assailed and they're badly wounded." Though he was convinced the woman in the alley was dead, he didn't want to be the one to break the young girl's heart. Thankfully the constable didn't ask any questions but hastily followed them back to the alley. Once they neared it, Brenna ran ahead a bit. As soon as she hurried around the corner, she froze in her steps.

Why is she just standing there? The young man thought, that is until he also came up behind the girl. It was indeed the very same alley, but there was no sign of the older woman.

"Where did she go?" Brenna took the words right out of his mouth. It was then they were reminded of the officer's presence.

"Did you happen to see who did this?" his snide remark was unmistakable.

"It was two awful men. She was lying right there," Brenna pointed further inside.

"Right…and what did you say your name was?" the constable slowly turned to face the boy, but he also seemed to vanish into thin air. "Now, where did he go?" he swiftly glanced down at Brenna, but she seemed just as surprised as he was. As he wandered out a bit to see if he could see where he had gone, Brenna slowly approached the spot Hephzibah had lain.

Where could she possibly have gone? Was she an angel or something? A thousand thoughts reeled through Brenna's mind as she gazed at the ground where she thought she saw some blood. "What's to become of me now?" she whispered to herself.

"For thou art my lamp,
O LORD: and the
LORD will lighten
my darkness."

2 Samuel 22:29

CHAPTER EIGHTEEN

April 1840

oseph gazed over the bow of the ship longingly. He wanted so badly to see land, yet there was nothing but blue waves that met the clear sky.

A year had passed and now he finally had enough means to return and marry. When he had asked Audrey to wait for him, he didn't realize then how difficult it would be. His determination had kept him going strong, but he wanted the waiting to be over now that he had made enough for them to live on.

Joseph sighed deeply as someone approached.

"Ah, you're thinkin' on your bride to be, aren't you?" Joseph turned to see Jake Harper grinning at him.

"Is it that obvious?"

"It's quite alright, my boy," Jake patted him on the back, "You've waited a long time. I dare say, the homecoming will be all the better. Have you given any thought about Edmond Thomas' offer?"

"Aboyt workin' for him permanently as second mate? Well…a bit. I don't nu if I can 'andle workin' directly under yer," Joseph joked.

"Hey, I'm not that bad, am I?"

"Naw…I've tart on it a bit. I nade ter pray on it more an' blather ter Audrey aboyt it. I wud enjoy it, yet at the same time, I wud be gone a lot."

"True. There's been talk that Edmond is lookin' into an offer to ship something different. Maybe the distance will be less or closer to home," Jake informed.

"Maybe I'll talk to him aboyt it." Joseph replied then looked out into the distance again.

"We'll be there soon enough." Jake knew his encouraging words wouldn't make the time pass any sooner. He could only chuckle at the young man's lovesome behavior.

"I'm glad I can amuse ya," Joseph smiled, partly embarrassed, "I'll git back to work nigh so as not to distract ya anymore." This only caused Jake to laugh all the more.

"Why hello, dear," Colm greeted when he looked up and saw Laura enter the shop. "What brings you 'ere? I'm just cleanin' up before locking up the shop an' comin' home," he wiped his hands on his apron. When she didn't say anything in reply, he glanced at her again. To his surprise she had tears in her eyes. Her arms were folded and she looked troubled.

"Laura, I'm sorry," Colm immediately came around the counter to her side. "What's wrong?"

"Nothin'...really," she sniffed. She finally met his gaze as her tears fell. "I wus in town today buyin' sum things...and...." Laura couldn't finish. She wiped her eyes but her hand lingered over the wrinkled, uneven skin at the edge of her face. Colm now knew what this was all about and it pained him.

"Dear," he gently put his hand on top of hers.

"People gawk at me. I'm nathin' more than a monster to them. How can you love me?"

"That's not true. Yer needn't struggle so. I thank God every day that you're alive. I almost lost ya."

"Why did ya marry me? I'm nathin'. I 'av nathin'...I had no means when we met...I'm too old ter give ya laddies."

"Laura, I didn't marry ya for children. I love you...no one else." Colm grasped both her hands. His words seemed to finally get through to her for a small smile broke through.

"I'm sorry," she then gave a quick laugh in embarrassment and finished wiping her tears. "Foolishness," she sighed as she regained her composer.

"Did you also go and see your ma today?"

"Aye, she's doin' pure well and enjoys workin' for the landlords. They are pure gran' to her."

"They're good people."

"I didn't think she wud ever allow 'erself to be happy

anywhere other than the place she lived. Once she realized an' accepted he wasn't comin' back…it's been nearly seven years, ya nu."

"Does she brin' him up at all?"

"Only rareley nigh. She often wonders what's ter becum of him if he ever did return cos he wouldn't nu where to find her. I told her surely if he did, he cud ask raun. I think it's better to accept him as gone, as hard as it might be."

July 1840

"Lord, as I just read in Your Word, I will do. 'I will commit my way unto the Lord. I will trust also in Him and He will bring it to pass,'" Audrey quoted out loud, "'And He shall bring forth my righteousness as the light…I rest in the Lord, and wait patiently for Him.'" She gazed up at the sky for some time, going over the wonderful verse. She eventually closed her Bible and stood with renewed purpose. She even felt lighter after giving her way and burden to her Heavenly Father.

Audrey had finished her devotions in the Primrose garden as she always did. Before going inside, and because it was such a beautiful day, she decided to go for a walk.

"Thank you, Lord for helping me to be patient. I could never have made it without You," Audrey prayed and let her feet carry her through the woods. Since she didn't have a planned destination she wandered further until the sea came into view. How beautiful it looked as it reflected the clear sky. She finally stopped and leaned against a tree as she looked out over the water. Because she was near the fish market, the same market she and Lanna had been forced to visit while captured by two St. Carlin sailors over two years earlier, Audrey spotted three fishing boats.

Most likely also taking advantage of the fair weather, she mused. She didn't know what kept her there, watching the boats. On this type of day it was hard to think of leaving for home.

I suppose I should go…if I'm to send Lanna's letter today. Audrey was about to leave when, out of the corner of her eye, she saw something white on the sea. Audrey squinted to get a better look at the large schooner. Her heart seemed to flutter at the thought that she might know the ship. For the past long months, Audrey thought every schooner she saw was the one she longed for above all others. Now she couldn't leave. Not until it came closer so she could distinguish the name or something that stood out to her. Because it was going at a fast speed she didn't have to wait long.

It is The Olivia! Audrey nearly jumped for joy. *He's here! Joseph has returned!* She quickly gathered her skirts and ran all the way back to Primrose.

Only a little while later, Audrey was on her way to the harbor. She was surprised to find that her mother wished to accompany her to meet The Olivia.

Audrey sighed and peered out of the carriage nervously. The last time she remembered being so impatient while traveling somewhere was when she sat in the exact same carriage with her grandfather. They had rushed to catch Joseph before he boarded a ship to leave for good, only to find him already gone, or so they had thought. They were pleasantly surprised later on.

Joseph could barely keep his thoughts on what he was doing when they let down the anchor in the tiny harbor. He was finally on his way to go to Audrey, who comsumed his thoughts, just as soon as he finished up his duties on board. He was in such a hurry to finish that it felt like a blur, that is until he saw her. Joseph, Jake Harper, and a few others were rowing to shore in a longboat when he caught a glimpse of two women emerge from a carriage. Joseph knew it had to be Audrey and her mother for they were practically the only women present at the harbor. His hopes were confirmed as one of them eagerly waved at him.

Audrey couldn't wait a moment longer and ran down to meet the boat. She could feel her heartbeat quicken in her redening face when Joseph met her gaze and smiled.

"Joseph, how are you?" she asked as soon as he set foot on land. They weren't aware of anything or anyone around them as they covered the distance between them.

"Grand nigh! I've painfully missed ya," Joseph grasped both of her hands. He fought the urge to do anything more than that for it wouldn't be proper. Furthermore, it had been awhile since he'd been able to clean himself up.

"I have missed you dreadfully as well."

"I am a witness to how much he's waited for this day. He's talked of nothing else the entire trip," Jake Harper stepped out of the boat and came behind Joseph.

"Is dat so?" Joseph looked at him as Jake ruefully winked.

"It has been no different here," Rose put in and also approached. They couldn't help but embarrass the couple. "You both must be exauhsted. Why don't we all go to Primrose so you can get rested and cleaned up a bit for dinner, for we have much to discuss." They readily agreed at her suggestion. Before Joseph had left a year earlier, he had made it clear what his intentions were towards Audrey and that he was leaving to earn enough to start a life on and to marry Audrey as soon as he returned. In Audrey and Joseph's oppinion, it couldn't be soon enough.

PART III

CHAPTER NINETEEN

Kenwood ~ Boston, Massachusetts   *June 1843*

see you're still hard at work, Brother," Theodore entered the study to find Edwin pouring over his books.

"Yes, can you believe the miser just left? I didn't think he would ever leave." His jovial reference to Professor Neylton, Edwin's private tutor, didn't get the simplest reaction out of Theodore. But what did Edwin expect? Everything had changed since that day nearly three years ago. All he'd attempted to do to rid themselves of their sister and the misery of knowing she was the only one who held their father's love had backfired. Edwin still would never admit it to be a mistake. It was too late anyway. Nothing could be done to change it. Edwin just wished his brother would realize this and put the past behind him. All he ever did anymore was attend Harvard University, then come home, greet Edwin before either sitting down somewhere, doing nothing but staring out the window, or retiring to do the same alone in his room. He was lifeless and appeared years older than his mere nineteen years.

Edwin was about to enquire as to his brother's day when Sedrick, Kenwood's butler, entered the room.

"Excuse me, young sirs. I'm to inform you that dinner will be served in the main dining room promptly at six." At this, both young men quickly looked at each other, then at Sedrick in question.

"I must have heard wrong," Edwin blurted.

"I assure you, tis true."

"Is Father to join us?" he asked again in disbelief.

"Yes," Sedrick couldn't help but smile. The Dorcet's had hardly spoken a few words to each other since Kylene's death, much less have dinner together other than special occasions with important guests.

Maybe there's hope for them yet, he thought and took his leave, shutting the door behind him.

Why now...after all this time, and now Father wants to dine with us? Edwin quickly stood and began to pace the room as his temper slowly rose.

"Well, I think he's lost his chance with us years ago. The minute he married that Irish—" Edwin abruptly stopped when Theodore suddenly spoke, "What if he's learned the truth?"

"What? Impossible."

"How can you be so sure?" Now it was Theodore's turn to stand, "We should've told father the horrible thing we did straight away, instead of ruining our lives with this guilt," he confessed fervently, with obvious pain in his voice. As much as Edwin disagreed with his brother, part of him was glad to see some life in him. He wasn't about to let this opportunity pass him by.

"You wouldn't dare reveal the truth to him now, after all this time. She's long gone now," Edwin knew he'd gone too far for Theodore marched up to him and looked like he was about to pummel him. He was within reach when he stopped and just glared at him.

"If I would have told the truth, like I should have, Brenna would be here safe and sound. All our lives would be far different." Theodore turned to leave without another word.

The clock finally struck six o'clock. Theodore sat up on his bed and sighed. Ever since he went to his room after talking with Edwin, he had tried to lie down and fall asleep, but sleep wouldn't come. All he could do was think about his past. Every thought was consumed with regret. For so long Theodore was certain he could do nothing to fix it, but now he even doubted that.

He was surprised at how nervous he was as he stood and washed his face. He then made his way downstairs, with every step his heartbeat quickened. What would he say? What could he say? William would never forgive him.

But at least the hidden truth won't torture me any longer, Theodore breathed in deeply before entering the dim dining room. To his surprise, Edwin and their father were already seated and actually holding a conversation, though it was one merely surrounded by The Dorcet Bank happenings, William hadn't discussed anything with his sons for years, other than Brenna and the lengths he had gone in his search for her.

"Sorry to keep you waiting," Theodore finally spoke as he nervously walked around the long table and took a seat. He could feel his brother's eyes on him the entire time. It was as if Edwin could read his thoughts.

"It's quite alright...son," William awkwardly replied. He couldn't believe how hard this was. *Since when is having dinner with my own sons so uncomfortable?* But William knew fully well that he was the only one to blame for it. Since he was at fault, only he could fix it and this dinner was the very start of his plan to do just that and more. He wasn't sorry for spending his every waking hour in attempts to find Brenna all this time, yet he regretted how he'd left his sons behind. They had never been close, but he somehow wanted to change that. He knew he had to be the one to mend things, but apologizing had never been easy for him.

"Is Benjamin to join us as well?"

"Well no. I wanted to dine with you and Edwin tonight."

"I see," Theodore stiffly replied.

Once the servants began to serve the meal, William was still having a hard time coming up with conversation. He could tell that his sons felt the same as they silently began to eat.

"Theodore, how are your studies faring?" Theodore nearly jumped at his father's question before glancing up from his plate.

"Oh, uh...just fine. It's going just fine," he stuttered and quickly took a drink of water, just about choking in the process. At first William thought it was just him, but when he looked in Edwin's direction, he found a bewildered expression on his face as well. He then returned his gaze to Theodore. It was the first time he'd really looked at him in quite a while.

When did he become so thin and sickly looking? William mused.

"My studies are going quite well," Edwin spoke up, trying to help the tense atmosphere, but William wasn't listening.

"Are you feeling alright lately? You're slightly pale." He decided to just ask instead of wondering about his son any longer.

"No…it's not that," Theodore's gaze never left his untouched plate. In truth, he was trying to ignore his brother's glare. He could hardly breathe as the familiar sickening feeling in the pit of his stomach came upon him. Theodore had suffered this as a result of guilt every single day since, yet this time it was far worse, for he knew there was no turning back now.

"I…have something to tell you," he finally spoke, but Edwin quickly cut in, "Theodore, no!" William's gaze quickly shot to him. He appeared to be so unsettled about something that he nearly came out of his chair.

"What is going on here?" William put down his fork on his plate with a little more force than he'd intended. The act caused a cold sweat to come over Theodore.

"It has to do with Brenna's disappearance." Now it was William's turn to fight the urge to stand to his feet. "Three years ago, we were down by the harbor. We locked Brenna in a trunk and left for a while to teach her a lesson. When we returned to let her out, the trunk was gone." There, he'd said it. The truth he'd miserably kept hidden for so long was finally revealed. It did nothing to make him feel any better.

"What are you saying?" William stood up so quickly that his chair fell over. He angrily pointed at Edwin, "Did you have a part in this as well?"

"No, it was Theodore's idea and he forced me into helping him," Edwin replied and boldly met his father's enraged stare. Theodore marveled at his brother's ability to blatantly lie to William's face.

You knew this would happen…that Edwin would lie and put the blame on you, Theodore told himself, *I might as well face this head on and take what's coming to me. Being spineless got me into this mess, but it will stop here,* he took a deep breath and forced himself to glance up.

"The trunk was cargo, so it was taken aboard a ship...bound to England," Theodore waited for William to explode, but he didn't move or say a word. He just stood there in shock. Theodore couldn't believe he was thinking this, but he almost wished his father would rant and shout at him instead of this. He couldn't bare William's distraught expression.

"We...I didn't mean for it to happen, truly I didn't," Theodore swiftly looked over at Edwin, who held his head in his hands. William never did say anything, instead he stiffly walked out of the room. However, he had never been more outraged. If only his sons knew how close he was to losing all self-constraint and taking all of his anger, which had been held for far too long, out on Theodore.

William hurried up the stairs, planning to lock himself in his room to think, when he passed Brenna's room. It had been untouched since the day she disappeared and William had shut the door to it nearly a month later. It was far too painful to look inside as he passed. Even to the day, William had to continuously keep himself from stopping in front of it. But not today, not when he finally learned the horrible truth.

He approached and slowly opened the door. Tears immediately blurred his vision. He'd been searching for so long, all in vain. The horrible fact seemed to echo in his mind as he moved to the large white vanity. William carefully picked up Brenna's hairbrush that used to belong to Kylene as if it was glass. Some of Brenna's beautiful dark hair could still be found on it.

If I would've known the truth right away, I could have saved her. At that moment, an urge to pray and ask God for help came from somewhere deep within him. *It's what Kylene would do if she was alive.* Unfortunately, William's anger quickly overshadowed everything else. *How could Theodore keep Brenna's disappearance from me for so long?* As he continued to scan the grand bedroom, William found the answer to his question. He wouldn't deny that he loved Brenna above his sons.

"I will find her!" he told himself. *And if I find out that any harm has come to her, Theodore...and Edwin will suffer the consequences!* William suddenly realized that in his temper, he was about to brake Brenna's brush. He swiftly set it down and made his way to the hall. He had to start making plans to travel to England as soon as possible.

But where should I start? Oh Brenna, where could you be after all this time?

"Then spake Jesus again unto them, saying, I am the light of the world: he that followeth me shall not walk in darkness, but shall have the light of life."

John 8:12

CHAPTER TWENTY

*t seemed like an eternity before dawn. At least it did to Theodore. He had tossed and turned all night, but he was used to it by now. He hadn't slept through the night for years now. Part of him thought he would feel better once he was able to get the truth off his chest.

Although he sought morning, Theodore dreaded leaving his room. His father hated him, along with his brother.

But the worst is already over, right? I've already broken the worst to him. Perhaps now we can put the past behind us and finally move on...perhaps one day with time, Theodore forced himself to open the door and make his way downstairs, but not before noticing that William's door was open and the room empty. Theodore's plan was to quickly eat some breakfast alone, then leave for the university. As soon as he neared the dining room and heard commotion, he abruptly stopped. He slowly peaked around the corner and saw Edwin reading the morning paper while finishing his meal.

Do I dare go in and face his wrath or should I just leave now? Theodore stood in indecision until he finally gained enough courage. *I have to face him sooner or later...I might as well get it over with,* he crept into the room as if his brother wouldn't notice him if he was quiet enough. Theodore was about to sit, but decided against it. He could already sense the animosity Edwin felt towards him.

"Uh, have you seen Father?" There, he'd sliced through the tense silence like a knife.

"Why, so you can tattle even more?" Edwin snapped, momentarily putting down the paper to glare at him. Suddenly Theodore felt very foolish. How could he think Edwin would treat him any different? Edwin was Edwin and he would never change. Since he knew fully well what his brother was like, Theodore wouldn't even try to argue.

"Have you seen him or not?"

"I must know one thing. Why bring it up…after all this time? Why now?" Edwin slammed the newspaper down on the table.

"You of all people wouldn't understand," Theodore sighed heavily and turned to leave, "It was the right thing to do and something I should have done long ago."

Just as he was about to open the front door to leave, William burst in without warning. He appeared to be excited about something, for he could barely stand still.

"I need to talk to you and Edwin. Where is he?" William didn't wait for a reply as he rushed past him and down the hall where he obviously found who he was looking for. Theodore dutifully followed, all the while scolding himself for not departing straight away. He would have missed whatever was about to happen.

"Edwin, there you are. I have something to tell both of you," William hurriedly took a seat. Edwin froze, worried that his father had somehow learned the truth. Again, William didn't wait until Theodore was seated before he began.

"I've hired a ship to take us to England," he swiftly got to the point as if it was the simplest of things.

"What?" Both young men blurted in shock.

"It will set sail for London in three days' time. I've already posted a letter to a British Private Detective. It is my hope that it will arrive before we do so we can begin our search as quickly as possible," William stood without giving them time to process what he'd just told them, and continued. "Pack your things quickly…I'm off to the bank to speak with Loren."

"Wait! Isn't this a little sudden?" Edwin stood also. Theodore on the other hand, just sat there stunned. He never thought this would happen. Anything but this.

"Can't we discuss this more?" Edwin's request was completely ignored when Sedrick entered.

"Mr. Davis is here, sir."

"Perfect, just the man I wanted to see," William quickly followed the butler to the door.

"Look what you've done!" Edwin moved closer to Theodore, who starred at him blankly. Thankfully he didn't say more, but instead went to see what Loren would have to say about this.

Father has gone mad...completely mad, Theodore slumped in his chair and buried his face in his hands. His brother's words played over and over in his mind. He thought once he confessed everything would get better. Now he regretted his actions even more.

We'll be searching all of England for someone who might be dead.

"Loren, just the man I want to see," William greeted his brother-in-law, as Edwin silently approached.

Surely Uncle can talk some sense into him. He's the only man he trusts, his musings were swiftly interrupted as Loren spoke.

"I came by to see if you're alright, since you weren't at the bank this morning," he momentarily glanced over at Edwin as if to gauge the situation by his nephew's expression. Like William's late wife Harriet, Loren had been strategically picked to marry Elizabeth Dorcet by none other than William's father. All for the gain of the Dorcet Bank. But William always thought the arrangement far more fortunate because Loren and Elizabeth had loved each other from the start. Unlike his own miserable marriage, even if it was only for a brief time. Even since the arranged marriage, Loren and William worked side by side. They were like brothers.

"I'll explain everything," William put his arm around Loren, "In my study," he then led him away, not even acknowledging his son's presence.

Blast, now I won't hear what Loren will say about the matter, Edwin thought as he watched them walk down the hall. However, just when Loren was about to disappear into the other room, he caught Edwin's gaze and winked. In other words, Loren would talk to him later.

It wasn't long before Theodore heard voices emerge from his father's study. Theodore still hadn't moved from his place in the dining room. He had been contemplating what his next move would be, but it was no use.

"Where are you off to now?" He heard Loren ask William.

"I must go to the bank to obtain enough means to purchase supplies quickly if we're to leave in three days' time," William informed then rushed out the front door. Once he was gone, Loren headed into the dining room to find Theodore.

"I heard father leave," Edwin also entered and walked to the other end of the large table to sit as far away from his brother as possible. Loren however, moved closer to him and put his hand on his shoulder.

"Is everything William told me true?"

"I'm afraid so," Theodore quietly answered, but he couldn't make himself look up at him. "What else did he say?"

"Well, after telling me about hiring a vessel, he wants me to oversee all of his affairs here at Kenwood and at the bank until you return. If truth be told, William's exact words were *if* you return. He left to gather funds from the bank before I could question him further."

"So, what are we to do now?" Edwin asked with a sigh.

"I tried to talk some sense into him, but the one thing I know about your father above all else is, once William is set on doing something, it's impossible to change his mind," Loren paused for a moment and glanced back down at Theodore. He could tell just by looking at his nephew that he was torturing himself about everything to no end. "I'm afraid we most likely won't able to stop William from going to England, although I will keep trying to reason with him. I might have an idea so that he would at least let you two stay in America."

"Why not let Theodore go…seeing it's his fault we're in this mess," Edwin grumbled and scowled at his brother yet again.

"Now, now, this isn't the time to put the blame on anyone." The minute Loren said this, Theodore sighed, but there wasn't the slightest bit of relief in it. "If we're to come up with a worthy plan, we must put the blaming aside and focus. Now, here's what I'm thinking…."

CHAPTER TWENTY-ONE

"We know you want to find her, of course you do, any father would. But we just feel this to be a little extreme," Loren took Elizabeth's hand, who sat next to him on the settee, to gain some support as he tried yet again to change his brother-in-law's mind. William was proving to be immovable as time went on.

All the Dorset's had come to their home to have one last meal together before they were to set sail in the morning. Throughout the evening, Loren and his wife hinted and tried everything they could think of to convince them to stay. And now that Benjamin had fallen asleep playing in front of the fire, the Davis' could get down to the matter since it would be their last chance. Sadly it wasn't going according to plan, for the minute they had retired to the sitting room, and Loren opened his mouth to speak, William set his jaw in stubbornness.

"William, surely you can see that Loren speaks the truth." Elizabeth took her cue when Loren squeezed her hand gently.

"You can't expect to arrive in London and see Brenna walking down the street. England is very large. Furthermore, it's been some time. How can you be certain you'll recognize her?"

"Of course I'll know her! I would know my Brenna anywhere!" William angrily replied. His annoyance was apparent.

"I know you love her dearly, we all do," Elizabeth momentarily wavered. She knew she had touched a nerve her brother had managed to keep hidden. *Maybe we are being too hard on him.* Thankfully, Loren came to her rescue.

"We just want you to clearly think this through. Why move your entire family across the ocean when there are so many factors you don't know. Where could a young girl have gone once the ship arrived in England? What if the ship did what they usually do to stowaways…perhaps the trunk didn't get loaded onto the right ship? What if the ship didn't even make it or what if they didn't find her in the trunk?" Loren glanced over at the very silent Edwin and Theodore. For a moment he'd forgotten they were in the room. "I know it's horrible to think this way, but—"

"Enough!" William quickly got up and shouted, "I don't want to hear anymore! Why did I come here?" he then stormed out. The uncomfortable, yet familiar tense silence filled the room.

"Loren," Elizabeth wiped a tear from her cheek.

"I know, but I had to speak the truth," he sighed and turned to Theodore, who looked as if he was about to be sick.

"Well, the time for our plan is now or never, son. I've tried all I can. Now you must stand up to him." Theodore felt frozen with fear. It took all the strength he could muster to get to his feet and slowly leave to find his father.

We come to say goodbye and have one last meal together, and they had to ruin it. Why did we even come? He didn't have much time to think as Theodore quietly came up behind him. William swiftly composed himself before facing his son.

"We're leaving now, so get your brother and wake up Benjamin." William started to move toward the door, but Theodore stiffly stood in the way. He met his son's gaze, planning to tell him to move, when Theodore spoke.

"Wait…a moment. I just have to say…I don't have words to express how sorry I am and how much I regret what I've done," his voice was hoarse and filled with emotion. William was completely taken aback by it. It was the last thing he ever thought he would hear. However, the refreshing, yet at the same time sorrowful confession quickly became distasteful as he continued,

"As much as it's difficult to hear what Loren and Elizabeth speak of," Theodore gulped, "I agree with them." William grimaced and quickly looked away in disgust. His father never looked him in the eye, and now that he finally did, although for a brief moment, Theodore began to doubt the plan. He knew fully well that what he was planning to say next would not bode well, but he had to. This was his only chance to spare himself and his brothers from searching all over England for someone who was most likely deceased.

"Well, it doesn't matter who or what you agree with, now does it? No one is asking for your opinion," William then approached and strangely enough touched his son's arm, but it wasn't an act of affection. He was merely pushing Theodore aside so he could pass by and leave. "Come along, we're leaving straight away." He began to walk away, so in a desperate act to stop him, Theodore forced himself to swiftly continue.

"I won't be going with you in the morning." William came to a halt just as he had hoped.

"What?" At his cold tone, Theodore almost wished his father wouldn't have stopped and turned to face him. "I say, what was that?"

"Seeing as I'm…of age, I would like to remain here and finish my education." He was doing a horrible job of standing up for himself, but he couldn't back down now.

"And what if I was to disown you and have you thrown out of Kenwood?" By William's furious tone of voice, it was obvious that he was seething. Theodore was glad he hadn't revealed more of the plan that Edwin wasn't to accompany him either. At least he wouldn't mention it just yet.

"Loren has offered to let me stay with him and Elizabeth," Theodore braced himself, but William didn't move. He slowly began to shake with rage. Theodore looked down for but a second. When he glanced back up, he didn't have time to think for his father charged towards him and didn't stop until he roughly pinned Theodore against the wall.

"Don't speak to me with such insolence!" It wasn't until the pain in his back momentarily subsided that Theodore realized William was only inches from his face and his hand around his neck. "It's because of you we're in this unspeakable mess, so you are going to do everything in your power to get her back!"

William's grip was slowly getting tighter. It took everything in him to finally release Theodore and walk away, leaving his son gasping for air and feeling like a hopeless coward.

CHAPTER TWENTY-TWO

*T*he morning came bright and clear. The calm winds promised that the sailing would be easy. The crew had been working long before dawn, loading the necessary cargo to make sure they'd be ready to leave as soon as possible. William and the boys were just finishing up directing the crew as to where to put the rest of their belongings when they saw a carriage approach. William immediately recognized it and was surprised to see Loren and Elizabeth emerge from it after it came to a halt.

"We had to come to see you off," Elizabeth forced a smile as she walked over to embrace the somber Theodore, Edwin, and Benjamin as Loren slowly moved to William's side.

"I didn't think you would come," William stiffly spoke but didn't turn to shake his brother-in-law's outstretched hand. Instead, he continued to stare at the busy ship before them.

"I'm fully aware that you think I'm heartless, but I'm not entirely unfeeling. You're like a brother to me." When Loren placed his hand on William's shoulder, he finally glanced over at him, his gaze still guarded.

"I think of you dearly as well. I only wish you weren't trying to continually change my mind when I'm immovable. Why couldn't you have supported my decision? Our last moments together could have been far different."

"But can't you see you're making a mistake?" Loren tried to interject, but William continued on.

"Instead, you go behind my back which you had no right to do." Loren was dumbfounded. As much as he knew William spoke the truth, he hated the feeling of being caught in his own scheme. "I would have embraced you and thanked you for your help, but now I don't know what to say other than, never make plans with my son behind my back." With that, he walked away from Loren and made his way to his sister.

"Goodbye, dear."

"Goodbye," Elizabeth replied and quickly kissed his cheek. Tears streamed down her face.

This was the scene that Captain Vincent Pearce came upon. He didn't want to intrude on this solemn family gathering, but he had to. William made it very clear that he wanted to leave as quickly as they could.

"Sir, the ship is completely readied and waiting for you to say the word."

"We'll leave straight away." William quickly replied. "Edwin, Theodore, come along." He then took Benjamin, who was crying, by the hand and followed the Captain up the gangplank, never looking back to Loren or his sister. Benjamin on the other hand, waved goodbye to them.

Edwin and Theodore shook their uncle's hand while he tried to offer them one last word of encouragement.

"I'm sorry we couldn't change your father's mind, but I'm sure everything will be alright. It will all work out in the end as soon as he realizes his decision to be foolish." Unfortunately, as they slowly made their way to the ship, Theodore knew it would be a long time before William would ever admit to being wrong. It was then that Edwin spoke to him for the first time in days.

"I've never hated anyone more than I loathe you at this moment," he said through clenched teeth. Theodore would have preferred his brother's silence rather than this, especially when he was helpless to change anything. Edwin quickened his pace to rid himself of Theodore and once on deck, he followed his father into Captain Pearce's quarters.

"Papa, can't they come with us?" Benjamin whimpered when they were seated across from the large desk and William lifted him onto his lap.

"No, Son. Loren and Elizabeth must stay here." William swiftly answered and glanced at Edwin as he also took a seat.

"Where is Theodore?" Edwin didn't reply and pointed toward the door.

"Proceed, we've already set sail so we have more than

enough time to go over things," the captain calmly sat back as William rose.

In the back of his mind, William wouldn't have been surprised to have found that Theodore had jumped overboard in one last desperate attempt to try to stay in America. However, once William emerged, he immediately found Theodore leaning against the rail, gazing at the ever decreasing Boston. For the first time since finding out the truth, William felt a pang of guilt, although very small. He was after all taking his family from the only home they'd ever known. Before William could remember that it was his son's fault for everything, he slowly, almost timidly approached until he leaned on the rail right beside Theodore. He didn't look at him, but out of the corner of his eye, William could see that his son wouldn't acknowledge him in the least. He just kept his gaze outward. While trying to think of what to say, William nonchalantly looked over at him without turning his head. It was then he noticed small bruises on Theodore's neck, just above his collar.

Most likely where I took ahold of him last night, William shamefully recalled. Sometimes in his rage, he would forget his exact actions. Now he really felt chagrined.

"I want to apologize for my actions last night. I again lost my temper…something I promised myself I would never do again." For the first time in years, William placed his hand on Theodore's back. He didn't notice his act caused his son to nearly wince in pain. The bruises on Theodore's neck were nothing compared to his back that had hit something like a doorknob when thrown against the wall. Theodore tried his best to hide it from his face. His father's touch brought on something stronger than his pain, unfortunately, not stronger than his hate.

"I am sorry." Theodore never did move or say anything as William repented again before going back to the captain's quarters.

"And this is the condemnation, that light is come into the world, and men loved darkness rather than light, because their deeds were evil.

For every one that doeth evil hateth the light, neither cometh to the light, lest his deeds should be reproved.

But he that doeth truth cometh to the light, that his deeds may be made manifest, that they are wrought in God."

John 3:19-21

CHAPTER TWENTY-THREE

July 1843

dwin awoke with a start. For a few moments he gazed at the close ceiling, trying to remember exactly where he was. It swiftly came to him as voices from the crew came from outside, just like the noise that had awaken him. They talked loudly as they passed by his cabin. Edwin heard them saying something about all hands on deck. Because of his curiosity, he quickly dressed and emerged from his cabin.

By the time he arrived on deck, the commotion was right before him. Most of the crew was gathered in front of the quarter deck, including the Dorcets, looking up at Captain Pearce.

"You all know that I don't tolerate thievery on my ship," his booming voice was quite intimidating as it echoed over the deck. "If anyone knows who has done this, you have until eight bells to confess or tell me. Otherwise we will begin searching your things."

Fear rose up in Edwin, something that happened very rarely. After glancing over to Theodore and his father and saw they were preoccupied, he slipped away unnoticed. Once he shut the door to his cabin, he rushed over to his trunk and knelt down by it. Digging through his things, he eventually found it and slowly lifted it out. The jewels surrounding the golden pocket watch were so large they glistened in the meager light from the small cabin. It was the most beautiful and costly watch he'd ever seen. Even the fob was gold and had small gems on it. It wasn't as though Edwin had to steal it from the Captain's desk drawer only the previous day for mere greed, want, or need. He and his family were of great wealth and Edwin had more than he could ask for. He stole it for the one and only reason that Edwin was Edwin. He wasn't really certain why he wanted it for himself. Even as Edwin stared at the precious token he asked himself why. Was it the thrill that he could get away with something so devious? Perhaps boredom? Or was it something deeper like gaining his father's attention? However, Edwin never thought things through for very long as his brother did. Who cared why he'd stolen it? Now it was a matter of what he should do with it? Never did he regret his actions. He just knew he couldn't leave the watch with his belongings.

I'll just have to keep it on me at least until I can come up with a better plan.

Just as soon as he carefully slid the article into the inner pocket of his vest, the door opened and in walked Theodore. Edwin tried to keep calm as he turned to see his brother eying him.

"What do you want?" he lamely asked. *Did he see the watch?* Edwin wished he knew if Theodore was suspicious or not.

"It's time for breakfast. Didn't you hear the bells?" Theodore slowly asked.

"Oh, right," Edwin nervously walked to the open door before Theodore could say anything else. He almost escaped when his brother did indeed question him.

"What were you doing in here?" He glanced around the room, looking for anything out of place.

"Doing what anyone else does in his cabin." With that he left with a little more speed than usual.

It was nearing twelve o'clock and Edwin still hadn't decided what to do with the pocket watch. He nonchalantly roamed the deck in hopes of an idea and to stay away from his inquisitive brother. Suddenly he saw it! Tripped over it, to be exact. A worn jacket lay against some rigging where Edwin was walking.

How easy is this? He looked around to see if the owner was nearby, but everyone was about their duties and completely ignoring the guests that usually spent time on deck. Without any hesitation whatsoever, Edwin took the watch from his pocket and placed it in the pocket of the jacket.

Quite easy indeed, he smiled to himself and moved away. He stayed on deck to see how it would all work out. Would the captain keep his word about searching everyone's things? Edwin didn't even know which unsuspecting victim owned the jacket.

Sure enough, as soon as the bells rang, which usually meant lunch time, Captain Pearce, along with his officers started to search through everyone's belongings. Even their own things were gone through. No one was exempt, other than the captain of course.

Nearly an hour later, the officers reappeared on deck empty handed. That was the first time Edwin saw someone wearing the jacket! It was the first mate of all people.

When did he get his coat and how did I miss it? The only other thought that crossed the boy's mind was curiosity as to what would happen next.

The captain was speechless when he found his officers without anything. His only question was incredulous.

"Have you searched your own pockets?" The six officers looked at each other solemnly, but since they had nothing to hide, or so they thought, they heeded the captain. The first mate froze while his face grew pale. Other than Edwin, no one seemed to notice his fearful expression. Edwin could tell the sailor didn't know what to do. He remained stiff with his hand in his pocket, trying to avoid the captain's gaze at all costs. For a brief moment, Edwin thought he saw the first mate look at him, almost locking his gaze with his.

Impossible...no one saw me touch his jacket. When the men were finished searching themselves, the first mate could hide no longer.

"Nate, what are you hiding?" Everyone's eyes were on the pocket watch as he pulled it out.

"I don't know where this came from! I tell you the truth, I didn't take it or put it in my pocket of all places. I'm not daft!" He was completely ignored as Captain Pearce motioned for the officers to hold him. Nathan kept on and only got louder as the captain spoke.

"Let this be an example to anyone who thinks I will abide larceny on my ship." He then turned to Nate, "Flog him."

"No! I didn't steal anything!" As the sailors carried him away, Captain Pearce swiped his pocket watch from Nate's hand.

"I could do far worse or throw you off my vessel to be rid of you."

Any ordinary person with a conscience would have cringed at the painful cries coming from the other end of the ship. Everyone on deck was silent as they were forced to listen to the wails over and over. Edwin didn't say anything either, though his thoughts weren't on the poor first mate, but on his own skin, thankful that he'd rid himself of the watch when he did.

Twenty lashes was the customary amount for theft. When it finally ended, two men brought Nate back to stand in front of the captain. Everyone pretended to go about their business, yet remained quiet so they could hear what he was about to say.

"You no longer carry any rank. Broic Forester will take your place as first mate. Now get back to work, for a theif doesn't deserve to rest." *thief*

That night, as Edwin made his way to his cabin from the dining room. He still hadn't one ounce of remorse over the whole matter. However, he was beginning to feel a bit nervous for Theodore was getting more suspicious as the time wore on. It was as if he knew he'd been up to something.

He's gotten involved in enough of my business. Edwin was just rounding the corner when he heard something. At least he thought he heard someone's whisper. He momentarily stopped but didn't turn to see who it was. That part of the hall happened to be one of the darkest of the ship. He couldn't have seen anyone if he tried.

Is this what a guilty conscience is? A whisper? It was only a fleeting thought for whoever it was spoke again.

"I know it was you." Edwin's eyes widened, but he kept

completely still.

"It was you who did this to me. Well, you'll be sorry. You'll be sorry for what you did!" Nate stepped forward into the dim light and smiled as the young man broke into a run and was gone.

CHAPTER TWENTY-FOUR

August 1840

"No! Let me go!" she screamed until one of her brothers covered her mouth. As much as she struggled, they easily threw her inside the trunk and shut the heavy lid, leaving her engulfed in darkness. "Papa! Save me, help…someone!" It was a darkness so dense it seemed to smother her. Brenna cried until she was hoarse and pulled her knees closely against her. A dim, eerie light eventually shone before her out of nowhere. She was drawn to it like a moth to a flame until she recognized where she was. The dingy alley, filled with heavy fog, beckoned her to enter. Because Brenna knew what lay within, she quickly tried to turn away from it, but only ended up moving deeper into the alley. She felt herself break into a sweat when she neared the horrible place. Her desire to look around swiftly faded when out of her peripheral vision laid a figure, crumpled on the ground, deathly still. Brenna knew fully well who it was. Right at that moment, something up ahead caught her gaze. Out of the thick shadows someone held out their hand, strong and sure. It wasn't reaching for her, but waiting for her to grasp it. Although she didn't know who it was, she was persuaded that it held her only protection. Urgency rose up in her to go to it. Brenna apprehensively stepped forward. While at first she thought it was her own steps she heard, something or someone else was following her and it did not bode that same feeling. It felt as if fear itself pressed in behind her. She was almost to the hand! If only she could move faster! Brenna desperately reached out to it when the darkness from behind overtook her. The presence was all too real as it placed a hand on her shoulder, sending shivers through her. Brenna was now only inches from the hand when the shadow pulled her back. She screamed and thrashed but was overpowered by the darkness.

127

The morning was calm, much to the relief to everyone on board The Florentine.

"Thank goodness," William breathed as soon as he awoke and realized the room was no longer being pitched about as it had for the past three days. He could barely contain himself as he quickly got out of his bunk and woke up Benjamin, who slept in the bunk directly above him.

"Son, the storm is over! Time to get some fresh air." Needless to say, their cabin seemed to have closed in on them. Especially the smell that followed the seasickness they had been cursed with.

Though a considerable amount of damage had been done, things seemed to be in order as far as William could tell. He and Benjamin emerged from the hatch, wove their way through the crew, who worked tirelessly to repair everything, until they made their way to the quarter deck.

"Captain, how did we fair through the tempest?" William called from their place on the lower deck. He didn't even try to climb the stairs to where Captain Pearce stood by the helm, for there was far too much commotion. He didn't want to get in the way.

"As well as can be expected. We're not too far off course. We had to let it drive when the main and trysail were damaged." Pearce motioned upward. William followed his gaze to find two sailors towering over them, working on a sail.

Theodore and Edwin were just as eager to escape their stuffy cabin. As soon as they arrived on deck, someone suddenly shouted.

"Watch out below!" At first, the boys didn't know where the warning came from. Out of nowhere a large sail seemed to fall from the sky! Immediately following the loud crash was a child's scream. Theodore and Edwin knew the only child aboard was their brother. They both rushed across the deck. The closer they got, the clearer they could hear what exactly Benjamin was crying.

"Papa, Papa!" William unconsciously laid under the sail that looked ten times larger up close. The captain and several crewmen quickly approached and lifted it off of his lifeless body.

"Poor bloke, hit 'im right on the 'ead," one sailor said.

"Still breathin'," another put in. Captain Pearce glanced up from William, then to the three young men. Theodore was trying to comfort Benjamin, while Edwin just stood there staring at his father blankly, almost unfeeling.

"Take him to his cabin…take heed to do it carefully," the captain chose not to say more. At least not in front of William's family. In truth, he didn't think Mr. Dorcet would ever come to from such a blow. Then what would he do? They were almost to England.

All we can do is wait. Time is all we have. Pearce mused as he solemnly watched the three young men follow the sailors, who carried their father away.

As they laid William on his bed, Theodore couldn't help but think this was some kind of punishment from God. He had done some horrible things and so had William.

I don't even dare ask God for mercy. Maybe He will spare Benjamin. What will we do if he dies? Theodore gazed down at his father and took Benjamin's hand when he started to sniffle again. William was breathing but very shallow. Although he was sorry this had to happen, Theodore was waiting for some kind of feeling or emotion to rise up in him. He almost envied his little brother. Had all that had happened numbed him somehow? He then noticed Edwin standing behind him, by the door.

Well, I know he doesn't have any feeling…no conscience at all. Theodore didn't know what to think about his brother anymore. Only that he was hated by him and that he was up to something, for he was much more silent than normal.

"But the path of the just is as the shining light, that shineth more and more unto the perfect day.

The way of the wicked is as darkness: they know not at what they stumble."

Proverbs 4:18-19

CHAPTER TWENTY-FIVE

athan slowly made his way down the lay board side of the deck, going about his now meager duties. He grumbled to himself nearly the entire time while swabbing down the weathered plank flooring. He neared the quarter deck when he glanced up and saw Broic Forester, doing what should have been his job. The way the younger sailor pompously held the wheel made Nate cringe with disgust.

If I ever get my hands on that boy, there's no telling what will become of him! Nate scanned the deck for any sign of Edwin Dorcet, but he knew he wouldn't find him. He stayed close to his still unconscious father's side. *Hiding for his life, no doubt.*

"Lay there, Losce," Broic called to Nate, obviously taunting him with his new rank. Nate looked around him for any sign of Captain Pearce before voicing what he thought of Brioc's insolent command. The captain was nowhere to be seen.

It's strange for him not to be on deck at this time of day. He held his fury in check with his newfound curiosity. "Where is the captain?" Broic didn't answer straight away. *Probably too good to speak to the likes of me now.* "I say, where is the captain?" Nate asked again.

"He's ill—"

"Oh...so you are in command...I know," Nathan finished for him. *No need to remind me.*

"You did this to yourself, not me," Broic calmly replied.

"What? No I didn't. I didn't do anything I tell you!" It was no use arguing with Nate, so Broic said nothing and turned back to the helm.

Nate walked away in a huff, when suddenly an idea came to him.

With the captain sick, how easy would it be to get rid of the troublesome family and take their means? Nathan, as the first mate, had watched Pearce lock up the Dorcet's hefty amount in his quarters. *William Dorcet most likely won't wake up. We could easily get away with it.* However, he knew the only way to pull off something like this was for Broic Forester to go along with it. *I'll just have to see if I can convince that dog to go along with me and find out just how ill the captain truly is.* Nate walked a little taller as he finished up. Maybe all wasn't lost.

Days had passed and Captain Vincent Pearce was still confined to his quarters. In fact, a sailor, who doubled as The Florentine's physician was tending to him more and more frequently which told Nathan it was quite serious. It was just as he'd hoped.

Now to approach Broic. He would have to go about it carefully for it could turn out horribly wrong. Nathan didn't want to be flogged again.

Broic passed by right at that moment, as if he knew Nathan's thoughts. He still wasn't quite sure what to say, he quickly crossed the distance between them.

"Forester." Broic spun around and was surprised to see who had called him.

"I have some information that might be of interest to you.

"And what would that be?" Nate looked around then lowered his voice.

"Over here…this is only for you to know." Both men moved to the corner by some rigging.

"Quickly. I have to get back to the helm."

"Alright, alright, listen. Mr. Dorcet hasn't come to yet, has he?"

"No."

"If he doesn't, what becomes of his means?" Broic said nothing at this. Nate leaned in a little closer.

"When they first arrived, I saw what the captain locked into his safe."

"What are you implying?" the first mate finally spoke. This was the last thing he wanted to be a part of, but something wouldn't let him leave.

"What I'm saying is, what's keeping us from…taking it? It will only go to waste otherwise." Nate made himself stop and wait for a reply. He could barely contain his excitement and thought Broic felt the same. It seemed like forever for him to speak.

"Are you daft?" Broic almost gasped and Nathan's excitement vanished. "You think we can just leave with everything? What about the Dorcets? What about—"

"We get rid of them. The father is as good as dead…the rest are mere children. Nothing is in our way, man!"

"You're daft!" Broic quickly turned away, "I want no part of this. We never spoke of it." Nathan could do nothing more than to watch his only chance walk away.

Nathan spent the rest of the day trying to find a way around the worthless first mate, but it was useless.

And now that he knows of my plan, there's no telling if he'll tell Pearce about it. Nathan sighed heavily as he plopped into his hammock in the steerage. He had just blown out the lantern when someone spoke.

"Alright," Nate didn't have to relight the lantern to know who it was. Instead, he sat up and rested his elbows on his knees.

"I knew you would see it my way," he tried to keep his tone calm, "So here's my plan. We carry it out tomorrow night…after the fourth watch. The sooner the better before anyone catches on or the captain taking a turn for the better by then." In the darkness, Nate heard Broic start to leave so he quickly stood and reached out to stop him. He grabbed the back of his collar. "Don't you be forgettin' whose idea this was. We split the funds." He couldn't see much, but he was close enough to see Broic nod. With that, Nate released him and went back to his bed. He never did fall asleep for he was much too excited

CHAPTER TWENTY-SIX

"Benjamin! How many times must I tell you not to jump on this bed! Just stay away." Edwin shouted at his younger brother after he'd pushed the door open and ran over to where William still lay, awaking Edwin in the noisy process. Theodore followed him into the cabin.

"I don't think it can hurt him. Might even make him come to," Theodore gently pulled Benjamin from the small bunk.

"Why do you even bring him in here?" Edwin sulked as he yawned and sat up to stretch. He'd slept in his father's room ever since William was injured and barely left his side. Theodore was beginning to think his brother might have a heart after all. In truth, Edwin was only there because he was frightened by Nate's threat. He was just waiting for William to wake up to ensure some protection. As every day passed and nothing changed, he was becoming more and more nervous, but not for his father's sake.

"Come on, Benjamin. You've said good morning to him. Let's go and have breakfast," Theodore urged. Whenever it was time to leave, Benjamin would get so upset that Theodore had to literally drag him from their father's side. Today was no different. As soon as Theodore took ahold of his hand, Benjamin began to cry until he screamed in objection.

"No! I want my papa! Leave me alone."

Benjamin is just like Brenna. They're both spoiled and stubborn, Edwin sighed.

Theodore was near the door when Benjamin somehow slipped from his hold and ran back to William's side. Before either young man could stop him, Benjamin leaped onto their father's bed in desperation, nearly landing on his bandaged head.

"Papa!" he shouted. As soon as Edwin reached him, he

roughly yanked him off of William.

"I told you to—" All of a sudden he froze. Out of the corner of his eye, Edwin saw his father move. William's hand slowly moved to his head, where the ship's doctor had wrapped it, and groaned. Theodore and Edwin remained completely still, as if too much commotion would hurt William. Benjamin on the other hand, crawled back onto the bunk and placed his hand on his father's chest.

"Papa! You're awake."

"My head hurts," William spoke hoarsely. Edwin and Theodore didn't know what it was exactly, but something in his voice sounded different.

"You were hit by a sail that had fallen." Theodore informed him.

"Where am I?"

"On The Florentine. We're sailing to England. Don't you remember?" He held his breath and waited for William to reply.

"Oh…yes, I remember now," he slowly sat up and looked around the room, "I'm hungry."

"You should lie back down. I'll go and get the doctor," Theodore turned to leave. No one could have prepared them for what came out of William's mouth next.

"Where's Mother?" Theodore's gaze shot back to his father. Surely he had heard wrong.

"What did you say?" Edwin asked before his brother could.

"Where's Mother?" William said again. This time louder. Benjamin sat up straight and could only stare at his father. Even he could tell something was terribly wrong. And it only got worse.

"Where's my mother! I want my mother!" William's voice grew louder until he was shouting it over and over, much like Benjamin had acted only minutes earlier.

Panic began to wash over Theodore, which was a usual occurrence as of late.

There is no doubt that God is punishing us for what we've done. What's to become of us? He didn't know what to do, only that they needed help quickly, for William was now trying to get out of the bed. Theodore went to go get the doctor, leaving Edwin and Benjamin with their hysteric father.

Edwin tried to get through to William that his mother wasn't there, but it was no use. He was a bit frightened himself. This was the worst thing that could have happened. Not only were they bound for a strange land with no family there or connections, but now he would be more vulnerable than ever before.

I can't hide in this cabin forever.

"How is he faring?" Broic asked Reid Matthias, The Florentine's sailor and physician, when he emerged from Captain Pearce's cabin.

"His fever is so high he's becoming delirious." Broic tried his best to appear concerned, yet he was far from it. He could see Nate down on the main deck fervently listening to them while working on some rigging nearby. Broic could feel his gaze on him.

"Well, just keep tending to him as best as you can." As soon as the words left his mouth, Theodore came running up to them.

"Dr. Matthias, my father has come to!" he cried anxiously. Broic and Nate swiftly exchanged glances. Their plans were ruined.

"Good. I'll go to him now." Matthias stepped toward the stairs, but the young man stopped him.

"No, you don't understand! Something is wrong with him…with his mind!" That being said, they both left. Broic followed, for he wanted to see the situation for himself.

Nathan waited just outside of William's cabin, but made sure to keep out of site in the hall.

"How long are they going to be in there?" he grumbled to himself. His eyes were fixed on the door. Several more long minutes passed before the door opened. Broic was the only one who came out. Nate waited until the first mate walked by before Nate took ahold of his arm and pulled him closer.

"Well?" Nate asked impatiently, "What went on in there?"

"William Dorcet has lost his mind indeed. But he has awaken...our endeavor is surely ruined."

"No it's not! This is perfect."

"And if his mind returns...what then?"

"Not if we go through with our plan tonight!" Nate was about to walk away as if his word was final.

"Wait," Broic spoke up.

"Wait?" Nate turned to face him again, incredulous. "Wait for what?"

"Well," he didn't know why he was ashamed to say it. After all, his rank was higher than Nate's. And Nate needed him. Not the other way around. Broic had to keep reminding himself of this, for Nathan was able to take over a situation rather quickly. He was guilty of mutiny by just coming up with such an idea, in which Broic had every right and responsibility to accuse him. Knowing all this, the first mate had to take back and maintain his role. He must stay in the position where Nathan had to ask instead of demand.

Take control and stop being a coward! Broic told himself and stood a bit taller, "The only way that I will go along with this plan is if we don't throw the Dorcet's overboard. Instead, we force them off the ship once we are in The Port of London." At first Broic had no problem with throwing them over, but after seeing the youngest Dorcet and William, who now had a mind of a child, it changed things.

Blast...he's found his spine. Nate thought. He was about to tell the first mate just what he thought of his absurd idea, when Broic spoke again. It was as if he knew what Nate was thinking.

"What difference does it make to you? The outcome will be the same and we still come away with what we want. We do it my way or nothing. As far as I can tell, we're only days from England." Nate grunted in return as he started to leave.

"Just bring them on deck as soon as The Port is in sight," he obstinately continued on his way. *I just hope the bloody Captain doesn't get better before then.*

CHAPTER TWENTY-SEVEN

heodore emerged from *William's cabin and slammed the door behind him. He drudged down the hall and onto the deck. He looked out over the ocean and ran his hand through his hair in frustration. When he had left, William was playing with Benjamin's toys, along with Benjamin himself. It seemed like things couldn't get any worse.

What are we going to do now? The single thought never left Theodore. He wished he could talk to Captain Pearce, but then again, he dreaded what he might say. He turned back and looked at the hatch that led to his father's room. It had become more like William and Edwin's quarters now, for Edwin still never left unless he had to.

Theodore was trying to decide if he should talk to the first mate. He had heard some of the crew say they would be nearing England soon, but yet no one had approached him about what they were going to do once they arrived.

Are they just going to leave us on the docks? Well, one thing was certain. He couldn't go back into his father's quarters. He could barely stand to look at him in his present state.

For the past few days, Theodore tried to ask him as many questions as possible to find out just how mad his father was. William knew they were his sons as far as Theodore could tell, but more like playmates than anything. He remembered Brenna and merely said she was lost. His mind was no older than Benjamin's five years of age and he only wanted his mother and more food. However, he didn't know where they were going or about the funds he handed over to the captain to lock up. In fact, Theodore wasn't sure if he was allowed access to the considerable amount. Since his father had been so angry with him, Theodore had no doubt that it might be the case.

The only thing to do is to ask the first mate about it.

Theodore finally made up his mind and went to the helm. Once there, he found Broic talking to another sailor. It looked like the man who used to be the first mate. Theodore thought it strange how they talked to each other in hushed tones.

The minute Broic saw the young man, he jumped in surprise and the other man immediately left.

"Young Mr. Dorcet," the first mate greeted nervously, "It's a fine day, is it not? What can I do for you?" Theodore had never talked to this man much, but he thought him to be quite strange.

"How is the captain?" *Perhaps I can talk to him instead,* he hoped.

"Not very good I'm afraid. Hopefully on the mend soon," Broic couldn't help but wonder if he had overheard them discussing their plans or not.

"I've heard that we are almost to England."

"Aye, that we should," Broic apprehensively shifted back and forth.

"Well, you know of my father's present state and because of that, I can't help but wonder what's to become of us once we arrive." Theodore closely watched Broic's expression as he tried to come up with a reply. His eyes revealed a mixture of fear and annoyance. Because he didn't know any better, Theodore pushed his suspicion aside and continued. "My father has a great deal of resources for us once we get there, but no one to meet us. We don't know anyone there. In the meantime, the captain allowed him to store them in his private safe."

"Yes," was all Broic could say as he was deep in thought.

"I believe the best thing would be to restock in England, then return to Boston where our family is. They'll know what to do about—"

"Indeed," the first mate finally found his voice and cut him off, "You are very wise for someone so young." Broic didn't notice Theodore cringe at the condescending remark. "I agree with you fully. I also am sure Captain Pearce would feel the same. We'll keep Mr. Dorcet's things safely in the captain's quarters until we arrive and only use what we need for the return journey. Now, rest your mind about everything. Let me take care of it and you see to your family's needs. I'll talk to the captain about our plans as soon as he's well enough." Theodore wanted to voice his thoughts to the snide sailor, that he wasn't a mere frightened child, but he didn't care to talk to him anymore than was absolutely necessary. Instead, he nodded and helplessly walked back to his own cabin. He thought he would feel better once he knew what would happen to them, but his concern hadn't lessened but only grew much worse. There wasn't anything that could be done about it.

"Does the boy know of our plans?" Nate quickly approached Broic when Theodore had left.

"No, no. Of course not," Broic's calm resolve didn't fool Nathan, for he had closely watched the exchange between him and the Dorcet boy. In fact, during his observance, Nate was now sure of his first impression of Broic, that he was no more than a coward trying to do a man's job.

The captain has to be just as much a fool for thinking him worthy of being the first mate. I can't wait to be rid of them both. "What did he want then?" Nate asked.

"He only wanted to know what was to become of them when we get to England."

"Is that all? What did you tell him?" Nate's demeaning tone reminded Broic of his place as first mate.

I don't have to answer to him. "It doesn't matter or concern you," he replied with a wry grin. Nate threw up his hands in aggravation as he began to leave.

"But the boy did say they don't know a single soul in England." Broic let the enticing words hang in the air. As much as both men hated to admit it, they needed each other to carry out the plan.

"Is that so?" Nate stopped and slightly turned back, "It seems this is too easy."

"Aye. They'll be brought to the deck as soon as we see port."

"Which have forsaken the right way, and are gone astray…who loved the wages of unrighteousness;

These are wells without water, clouds that are carried with a tempest; to whom the mist of darkness is reserved for ever."

2 Peter 2:15-17

In the Midst of Darkness

CHAPTER TWENTY-EIGHT

"*L*and ho!" What was music to the crew's ears only brought apprehension to Theodore. He opened the door to their cabin and peered out to see excited sailors walk down the hall to the deck.

"Have we arrived?" Theodore asked one man.

"Not quite. We're just coming to the entrance of the river. Still a few hours to London yet."

"Theo…Theo! Theodore," William shouted.

"What?"

"What does land ho mean?" he asked innocently.

"Oh, it doesn't matter," Theodore shut the door, turned to his father, and sighed heavily.

"But I want to know. Tell me! Theo, please tell me."

"No! Keep quiet for once and go away!" Theodore snapped. His father's whining and questions were endless. William's expression fell as he sadly shuffled away.

Theodore wished he could leave and go on deck for a while, but the last few days proved it to be a very bad idea. Every time he left, he would come back to a disaster. William and Benjamin would be quarreling about a toy or something and Edwin would solemnly sit by and stare at them. If truth be told, Edwin was beginning to worry Theodore. As if he didn't have any other worries. His usual active brother was no more. In his place was someone who refused to leave William's cabin and barely talked anymore, other than yelling at his father and younger brother to be quiet. He would sit day after day. It was as if he was being tortured with fear. Before, nothing whatsoever seemed to bother him.

Perhaps his guilty conscience is finally catching up with him, Theodore presumed.

It was nearly dusk when there was a knock at the door.

"I've come to fetch you to see if you want to get off the ship for a bit." Broic informed when Theodore came to the door. Although it sounded wonderful, Theodore thought it a rather strange hour for it. He figured Broic was merely coming to give him their funds from the safe.

"Where would we go at this time?" he asked. Broic was yet again at a loss for words.

"I…just…thought you would want to leave the ship for a while. I know I do."

"Me too! Let's go. Please?" William and Benjamin began shouting at once and jumping up and down. Theodore glanced over at Edwin. His expression was unchanging.

Maybe that's what he needs to come to himself, he thought and finally agreed.

As they walked onto the deck, Theodore grasped Benjamin's hand to keep him in tow. He knew his father should also, but he couldn't bring himself to do it. Their sad situation was still very hard to get used to, much less except. Theodore noticed more than one sailor glaring at them. Usually the crew hardly paid them any mind, but now they seemed quite interested by something.

Most likely my father. A grown man acting like a child.

Broic followed them very closely. Theodore tried to see if the first mate held anything like the funds. He knew he would most likely hand it to him at the last moment so no one would know of the substantial amount. However, the first mate held nothing.

Perhaps it's inside his jacket?

They were just approaching the gangway that led to the docks of the harbor. Because of the time of day, it was fairly quiet. All of a sudden, Edwin seemed to come to life. He shoved past Theodore and took Benjamin's arm.

"Come on, let's get off the ship," he nervously stated and tried to hurry them along. When Edwin had seen Nate, the sailor who had threatened him, saunter over to them, he knew this wasn't going to end well. They had to get off the ship and away from Nate!

"Hurry up!" Edwin now pushed William.

"Edwin, what has gotten into you?" Theodore put his hand on his shoulder, "There's nothing to fear."

"If you only knew," Edwin replied under his breath before pulling away from his brother. "Just listen to me for once!" he snapped and couldn't help but glance over at the sailor. He wore a wry grin as he helped lower the gangway. Couldn't Theodore see this was some sort of trap? As hard as he tried to stay calm, panic began to rise up in him. "Let's just go!" Edwin was almost finding it hard to breathe as some sailors seemed to close in.

Theodore still had no idea what was happening. Broic came up behind him and held up something. In the dimming light he thought it was a leather bag with the means when in truth it was a pistol.

"What are you doing?" Theodore asked Broic, but he said nothing nor moved like he was in indecision, fighting within himself.

"Time to leave," Nathan then spoke up for him. When Broic pointed the gun at him and slowly pulled back the hammer, it finally hit Theodore. There was indeed plenty to fear.

"Off you go."

"What about the funds?"

"I don't think you are in any position to be asking questions," Broic gave a quick nod to the sailors standing by. They swiftly came forward, grabbed ahold of all four Dorcet's, and dragged them down the gangway.

"You can't do this. Captain Pearce! Help, help!" Theodore shouted over Benjamin and William's shrieks. At that moment, another shout was heard that caused them to momentarily quiet down.

"Wait!" Edwin felt a hand clench his shoulder. His worst fear was coming to pass as he glanced up to see Nate smiling, "This one is mine."

"Captain! Captain Pearce!" Theodore frantically shouted as Edwin's panic broke loose. He thrashed about with everything in him and began kicking and biting. Anything he could think of, but there were too many strong men. They easily threw Benjamin, William, and Theodore onto the dock and quickly pulled the gangway away from it so they couldn't get back onto the vessel.

Nate took ahold of Edwin's face and forced him to meet his gaze.

"Now I'll make you pay for what you've done."

"Help, someone! Help!" Theodore scanned the harbor, but it was empty, other than a few people milling about, trying to ignore his cries. He fearfully gazed up at the tall ship. What was happening up there? Before he could reason further, a splash was heard. Whatever had happened, Edwin either jumped or was thrown from the deck and plunged into the sea. After the sun had set and the sky grew darker, the light made it nearly impossible to see where Edwin was or if he was even conscious. Then, seemingly out of nowhere, his head bobbed up over the water and he swam toward the dock. Once Theodore and William pulled Edwin out, Theodore instantly began the questioning.

"What happened up there?" he pointed to the ship. Some sailors were still watching and laughing at them from the deck. When Edwin didn't answer, Theodore moved his gaze to him. It might have been a shadow from the growing darkness, but it looked as if Edwin had a swollen and blackening eye. "Well?" he asked again, but his brother only wiped his face. When his hand moved away, Theodore thought he saw blood coming from his nose as well. "Edwin, what went on?"

"What does it matter to you?"

"You must have done something…you always do something. Anything to get a bit of attention!"

"You don't know anything!" Edwin angrily blurted. His teeth started to chatter from the cold, salty wind blowing against his dripping clothes.

All was quiet as they tried to think of what could be done. That is, until William moved closer to Edwin.

"Ed, you are bleeding. Why?" he reached out to touch his

face, but Edwin pushed his hand away roughly.

"Get away from me!" he wiped his face again.

"I think it's pretty clear we're being punished." When Edwin snorted Theodore went on, "Can't you see? God is punishing us for all we've done? How can it possibly get any worse for us? We're stranded, moneyless, we don't know anyone, and our father has gone insane."

"I have not!" William put in, but it only added to their misery.

"God's punishing us for what *we* did? What *we* did?" Edwin's voice grew louder, "We wouldn't be here if it weren't for you and you're babbling on. If you would've just stopped thinking so much and kept quiet, none of this would be happening!"

"You're the one who talked me into locking Brenna in a trunk in the first place!" Theodore shouted in return.

"Brenna." Something immediately caused their argument to cease. "Brenna," William whimpered, "Where is Brenna?" he looked at his sons earnestly. Neither Edwin nor Theodore knew what to say to the heartbreaking plea. It made both young men ashamed of themselves. "Where is she?" For a brief moment, Theodore thought he might have gotten his right mind back, but it wasn't so.

"The only thing to do is to try and get some help. Let's try to find a constable." He looked down the dark dingy street directly in front of them. It only came as a bleak reminder that they were indeed being condemned. *And it's only bound to get much, much worse,* Theodore thought as he grasped Benjamin's hand and made their way down the street. *Can I ever hope to be forgiven?* He presumed the bitter gust of wind that suddenly came up meant a cold, hopeless reply.

CHAPTER TWENTY-NINE

Caragin ~ Dolbury, England

*T*he door slammed loudly and they were left alone. Lanna sat down at the table and buried her face in her hands.

"Don't take it to heart, my dear," Stephen moved to his wife and tried to comfort her by putting his hand on her shoulder. "She must have had another dream to bring this on again. It seems every time she has this…episode, it begins with her peculiar nightmares."

"Jist when it seems loike she is doin' better and forgets her mysterious past, somethin' causes it to cum back on her worse than it was before. Stephen, what shud we do? Were we wrong to take her in?"

"No, I believe we were right. I know He wanted us to help her…and we have. We've done everything we possibly could, we even sent a letter to her so called family."

"Perhaps we were terribly wrong in not believin' her straight away and believin' the orphanage instead," Lanna glanced up at him and took his hand.

"Well, you've seen firsthand how orphans many times make up all sorts of stories of their past, until they begin to believe it themselves. But we can't know for sure. The only thing to do is to pray."

"Aye," They both shut their eyes.

"I shud go and talk to 'er. She needs to nu that we love her an' wud never lie to her." When they finished praying, Lanna stood.

"I agree. She needs to get her mind off things." They spoke a little further, then Lanna left.

She quickly found her amongst her other six children, playing in the side yard. It was quite a rarity to have a warm day, complete with sunshine. When they did, the whole family joyfully took advantage of it. As she approached, Lanna couldn't help but smile at the sound of her youngest giggle from being tickled by Brenna.

She has such a way with Tully. Why can't she be content here?

"Mummy!" Katherine, the next in line, eagerly ran up to Lanna as soon as she saw her. "Tully almost ate a worm!" she dramatically exclaimed.

"Oh dear! Is he gran' so?"

"Yes," she grinned proudly, "I saved him." Lanna glanced at Brenna, who looked up from the toddler and met her gaze. From her red, puffy eyes, it was evident that she'd been crying.

"Brenna, might we take a walk?" Brenna didn't say anything as she rose from the blanket they had put on the ground and solemnly followed.

They walked for some time without saying a word. In truth, Lanna was silently praying for direction. They were almost to the end of the spacious land, surrounding their large country home before she spoke.

"You nu I love you as me own. I want more than anythin' to please you. Not ter hurt you or brin' you misery. Least av all, lie to you. When Stephen and I see ya in such turmoil, we share it with ya. In a way, I think the whole family does," Lanna put her arm around the girl and pulled her near. "All any av us want is to help you...to fend peace," tears welled up in her eyes and Brenna as well.

"I'm sorry I accused you of lying. I just...I didn't mean to...."

"Did ye have another nightmare?"

"Yes," Brenna slowly pulled away and looked at the estate in the distance.

"Might I ask what it wus about?"

"I was being put inside a trunk...by my brothers. It was exactly as it really happened. Except, right before it was closed over me...before the darkness, I saw my father standing behind Theodore and Edwin. But he didn't stop them," her voice cracked

with emotion. It wasn't long before Brenna started to weep.
Lanna rushed to her side.

"It's alright, dear."

"Why didn't he stop them?" Brenna faced her, "Why didn't
he save me? Why didn't he save me?" she kept crying. Lanna's
heart went out to her as she took her in her arms again.

"I'm so sorry, Brenna. I don't nu all the answers, nor can I
alone brin' ya comfort. There is someone who can."

"God," Brenna sniffed and wiped her eyes.

"He is the God av all comfort an' He wants to take all your
pain and worry. He'll take them an' work them all oyt because
He loves ya."

"Yes." While Brenna fully agreed, her Heavenly Father
seemed so far away. "Sometimes it feels so hopeless...everyone
has left me."

"Brenna, ya ask why didn't your father save you? He already
has. God is your Father. All you have ter do is ask Him. Give it to
Him and trust Him. Everyone might 'av left, but He has never left
ya." Lanna could tell she had taken her words to heart for her
countenance already seemed brighter. "You mustn't think your
family isn't replyin' to the letter we sent. It most likely jist
arrived. It takes a few months for a letter to travel that far."

CHAPTER THIRTY

London, England

loody street urchins!" Theodore awoke and quickly sat up.

"Edwin, Father, time to get out of here!" Edwin was on his feet in seconds and frantically looked around the shed. Because he was still a bit groggy, he couldn't tell if anyone else was there at first. The morning light shined *shone* through the open door. Where should they exit the shed and was the owner inside? He hadn't heard the shout that had awakened his brother.

We could probably get away unseen if not for Father's loud snoring, Edwin glanced down at William.

"Father, wake up! Come on," Theodore nudged him until he finally roused.

"What? What's going on?"

"Be quiet and get up!" It was then that the owner made his presence known, holding a pistol.

"Get out of here before I...." he momentarily paused when he saw Theodore pick up Benjamin. It did little to soften him, for he often had to throw people out. When he had chased all of them out, he watched as they walked aimlessly down the busy street.

"Don't let me catch you in here again!"

"That was close," was all Theodore could say as he pulled his jacket closed to try and keep warm from the damp, foggy air.

"Well, it was worth a try. At least we got a few hours of sleep away from the cold. If father wouldn't make such noise in his sleep, we wouldn't have gotten caught."

"Hey, what did I do?" William asked.

"The whole city can hear your endless snoring!"

"Stop quarreling!" Theodore rebuked, but only looked sternly at Edwin for starting it. "I can't stand it anymore. I'm far too hungry."

"I'm hungry too," Benjamin spoke up for the first time and began to cry. Being hungry himself was one thing, but seeing Benjamin cry almost made him want to as well. It had only been a week since being forced off of The Florentine, but it seemed so much longer. They were cold, hungry, and completely hopeless to ever help their situation. The homeless were not taken to kindly for London was overrun with them. The minute people saw their tattered clothes or smelt them, they either chased them away or turned their backs. William's strange behavior did little to help things.

What are we going to do, other than die in the streets with sickness or starvation? Theodore thought as Benjamin began to cough uncontrollably. Then, as if on cue, they walked past an orphanage. From what Theodore had heard and read of most orphanages in London, it was less than pleasurable. *Unless someone is desperate and starving.* He looked down at Benjamin. If he didn't get some food soon, Theodore feared the worst. He went back and forth within himself as they trudged by. His gaze was fixed on the stately brick building. *It would only be temporary until we can find some help...or food.* When Benjamin started another bout of hacking, it made up Theodore's mind for him. "That settles it."

"Settles what?" Edwin glanced over at his brother, but he wasn't beside him. He turned to see him walking up to the tall iron gate of an orphanage.

"Where are you going?"

"Just wait here. I'll be right back." Theodore replied without looking back.

He marched up the steps and rapped the door with the doorknocker. He could still hear his younger brother's coughing from the street. *This is the only way to save his life,* he reassured himself as the door opened.

"Yes?" the maid asked.

"I need some help...my brother, he—" Without waiting until he'd finished, the maid walked away. *A lot of good that did,* he first thought.

"Follow me," she then beckoned for him to come in. Theodore took off his hat and caught up to her.

As she led him down a hall, he looked around at the plain, but fairly well kept rooms along the way.

"Mr. Thordon, someone to see you, sir." The maid showed Theodore in to a large office, then quickly left and closed the door behind her. The office seemed much grander than what little he had seen so far.

"Yes?" Mr. Thordon, a short and well-rounded man looked up from his desk.

"Sir, I need your help. My brother, he's...I fear he might die from...anyway, I came to ask if he could stay here in your care. Now, I don't have the means at this time, but I will as soon as I can," Theodore blurted without taking a breath and continued to hold it as he waited for a reply. Mr. Thordon adjusted his spectacles and leaned back in his chair.

"You're not from around here."

"No, sir," Theodore nervously replied.

"You're a long way from America," his gaze moved back to the papers on his desk. Theodore was a bit disheveled. What was Mr. Thordon implying? Was he mocking him? Theodore wasn't used to his present state of being filthy, penniless, starving, and desperate. While he badly needed Mr. Thordon's help, he didn't care to make a bigger fool of himself. He was about to turn to leave when the man stopped writing and finally spoke.

"How old is he?"

"Nearly five, sir." Mr. Thordon looked up at him once again.

"Well," he stood, "I think we should be able to find room for him. I'll just have you sign here for the release." Theodore marveled as he then put his arm on his shoulder and walked him out.

"What about some kind of payment? I can't promise—"

"Don't worry about it, my boy. I know you've fallen on hard times...many have. You just pay whatever you can spare once you are able to. Where is the lad?" They stopped in front of the entrance.

"He's out on the street...he doesn't know of this yet."

"I'll have an attendant go out with you."

"I'm very grateful. Uh, would there happen to be any work that you need done? My other brother and I are hard workers. You could pay us anything you like."

"No. Like I said before, I've fallen on hard times also. I don't have any work for you, I'm sorry."

"Alright…thank you," he would have said more, but Mr. Thordon already made his way back to his office.

"There's Theodore!" William excitedly stood up and pointed at the orphanage.

What is he doing now? Edwin thought as Theodore called for them to come to him. There was another man standing beside him.

Theodore knelt down before Benjamin and forced himself to smile.

"Benjamin, now this is just for a little while. As soon as we can, we'll come and get you."

"What?" A frightening look crossed the boy's face. Theodore could only sigh. This was turning out to be much harder than he first thought.

"You have to stay here just for a little while."

"No!" he shrieked before Theodore could finish. "No, I want to stay with you!" he started to cough again as he reached out to Theodore.

"You can't. You're too ill. This is just for a while." Theodore stopped Benjamin before he could cling to him. The attendant placed his hand on the boy's shoulder, which only caused him to cry louder.

"Theodore, don't leave me!" he screamed hoarsely as Theodore stood. He had to make himself look away from the heartbreaking scene of the attendant pulling Benjamin toward the front entrance. "Theodore, no! Papa, Papa! I want to stay with you!"

What Theodore and Edwin, didn't count on was their father. He might have lost his right mind, but he still obtained his fatherly affection for Benjamin, even though they presently were more like playmates. Something rose up in William when Benjamin desperately called out for him between sobs.

"Let him go!" he shouted and stepped forward.

"Father, stop. It's for the best." Both young men had a difficult time holding William back.

"Papa! Don't leave me." Benjamin's cries, which made Theodore cringe, continued on until he was taken inside and the door was closed. When Theodore and Edwin didn't think they could hold their father back any longer, he suddenly stopped and began to weep. Seeing William so upset caused Theodore to doubt his decision.

Maybe we could have found help if we just kept looking. Should I go and get Benjamin back? Theodore had to cover his face to hide his own emotion. *No. It would only cause father more pain. This is the only way to save Benjamin's life,* he repeated to himself. When Theodore realized that it was no use to try and hold back his tears, he stood and forced himself to start walking again. Maybe the further they got from the Orphanage, the hopelessness they felt would somehow lessen.

"Why did you let them take Ben? Why?" William demanded. He gazed at Theodore with tears streaming down his face and into his beard. At first, Theodore couldn't speak, but William wouldn't relent as they continued down the street.

"Go back. Get him back!" he was starting to get upset again, "Don't let him go away…like Brenna!"

"We had to leave him!" Theodore couldn't stand it anymore, "Otherwise he'll starve! We'll come back for him." William wept for some time, when the fight in him dissipated, but at least he didn't say anything more.

Edwin remained completely silent through the entire ordeal.

"Papa, save me! Help, someone!" The trunk lid slammed shut leaving her in the lonely dark. Brenna cried until she was hoarse, even though she knew what was coming. Sure enough, the light came towards her. The dreaded alley, filled with fog, lured her in. Brenna didn't try to pull away anymore for it was no use. She moved deeper inside. As she did, she kept her gaze straight ahead, yet still grimaced as she past the frightening figure that lay unmoving. Her eyes were fixed on the shadows before her as she frantically waited for it. Brenna held her breath until finally the hand reached out to her. It was her only rescue from this nightmare. It had happened so many times and unfolded the exact same way, but this time Brenna would not stand by and wait for whoever or whatever it was behind her to make itself known. She would do whatever it took to get to that hand. Brenna instantly broke into a run like never before. The horrifying sound of someone following her, above her own breathless huffing, did nothing to slow her steps. It only caused her to quicken her pace. Everything in her told her to look back. Who was it? Why was it after her? But she couldn't turn back. She was too close to reaching the end! For a moment it sounded as if she might outrun it, which made her want to see what it was all the more.

I made it! I'm safe! Brenna reached for the hand and nearly touched it when suddenly the fearful darkness urged toward her from behind. In one loud whoosh it overcame her and her screams, pulling her from the hand and into the shadows.

Brenna sat up and grasped the air, where the hand should have been. Instead of the roaring and darkness that surrounded her, all was quiet other than her panicked breathing. She tried to calm herself as she looked around to find that she was safely in her and Scarlette's room. Thankfully she hadn't screamed out loud to awaken Scarlette, like she'd done before and nearly scared her out of her wits. Even though Brenna was completely safe, fear still closed in, letting the nightmare seem all too real. She pulled her blankets around her, also using it to wipe away her tears and perspiration.

Why does this keep happening? How many times do I have to go through this same horrible dream? Brenna shut her eyes tightly to keep out the remaining shadows that lingered from the dream. Every time this happened, it seemed like it took longer to rid herself from the feeling of panic and being watched from the dark presence.

She assumed that the hand stretched forth was Jesus, trying to save her.

Why can't I get to it? No matter how hard I try to reach it, it all ends the same terrible way. "Lord, what do I need to do?" Brenna whispered desperately, "Help me."

"For I know nothing by myself; yet am I not hereby justified: but he that judgeth me is the Lord.

Therefore judge nothing before the time, until the Lord come, who both will bring to light the hidden things of darkness, and will make manifest the counsels of the hearts: and then shall every man have praise of God."

1 Corinthians 4:4-5

CHAPTER THIRTY-ONE

September 1843

*T*heodore turned to see Edwin at it again. *We'll be arrested in no time if he keeps this up,* he sighed as Edwin inched closer to the unsuspecting, fine dressed man, who was doing business with a storekeeper. He reached for his pocket, when William must have seen him as well.

"Ed, what are you doing?" he nearly shouted in question. Edwin immediately backed away as the man spun around. The only good thing about Edwin was that he was fast and quite sneaky as he slyly began looking at some of the merchant's wares. Theodore sighed with relief as the man went back to his business with no harm done.

He waited until Edwin made his way back to them before he spoke.

"Will you stop this foolishness before you get us all in trouble." They started down the street.

"Me? I was doing just fine until he started hollering," Edwin pointed at his father. Theodore could only sigh again. "We can't just keep doing nothing but walk. I've got to eat!" Edwin placed his hand on his rumbling stomach as they continued to wander. All along the street Theodore would humbly approach shopkeepers to beg for work. However, as soon as he spoke, they'd only brush him off. Theodore and Edwin were beginning to get the impression that the true reason no one would hire them was William. If anyone seemed interested in hiring the young men, they would rudely change their minds the minute they saw William, doing anything from trying to catch a stray cat to skipping like a child.

The further they walked, the busier it got. It also smelled worse and the buildings slowly became more rundown. The whole atmosphere felt dreadful.

What or where are we getting closer to? Theodore asked himself. It was fairly easy to get turned around in such a city. And yet, within the grandness, the smells, thieves, sickness, and slums were anything but grand. It was a grim place for the most part. Boston was bad enough around the docks, but this was much worse.

What they were approaching eventually came into view. It was like nothing they'd ever seen before. Standing before them was a large bridge and in the distance hundreds, possibly thousands of vessels arriving and departing from a seemingly endless port on the river that led to the sea. Besides the loading and unloading of cargo, various markets lined the harbor. The vastness of it all took a person's breath away. While Theodore took in the sights, Edwin had a very different idea.

It's so crowded and busy that stealing will now be easier than ever! He was already eyeing people he presumed to be easy prey. It wasn't long before another scheming idea presented itself. One large market was so busy at the moment that Edwin couldn't even see where the owner was. His stomach growled at the sight of it, especially the crates with heavy bread and cheese.

Just waiting for me to take. He casually left his father and brother and roamed closer to it. *This is too easy,* he lifted the largest loaf and shoved it between his vest and jacket. Without looking around, he moved to where the cheese was. He reached out for one only to have someone to catch ahold of it tightly.

"Gotcha!" Edwin's gaze shot up to find a burly man, wearing an apron, glaring back at him. His hold tightened as he ripped open Edwin's jacket with his other hand and the loaf fell to the ground. "Filthy thieves! I've had enough of you!" he shouted as if everyone within earshot held the same motive as the young man.

Theodore could only hope the angry man wasn't talking about his brother as he turned toward the commotion in apprehension. Sure enough, it was Edwin.

"Let go of me," he winced and tried to pull away.

"Someone fetch a constable."

I told him to stop! Theodore could only watch as if he didn't know his brother at all. In truth, he was tempted to leave and let him try to get out of it all by himself. There was nothing he could do anyway. *I just hope father will keep quiet.* Theodore tried to keep William preoccupied with anything he could as he saw a constable approach out of the corner of his eye. No one could have guessed what happened next. Instead of waiting to hear Edwin protest as he was taken away, an older woman's voice was heard.

"Sir, there's been a mistake."

"What are you talking about?" the storekeeper started to argue. Theodore couldn't help but remain close by to see how this would turn out. A short woman stepped out of the crowd and placed her hand on Edwin's arm. Even Edwin stopped squirming in confusion.

"I believe dis is enuff for this loaf 'n two mooar besides," she held out her hand with the coins and showed the storekeeper the other loaves she held. "And also sum of that cheese if ya will. Naw, will thou please release the lad, for I surely can't lug all of this." At first, the man didn't know what to say. He looked at Edwin, then the lady.

"What's the meaning of all this? This no good thief was stealing! I saw him."

"Are theur garn ter take this payment or not? Ye have customers waitin'," she remained calm.

"No. I want him taken away. I don't—"

"It's not stealing if she's paying for it. Let 'im go," the constable, who stood by, finally put a stop to his ranting. It was some time before the storekeeper eventually released Edwin. If he hadn't been so taken back, Edwin had all the intentions of running away, but something about this mysterious woman held him there. Plus she had bought him some food, or so he hoped.

"Alright now, you take these," she trustingly handed him the box of food and they were off. Edwin quickly glanced back at the storekeeper, who still gazed angrily at them until they were out of sight.

Theodore forced himself to wait until it was clear that Edwin
was truly free before marching up to him with William following
close behind.

"What were you thinking? I told you to be stop this
nonsense."

"Oh gran'," the lady dropped a package in Theodore's arms,
then in Williams. It was as if she had known them forever.
William immediately began to drool over the lovely food placed
before him.

"Theodore!" he gasped and was about to eat some of the
bread when she kindly, but at the same time, boldly stopped him.

"Now, now…na eatin' yet."

"But why? I'm hungry!" Theodore could tell that the woman
quickly discerned the situation when tears brimmed in William's
eyes. Strangely enough, she didn't back away in fear like
everyone else had as soon as they realized he wasn't in his right
mind. Instead, she changed her tone as if talking to a small child.

"Well, don't fret. We will eat in just a moment. But fust, we
must thank t' gran' Lord for dis glorious scran food. But even
afore that I 'ave something ta say," her voice grew stronger as
she turned to look at Edwin and Theodore. "You boys ought ta be
ashamed o' yourselves," she scolded. When she saw that Edwin
wasn't looking at her, like he'd done nothing wrong, she marched
right up to him. "Stealing! Of aw things." The fact that Edwin
was feet taller than her didn't make her waver in the least
"You're garn ta get yourselves thrahn into a workhouse if ya
keep on," she clicked her tongue, "A reeight sad and 'orrible
place indeed. Ya need ter get yourselves an 'onest job."

"We've tried, but no one will hire us with him the way he
is," Edwin nodded in his father's direction. As if on cue, they all
looked at William right as he was trying to wipe the drool from
his beard and still hold the crate at the same time. If the sight
wasn't so pathetic, it might have been humorous. But the
seriousness of their situation weighed heavily on the young men.

"Well then…we'll just 'ave ta do something abaht that na
won't we? Folla me," she started to waddle down the road.
Theodore and Edwin exchanged glances. They both asked

themselves what power this woman had over them that she could take charge of them and their situation so easily. Although they didn't quite understand why, they followed her for they had no one else to turn to.

The four weaved through the busy markets and harbor for only a few minutes before William shouted to the woman who led the way.

"Hey, when are we going to eat?"

"Just as soon as we get theear," she simply replied without looking back at him or slowing. Theodore couldn't hold back his curiosity any longer.

"Wait just a moment," he caught up to her and she finally came to a halt. "Who are you, and why are you helping us?"

"Naw, wot a daffy dahn dilly thing of me...to forget ter introduce missen. Forgive me. I'm Hephzibah Melling. And ye are?" Theodore couldn't help but smile at her queer words and ever stranger name. He'd never heard anyone talk like her.

"Theodore Dorcet. This is my brother Edwin and my...." When Theodore looked at William, he was just about to take a bite of the loaf of bread. "Father!" William gasped and glanced up in surprise.

"But I'm hungry!" he whined.

"You can wait a little longer," Theodore turned back to Hephzibah and sighed in frustration. "And this is my father...William," he felt ashamed. Not so much because of William, but by fact that he was ashamed of him. William couldn't help his present state.

"Why are you helping us when we have no hope to repay you?"

"I 'elp because of Him who 'as helped and saved me. Ah love 'cos I am loved by me Heavenly Fatheur." Theodore didn't know what to say to that. What did she mean?

"Where are we going?" Edwin then asked.

"You'll clock once we get there. We'd betta 'urry sa Mr. Dorcet dunt faint." Hephzibah continued on.

"Well, Hephzibah Melling…what are you doing in the likes of this place?" They stopped in front of a large, well-used building across from the docks in the busiest part of The Port. Countless men were loading and unloading crates from the building to a grand vessel. Out of all the bustle, an older man holding papers, stepped out onto the platform. The minute he saw Hephzibah, he smiled and quickly approached.

"How are theur?" she asked.

"Good. I 'aven't seen you or Weston in ages."

"I know…wha' a shem it is. How is business?"

"Very good! So what brings you all the way over here?"

"This is Mr. Dorcet, Theodore, and Edwin," Hephzibah glanced at the Dorcets.

"Hello. I'm Howard Morrison." Though he appeared a little gruff from years of hard work, his eyes were kind as he took time to shake each of their hands.

"We met…just this day's dawnin' and I thought ye moight be in dire need o' some pin' pong strong, hardworking young men."

Theodore was trying his very best to keep up with what she was saying. He kept asking himself if she was even speaking English!

"Let me see here…I think we can do something about that. Since Hephzibah here is such a good old friend."

"Old is t' word!" Hephzibah laughed. Theodore breathed a sigh of relief at the good news.

Maybe things are finally looking up, he hoped. "Thank you very much, Mr. Morrison. We won't let you down." Theodore tried to get Edwin's attention to also thank him or at least say something. He only stood there, looking unappreciative. *What will it take to make him thankful for anything? We have food and a job now! What more could he ask for at the moment?*

"I had betta get back hammer and tack before Weston begins ta worry. All the scran in the crates are for thee."

"Can we eat now?" William eagerly asked.

"Yes, dear."

"I don't know how to thank you for all you've done,"

Theodore said.

"I'm glad I could 'elp. Naw I don't wanna see any of ya tryin' ta tek things that don't belong to thee," she chuckled. Theodore smiled, for the first time in weeks.

"Howard, thank ya roight much," Hephzibah moved closer to Howard as the Dorcet's dug into the food, "I kna fully well that you didn't need more workers,"

"Like you, I'm also glad to help. I think they'll do well here. Give my regards to ol' Weston. And don't be such a stranger yourself." Howard shook her hand.

"In him was life; and the life was the light of men.

And the light shineth in darkness; and the darkness comprehended it not.

If we say that we have fellowship with him, and walk in darkness, we lie, and do not the truth."

John 1:4-6

CHAPTER THIRTY-TWO

Caragin ~ Dolbury, England   *April 1844*

"Why can't I go, Lette? I want to go!"

"You're too little," Scarlette replied, but kindly. That did nothing to stop Katherine's begging. She would only find someone to side with her.

"Mummy! Why can't I go? I'm almost six," Katherine released her sister's skirt and ran to her mother as she approached the group.

"All ready, sir. Packed securely," the driver came around the corner and announced.

Just as Brenna finished putting a basket in the carriage seat for the journey, she turned to face the Kinsey family she'd grown to love. It wasn't until the talk she had with Lanna several months earlier when she finally realized how much this kind family loved her. Before, her focus had only been consumed with trying to get someone to believe her. But after sending a letter to her family in America over a year ago, without any word, Brenna had lost hope in them. She couldn't help but think that her family wasn't even looking for her.

After all, it has been nearly five long years since I've been gone," Brenna forced a smile as she watched Lanna try to calm Katherine down by comforting her. *Father probably gave up long ago.* It was then that she caught herself. After talking to Lanna, she'd made the decision to put all the sadness behind her and try to allow herself to enjoy the present. Try as she might to hide it away completely, her persistent dreams would not let her forget. *Perhaps this trip will help me to finally put it aside.* Brenna turned her attention back to the Kinsey's.

"We had better say our goodbyes and get started. We don't want to arrive too late," Stephen came up behind Scarlette and put his arm around her shoulder. Scarlette stepped up to her family, who seemed to line up to wait for a farewell hug.

When Scarlette was finished with each family member, it was Brenna's turn.

"Goodbye, Stephen," she started at one end where Stephen Jr. stood. Though he was much too mature to give her a hug, he stretched forth his hand to shake hers.

"Be safe," he tried to sound like a protective older brother, but Brenna knew he was sincere. Next was Andrew and Philip the twins. No matter where they went or what they did, the boys would naturally end up together. Brenna hugged them both and promised them a game of tag when she returned. Following the boys was Katherine.

"Goodbye dear," Brenna stooped down to her level.

"Bye," she immediately gave her neck a tight hug and sounded as if she might cry. Their absence would surely feel like an eternity to the young girl, not to mention she would be sorely outnumbered by her brothers while they were gone.

"How many days will it be?" Brenna tried to come up with a satisfactory answer to Katherine's cute question. It would after all be the entire summer.

"About three months."

"Well, how many days is that?" she wrinkled her nose in confusion.

"Um...around ninety days."

"Oh my!" Katherine couldn't help but cling to her again. Brenna was sure the girl would cry now. She was close to tears herself.

"Don't worry, Brenna. I won't let the boys go into you and Lette's room...ever!" she exclaimed.

Finally, Brenna turned to Lanna, who held baby Audrey on her hip and Tully in hand. Lanna was already in tears since saying goodbye to Scarlette. She didn't know why she was so emotional. The girls weren't going far or overly long. The only reason she could come up with was that she was more than a mere mother to the two eldest. They were her best of friends. And oddly enough, Brenna reminded her of another dear friend she had, even though they were far different from each other.

Lanna tried to pull herself together as she watched Brenna hug Tully and ruffle his curly red hair, then stood up and took Audrey's little foot. The baby's face brightened as she grinned happily.

"Be safe me dear," Lanna briefly let go of Tully's hand to embrace Brenna.

"I will," Brenna choked.

"You will 'av so much craic in London. I remember whaen I went to the Season," Lanna slowly pulled away and placed her hand on her shoulder. "It's full av beauty and excitement ter be sure. 'owever, like I told Scarlette jist a moment ago, people an' things will pull you in al' sorts of directions. Ya must remember the most important thing in life." Brenna nodded knowingly at this. "God has a wonderful plan for your life. You must keep in mind what His will is for you at al' times. But don't fret. He is alwus with you. He's in you. Closer than any friend...or beau. You can blather to Him anytime ya like. He's alwus speakin' to you. I love you so much," Lanna smiled and sniffed.

"I love you," Brenna replied.

"Have a good time!"

"Bye!" Scarlette waved, "You probably won't recognized us when we return. We'll be so refined after being presented into society." All the Kinsey's laughed and waved as Scarlette climbed into the carriage, followed by Brenna and Stephen.

Although Lanna had told the girls many times all about the season, being presented to court, and debutante balls, they didn't exactly know what to expect. Scarlette began to talk about all the excitement they were about to have as soon as the carriage jolted forward. As much as Brenna enjoyed listening to such an excitable person, half the time she didn't know what she was talking about. Hyde Park, going to court, the races, and Rotten Row was all foreign to her.

I'll soon find out. And hopefully during all these things, I'll be able to put everything behind me and finally start anew. Brenna sighed and sat back against the plush seat as she gazed out the window to watch the passing scenery.

"And art confident that thou thyself art a guide of the blind, a light of them which are in darkness."

Romans 2:19

CHAPTER THIRTY-THREE

he carriage stopped in front of a large home in a wealthy part of London. Stephen emerged first then offered a hand to the young ladies as they stepped out next. Brenna gazed up at the tall town house and the others right beside it. The entire street was made up of rows of equally handsome and spacious homes, also several stories tall.

The door quickly opened to their long awaited guests before they even reached the front steps. The butler was about to speak when an older woman passed by him in the entrance.

"Bertram, they're here! They're here!" she called behind her then rushed down the steps. She was very finely dressed with dark greying hair neatly arranged in the latest fashion.

"Stephen, young ladies, you're here at long last." Stephen swiftly dropped the bags he held and turned to face her.

"Dear Aunt. It has been too long." They embraced warmly. Stephen had to almost bend down to hug the short woman.

"Too long indeed! Let me look at you!" she briefly pulled away to take him in and sighed in satisfaction.

"Well Stephen, you haven't changed a bit," Bertram came out and approached.

"Neither have you, Uncle," Stephen moved to him and shook his hand. Brenna couldn't help but smile when the woman giggled like a young girl.

"Stephen, it is quite rude to lie. I dare say, we've aged into two old coots."

"It has only been a couple of years. How much can a person change? The little ones do the most changing," Stephen put in.

"Well, you've only grown more handsome," the woman reached up to touch his reddening face. Now it was Scarlette's turn to laugh. The act finally gained the couple's attention.

"Brenna, this is Adelaide and Bertram," Stephen introduced

the newest part of their family to his aunt and uncle. Adelaide approached the two girls and took each of their hands to stand in a small circle.

"Oh, she is just beautiful. Just look at that lovely dark hair." Then she gasped, "And Scarlette! You've grown into an attractive and distinguished woman. So much like your mother!" Brenna quickly glanced at Scarlette, then to Stephen, trying to figure out what she meant. Scarlette hardly looked a thing like Lanna. Lanna had green eyes and very curly red hair. Nothing like Scarlette's straight auburn hair and dark eyes. She wondered why it had never occurred to her before. However, she didn't have much time to think it over, for they were ushered into the house.

"Mildred, will show you to your rooms," Adelaide took charge once inside. "After you get settled, we'll have dinner. The cook made your favorite," she smiled at Stephen. "Are you sure you won't stay the Season with us? I wished all of you could have come for a good long visit."

"Lanna wanted to come. You know I would love to stay, but Audrey is still very little and it's busy this time of year."

"Yes, of course." Brenna marveled at how Adelaide was so warm and bubbly but at the same time, she held herself gracefully with refined poise.

Brenna looked around at the spacious entry. For such a narrow building from the outside appearance, the inside was very roomy. The white marble floor and columns were very bright and welcoming. Not to mention the exquisite statues, among some greenery. It made Brenna wonder what the rest of the house would be like if the mere entry was so lavish. Scarlette moved to her side and linked arms with hers while the others took charge of their luggage.

"Isn't this place something?" she giggled excitedly.

"Yes!" she breathlessly replied. "And they seem so kind."

"They give several balls here during the season. Well, they used to at least. Probably less as they're growing older. And to think, this is only their town house! I've been to their home in the country only a few times that I can remember."

Brenna remained speechless as the maid led them through more magnificent rooms and to the grand staircase. From her first impression of the grand home, Brenna would have guessed that the owners were wealthy and most likely snide and pious. But because Adelaide and Bertram were so friendly and kind, it made it feel so much homier and comfortable. Brenna could now relax and put herself at ease during their stay for the summer.

When Scarlette and Brenna had unpacked and changed for dinner, they made their way to the dining room. Again Brenna was taken aback by the sheer detail in the large room. The dark walls were brightened by the molding that glistened with a sort of golden tint. It made a person's gaze follow it upward to the ceiling where it became lighter with whimsical paintings. The room was complete with two crystal chandeliers.

When Bertram and Stephen saw the young ladies, they both stood and waited for them to come in and be seated. Since the table was quite substantial, they all sat at one end to be together.
Even the dishes match the room! Brenna thought. It was then that Adelaide entered. Adelaide was dressed so elegantly that Brenna turned to Scarlette and whispered, "Are there others coming for dinner?"

"No," she replied with confusion. She soon realized what she meant. "Aunt always dresses this way for the evening meal."

"Even when it's just family?"

"Oh yes! Probably more so when she's here in London than at their home in the country."

"I'm so glad to have all of you with us," she smiled as she looked at everyone and gracefully sat down after everyone was seated. Bertram led them in prayer then dinner was served.

"You must tell us about young Tully," Adelaide glanced at Scarlette, "The last time we were at Caragin for a visit, he had just been born."

"He's like any other youngster. Very sweet at times,"

Stephen replied.

"But can get into trouble all too easily!" Scarlette finished her father's sentence and Adelaide and Bertram chuckled. Adelaide turned to the young ladies before asking her next question.

"And the newest Kinsey member…Audrey? What is she like?"

"Delightful and sweet. She has bright eyes like her mother and," Scarlette glanced at her father, "Her nose is like Father's." Everyone snikered again.

"Poor girl…if she looks anything like Stephen with his smeller!" Bertram smiled wryly as another round of laughter broke out.

"Well, now I'm not sorry to be leaving in the morning, rather than put up with this," Stephen joked.

"It's good to see you in such light spirits. I remember a time not so very long ago that nothing could lift you out of your sad place."

Brenna watched the family suddenly go from jesting to very solemn. What were they talking about? She gazed at everyone in confusion. Even Scarlette's face lowered in sadness.

I'll have to ask Scarlette later. Brenna thought. She dared not do it presently, for the family seemed close to tears.

"Yes…it wasn't very long ago," Stephen met her daughter's gaze knowingly. Brenna didn't miss it.

"But it does seem much longer. Lanna is such a joy. The children love her dearly and she them. It is as if they have all belonged to her from the start."

Adelaide must have noticed Brenna's muddled stare.

"I take it, Brenna doesn't know the lovely story." At first Brenna was surprised that she knew her thoughts. Though, she seemed attentive to everyone.

"Would you like to hear it? It's a wonderful story really." Brenna nodded.

"Lanna came to stay with us, oh…probably about five years ago. It started out to be a favor for a friend, Rose Wesley. She was to stay with us for the Season so I could take her under my wing and introduce her into society. It wasn't long before Bertram and I realized it to be no favor at all, but instead a blessing. Lanna was bright, cheerful, kind, and a Godsend. Especially during the hard time we had just experienced months before. Stephen's first wife had passed, leaving him to care for five little ones, Katherine only being a babe. We had raised Stephen as our own after his parents had passed on. During this troubling time, things weighed heavily on him," Adelaide purposely didn't look at Stephen for fear of losing her composure or causing him to. She knew he could very well tell this himself, but since he didn't say a word, she presumed it was still quite hard to speak of.

But talking about it brings healing.

Something inside her beckoned her to continue.

"He decided to leave his grieving family for a short time and come to us for help and guidance. Little did he know, the visit would change everything. I truly believe it was the hand of God Himself that brought you to us at that moment," Adelaide smiled and finally made herself glance over at him. Stephen's expression was still doleful, but he nodded in agreement. "Needless to say, he stayed longer than he planned. Lanna was and still is very strong in her beliefs. Her spirit surely shines with Christ's love. Why, her mere presence seemed to bring Stephen peace. Within a year, they were married." With that, the sadness that had swept over the room faded and in its place a warm feeling of love and the closeness this family had.

Brenna now knew why she liked the Cheverell's right from the start. It was obvious they were sincere believers. Thankfully all of her questions were now satisfied. She had always thought in the back of her mind that Lanna looked much too young to mother all seven children. At that moment, a maid came to take their empty plates.

"Enough about me," Stephen sighed, sat back from the table, and put his hand over his stomach. "What kind of things do you have planned for the next few months for I know you to be quite the planner?"

"Since you ask, tomorrow I will be sending in the application for these beautiful young ladies to be presented at court," Adelaide replied. Scarlette gasped with excitement and clasped her hands together. She turned to Brenna, who still didn't know exactly what it all meant, but grinned anyway.

"Then there is the hiring of two ladies' maids for them, fittings for complete new wardrobes including the debutant gown of course, etiquette classes for the presentation at the palace, luncheons, dinner parties, operas, portraits, soirées, balls, the races…" Brenna couldn't help but keep her gaze fixed on Scarlette. She thought she might faint with pleasure. It also made Brenna more eager when she saw their anticipation. They would definitely not be bored.

"Ah, yes. I forgot how busy the Season can be. It's been many years since I've been a part of it."

"I can see that you're enthralled with it all," Bertram sarcastically spoke, "I suggest we retire to the sitting room."

CHAPTER THIRTY-FOUR

"My Lady," All three women looked up from their reading when a maid entered. "Miss Trembley and Miss Voclain have arrived." Scarlette and Brenna exchanged puzzled glances when Adelaide happily replied.

"Oh good! Please have Terrance bring their things to their rooms and send them in." As soon as the maid left, Adelaide swiftly turned to the girls.

"What perfect timing."

"What is it?" Brenna and Scarlette asked in unison.

"Your ladies' maids. They came all the way from France."

"France? Aunt, are you quite serious? How marvelous!" Scarlette was aflutter and bounced up and down in her seat. However, when she remembered Adelaide's presence and what they had just been speaking about, she quickly calmed herself. For the past few days, before the balls and parties officially began, Adelaide had been hard at work showing them the correct etiquette such as how to present yourself with modesty and what was expected of them. Growing up, Scarlette had been trained in some of these things by her governess, but this was to ready them for marriage and being a proper hostess. Adelaide was very patient and kind through it all for Brenna and Scarlette were still fairly young. She was a perfect example of what the young ladies strived to become.

"France has the latest styles so they will be able to show us all the most fashionable attributes to attain," Adelaide gently set aside the books she'd been showing them and smoothed her skirt. "I hope they will be a good match for both of you...for years to come. Why, I still have my ladies' maid from my coming of age." Brenna thought of the maid she used to have at Kenwood. Sadly, the only memorable thing about it was how she used to boss her around the entire time. It wasn't just her maid. All the staff had to put up with her demands, even as a young girl. If they didn't give in, she would go running to her father. To this day Brenna was ashamed of how she treated everyone.

The worst part is, I'll never be able to apologize for my actions, she thought as the maid returned with two young women. Adelaide, Brenna, and Scarlette stood to greet them. Brenna guessed that they weren't much older than her. They both wore nice but rather plain dresses. It was obvious they weren't related for one was tall and very slender with light almost white blonde hair and sky blue eyes while the shorter of the two had shiny chestnut hair with hazel eyes. Both were quite handsome.

"My Ladyship," both ladies curtsied, "At your service. I am Eleta Trembley," the taller woman stepped forward.

"And I am Pensee Voclain," the other took her turn. Because her voice was lower, she seemed older than the other. Brenna and Scarlette smiled upon hearing their heavy French accents.

"Pleased to meet you," Adelaide approached and shook their hands before moving aside. "These are my great nieces, Brenna and Scarlette Kinsey, whom you will be attending." The maids curtsied again while the girls greeted them.

"Let us have a seat so we can go over things," Adelaide showed them in. Brenna noticed that she was more business-like now, but still a perfect lady.

"I hope your journey went well?"

"Yes, My Lady," Pensee replied.

"Good. We might as well get down to things straight away so you have time to rest. We already discussed compensation through our correspondence. I will give you three days' time to get settled before your duties are to begin. In the meantime, Brenna and Scarlette will be fitted for complete wardrobes. We don't know the exact date they will be summoned to be presented at court, but we will go ahead and have their court gowns made for the event. Anyway, I want to ask your opinions about the newest fashions and what we should have made or not."

"I vould say at leest a dozen evening gowns. Two silk afternoon dresses, a white Indian muslin dress for lawn parties, complete wiss hats and bonnets for each outfit. Parasols, mantles, and of course two dozen pairs of gloves," Pensee stated with enthusiasm then glanced at Eleta to see if she wanted to add anything.

"Perhaps one or two pale gowns of pastel silk for small dinner parties as well, no?"

"Excellent, I will keep all of that in mind. I will leave all of you young ladies to get acquainted and to decide who would like to attend to whom. I will have the housekeeper come in a few minutes to go over the last few details then you may retire." With that, Adelaide rose and left.

May 1844

Brenna was amazed at how busy London was becoming more and more each day with everyone arriving in anticipation of the long awaited Season to start. She had just stepped out of their grand open carriage in front of the Cheverell's home and patiently waited for Adelaide, Bertram, and Scarlette to follow. Brenna turned to watch the crowded streets with countless carriages, buggies, horses, and people taking a leisurely stroll.

"What a wonderful day it is. I'm so glad we went to Hyde Park," Adelaide sighed and reached up to hold her hat as a gentle breeze came up. Brenna also reached for her hat which was part of her new wardrobe.

"Yes, but the wind does seem to be picking up a bit," Bertram looked up at the sky, "Perhaps we should take the enclosed carriage to the luncheon," he glanced at the driver who nodded in return.

"Well, come along. We must change and then be off."

"Welcome home. Did you have a nice time?" James opened the door for them and stepped aside.

"Yes it was lovely," Scarlette and Brenna both replied and smiled. The butler enjoyed the two guests for they were always pleasant, polite, and graced everything they did with happy enthusiasm. The three women made their way through the entrance to the stairs when they heard a knock at the front door. They all stopped and turned to watch with curiosity as James answered it. They caught sight of a man dressed in regal attire. He didn't come in, but merely bowed and handed the butler something.

"The Lord Chamberlin, from Her Royal Highness' court, summons Miss Scarlette Kinsey and Miss Brenna Kinsey to be presented on June first," he stiffly bowed again and left. After James shut the door, Scarlette couldn't hold her excitement back any longer and clasped her hands and giggled.

"How thrilling! June first…just think Brenna, only one month and we'll be out in society," Scarlette grasped her hand and giddily sprung about until Brenna joined in. Adelaide and Bertram chuckled at the sight.

"June first it is. It's a perfect date. Not too soon with plenty of time to finish everything and yet not too late in the Season. Now off with you," she shooed them, "Have Pensee and Eleta help you dress."

"Through the tender mercy of
our God; whereby the dayspring
from on high hath visited us,
to give light to them that sit in
darkness and in the shadow of
death, to guide our feet into the
way of peace."

Luke 1:78-79

CHAPTER THIRTY-FIVE

he night Scarlette and Brenna had long awaited for since arriving in London had finally come. The first of many balls was upon them. After the ladies' maids helped them dress and styled their hair, Scarlette and Brenna finally came out of their rooms, where they'd spent most of the day readying themselves. They made their way to the drawing room where Adelaide and Bertram waited. However, before they presented themselves to their aunt, both girls made sure everything was perfect. Brenna reached up and put a stray hair back into its place while Scarlette pinched her cheeks for color. Brenna smiled when she turned and saw that Pensee and Eleta had followed them. She knew very well they also wanted to ensure that they looked their best. Both ladies' maids took their job very seriously. After all, Brenna and Scarlette were the direct example of their expertise and they wanted to prove their ability to the lady of the house, especially since this was the first ball.

"How do I look? Did I ruin my hair?" Brenna glanced at Pensee and sighed.

"You look magnifique! Our veree pride and joy, no? Eleta?"

"Oui, oui! Now, Miss, please don't pinch your cheeks anymore! You look quite flushed alreadee," Eleta approached Scarlette and readjusted the bow on the back of her dress. After a few more last minute adjustments were completed, Pensee and Eleta stood back and took in all their hard work and pronounced in unison, "All finished!"

Adelaide and Bertram stood as Scarlette and Breanna slowly entered. The ladies' maids peeked in to see their expressions and immediately breathed a sigh of relief when they appeared to be pleased.

"Oh my, you both look positively breathtaking!" Adelaide exclaimed.

"Very stunning," Bertram put in.

"Come and let me have a better look at you." The young ladies did as she asked and each turned around in a circle.

"Brenna, how that royal blue brings out your eyes! The netting on the skirt is delightful, as is the brocade."

"Thank you," Brenna replied and tried not to blush.

"And Scarlette, the print on your rose gown is lovely as well," Adelaide bent slightly and touched her skirt, "the embroidery is so intricate. What did Eleta call it? It was a strange name"

"Um…scalloped ecru," Scarlette recalled.

"Oh yes. My, what will they be able to do next?"

"It's truly all thanks to you, dear Aunt," Scarlette gave her a quick kiss on the cheek.

"Yes, we are very grateful for all you've done for us," Brenna meekly did the same.

"Well, we're glad to have you with us," Adelaide responded.

"But there is a bit of a problem," Bertram pointed to his cheek, "Where is my kiss?" He was swiftly joined by a round of laughter.

"Your hair is quite beautiful as well. Pensee and Eleta did a splendid job." Hearing this, the maids looked at each other in glee. They made their way back upstairs for their job was done for the evening, that is until Brenna and Scarlette returned home.

They took a short ride through the wealthy streets of London until the home of the Eldridge's came into view. The tall town house was brightly lit up as it warmly welcomed the carriages that lined the street in front of it.

"I can hardly wait to see Cora!" Scarlette peered out of the carriage as they patiently waited their turn in line.

"You know the Eldridge family?" Brenna asked.

"Ever since I can recall."

"Old family friends," Bertram went on to explain with a nod. "Cora is my age. In fact, she is most likely going to be presented at court this Season as well. She is the youngest of four brothers! Can you imagine?" A small pang of something Brenna had buried deep within seemed to stir. Sad thoughts of her own three brothers came to mind in torrents, tempting her to recall her past. The only other times it happened anymore was in her dreams and they would hold onto her for a long while. Brenna quickly stifled them as quickly as they had appeared. Thankfully, no one else noticed as they came to the entrance and stopped. A footman opened the carriage door and Bertram stepped out first, as was the polite thing to do so he could reach out and assist the women in climbing out in their full gowns.

Adelaide took Bertram's arm and led the way up the stairs to the grand entrance, greeting and nodding to people as they past. *passed* The inside of the Eldridge's home was just as becoming as the exterior. It was bright and cheerful with countless sconces that lined the wall, directing them to the main ballroom. Brenna didn't know why, but upon seeing so many people, her stomach began to flutter with a nervous excitement.

Before going further, Adelaide and the young ladies separated from Bertram and made a brief stop to the lady's sitting room. There they rid themselves of their warm cloaks, arranged their dresses, and made sure their hair was still in place. There were several mirrors in the room and maids present to offer any assistance.

Bertram was passively waiting outside the sitting room among other gentleman, who did the same.

"Are you ready, dear?" Adelaide quietly asked and Bertram nodded in return.

"Come along," she turned to look at Scarlette and Brenna and gave them a reassuring smile, "You look simply beautiful."

"Thank you," they replied. With that, they were off to the ballroom.

The friendly glow from the sparkling chandelier and sconces radiated off the soft pearl colored walls, edged with decorative moldings that framed classical figures and swags. Innumerable people were already busy milling about in light conversation. The becoming scene was complete as the orchestra began to play a waltz and people started to dance.

Scarlette and Brenna timidly followed Adelaide and Bertram through the crowd that had formed into small groups. They greeted several people in each group then continued on to the third. By the time they had just reached the next group of people, Cora Eldridge caught sight of Scarlette and rushed over to them.

"Scarlette Kinsey, is that you?" Brenna turned and watched a vibrant young woman quickly approach and embrace Scarlette like an excitable child. Scarlette laughed as she did. Once Cora released her, she stepped back and grasped both her hands.

"My, you look wonderful! Like someone who's to be presented at court this Season...am I right?" Cora asked and smiled from ear to ear.

"Indeed! And I presume you plan to as well?"

"Why yes!" Cora grinned.

"Miss Cora, how are you?" Adelaide came over at this point since Bertram was talking to another gentleman.

"Very well, Lady Millborrow," Cora faced her elder and curtsied, "I'm glad you could attend this evening." Right at that moment, another refined lady from the group began talking to Adelaide. That was the first time Cora seemed to notice Brenna, who stood beside Scarlette. Scarlette also must have noticed her inquisitive stare.

"Cora, this is my sister Brenna. Brenna, this is my dear friend, Cora Eldridge." Both young women briefly curtsied.

"I heard you had obtained a new addition to your family. But I never imagined someone so...sophisticated."

"It's so nice to meet you. You have a beautiful home."

"Thank you," Cora replied as she spotted a handsome young man causing her to fluster. "You must go and get your dance cards! There are many eligible and dashing young men present," her eyes never left the man as she spoke, "So we must get busy!"

Cora then leaned in closer to Scarlette and Brenna and giggled. "Have a wonderful time, dears," she bustled away.

Brenna couldn't help but laugh at how ecstatic Cora was.

"And I thought you were excited, Scarlette. Miss Eldridge is ten times more so!" They both chuckled loudly at this. That is until two young men walked by, causing them to quickly quiet down and act more ladylike. One of the men seemed to hold Brenna's gaze longer than any other, though she didn't know why. Something about his presence drew her attention to him. The way he carried himself across the ballroom floor made her wonder if he was some sort of nobility.

When the gentlemen moved out of ear shot, the girls finally realized that Adelaide and Bertram had moved on without them. They swiftly exchanged glances before catching up to them just as the orchestra finished the waltz.

After a light midnight supper had been served hours later, the dancing started up again in full force. Brenna and Scarlette had been introduced to a vast amount of people and danced with a few gentlemen, but not as many as Scarlette had hoped. She voiced her disappointment when she sat down next to Adelaide and Brenna after dancing a quadrille. She waited until the young man left before she sat back and sighed.

"I had hoped to dance much more. There are far more beautiful women present, I suppose." Brenna opened her mouth to disagree, but Adelaide spoke first.

"You mustn't worry. This is only the first ball of the Season, and only a private one, mind you. There will be plenty more. So many that you'll most likely tire of them before the end. And don't forget that you aren't officially out in society as of yet, which means you're not quite known yet," she reassured. At that moment, someone slowly approached.

"Will you favor me with your hand for this dance?" A young man stood before Scarlette at a proper distance and bent slightly.

Brenna glanced at him and saw it was the same man she'd been drawn to earlier that evening. What was it about him that intrigued her? With his dark hair and broad build, he carried an air of relaxed confidence and at the same time mystery. She watched Scarlette eagerly accept his request and followed him onto the crowded dance floor and continued to do so throughout the entire song, although she did her best not to stare.

It wasn't until the music ended and he led her back to her seat that Rylan noticed Brenna, who sat next to the empty chair, talking to an older woman beside her. He bowed to Scarlette then couldn't help but peruse in Brenna's direction again, for he had seen her somewhere before. Her face was fair, though a bit flushed from the warmth of the dancing and overcrowded room, but it only caused her blue eyes, framed with dark hair, to intensify all the more. If not for anything else, he was sure he'd seen her bright eyes, filled with childlike innocence, before.
But where?

As he slowly made his way back to some of his friends, he tried to watch his step and the young lady at the same time. He wasn't doing a very good job at it and nearly plowed right into an elderly woman.

"Pardon me," he nodded with embarrassment.

"Quenell, you need to mind where you're going!" A noisy man bellowed in the midst of a handful of other single men, who joined in the laughter. Rylan didn't say anything, but instead moved closer to them because he noticed one of the Eldridge's among them.

Surely he must know everyone who might be present, he thought hopefully.

"Daniel."

"Yes? Are you enjoying yourself?" the man no older than Rylan, turned to him and smiled roguishly, for he too had witnessed the mishap.

"Yes, yes…say, do you happen to know that young lady sitting over there?" Rylan leaned closer to him and tried to motion in Brenna's direction without having to point.

"I'm sorry, no. But I do know the one next to her," Daniel spotted Scarlette, "She's good friends with my sister, Cora."

"Good," Rylan grinned, "So then…."

"Say no more," Daniel snickered. He knew his duties well as one of the hosts of the house. "Follow me."

By now the lady of interest and the other she was with had slowly made their way to the refreshments on the far side of the room. Brenna saw the two men coming towards them just as she took a sip of punch. She quickly swallowed to keep from choking and nudged Scarlette, who stood next to her, to let her know they were coming while Adelaide was busy talking to a group of ladies nearby.

Rylan did his best not to appear too eager, but calm and collected.

"Miss Scarlette, how are you this fine night?"

"Very well. Thank you, Mr. Eldridge." Daniel looked over at Rylan, who confidently yet at the same time humbly stepped forward.

"I would like to introduce Lord Rylan Lennox, Earl of Quenell," Daniel's gaze moved from Rylan to Scarlette, "This is Miss Kinsey," then lastly to Brenna as he waited for Scarlette to present her mysterious friend.

"Pleased to meet you, Lord Quenell," Scarlette curtsied as was customary, especially to a member of peerage.

"This is my sister, Miss Brenna Kinsey. Brenna, Daniel Eldridge, Cora's brother." Brenna curtsied as well.

"Please to make your acquaintances," she felt her face grow warm when she exchanged a polite glance with Lord Quenell.

When Rylan heard Brenna speak, his fascination grew all the more. Her accent was unlike any he'd known from any habitant of England or any place surrounding it. It was even different from her sister.

How could that be? He wondered and wished he could question her, but alas, it wouldn't be proper. Along with his growing interest was the same thought as previously, that he indeed knew this woman from somewhere, but under far different circumstances. He continued to think hard on this as he and Daniel kindly parted ways.

Throughout the remainder of the busy evening, Rylan kept a keen eye on the beautiful young lady. She was different than everyone else he observed. Miss Kinsey wasn't desperately seeking to be noticed by the men as many other women strived to do, making the most distinguished acquaintances, or dancing more than their competition. She was merely enjoying herself and taking it all in. At first, Rylan thought he was only drawn to the mysterious lady to find out where he'd seen her prior to this, but he was beginning to realize that it was something more. Somehow there was more to this petite woman than one could see from her outward appearance, though he couldn't put his finger on it.

It was the wee hours of the morning before Brenna finally crawled into bed. In fact, it would only be an hour or two before dawn. Even though she was exhausted, sleep didn't come immediately as she reflected over the wonderful evening. It wasn't long in doing so when Lord Rylan came to mind.

Why is he different than any other? Brenna sighed as she lay back on her pillow. *It was nothing more than a polite introduction and swift glance.* The peculiar feeling came over her once again. It was the same as when she first beheld his ardent gaze, while she curtsied upon meeting him.

The last thing Brenna expected to hear was a soft knock at the door. She lifted her head to see Scarlette enter. Her long hair draped down the back of her white night gown. She smiled but didn't say anything until she tiptoed to Brenna's bed and giddily jumped onto it.

"I didn't think you'd be asleep yet. How could anyone after having such a marvelous night?" Scarlette sprawled out to get comfortable and propped her head on her hands. Although she was equally exhausted, Scarlette never seized to be excited, but

ceased

Brenna loved her because of it. She never looked for the bad in anything, and in turn never found any.

"It was quite fun, wasn't it?" Brenna moved onto her side to face her and thought herself foolish for saying it. It sounded as if she was surprised that she could actually have fun and enjoy herself. "I'm glad I got to meet some of your friends and acquaintances. I especially liked Cora!"

"She is a quip. Were you present when she came up to me right after we were introduced to Lord Quenell?"

"No, I must have been dancing at the time."

"Well," Scarlette gasped then quickly lowered her voice, though it wasn't likely than anyone could hear them in such a large house. "Cora said as soon as she saw that I was dancing with him, she knew she must inform me about him and his family. She said it was scandalous really."

"Like what?"

"I guess Lord Quenell and his family live in a large estate in Ireland and own a vast amount of land there."

"What is so scandalous about that?"

"Well nothing…yet. It has been told that one night his father, Lord Kerrich came upon a horrible sight. His brother was burning down the home of one of their tenants in the middle of the night for mere pleasure. The people who lived in the house were fast asleep. Lord Kerrich was going to try and save them, but his brother wouldn't let him. Although he didn't mean to, he killed his own brother to save the people inside. He later found out that one of the women who lived there was carrying his brother's child. To save the family from disgrace, Lord Kerrich married her and claimed the child as his own. He was soon caught for the death of his brother and was supposed to hang, but he somehow escaped. His son, Lord Quenell is the woman's child and has been looked down upon his entire life." Scarlette finished and waited for a response from Brenna. For a brief moment, she thought she had fallen asleep when she didn't say anything, but then she finally spoke.

"Do you think all of that is true?"

"Cora does. But…it is a rumor, I guess. Lord Quenell is sort of mysterious, don't you agree?"

"It would seem so. He seemed quite taken with you," Brenna glanced at Scarlette to see her expression in the moon lit room.

"I don't know about that," she replied and smiled dreamily.

CHAPTER THIRTY-SIX

ylan promptly walked to his carriage and was about to climb inside when he turned to the driver. "Yes, My Lord?" the driver, who sat atop the enclosed buggy, asked when Rylan didn't say anything, but instead looked past him.

"Uh…yes," Rylan stepped down into the street again. His gaze was still fixed on something in the distance. "I will be along in a moment." The driver watched Rylan walk across the busy street and approach someone coming out of the bank.

When Rylan saw Bertram Cheverell, a hopeful thought came to him.

Perhaps in talking to him, I'll find out more about the mysterious young woman. Ever since the ball, he couldn't stop wondering about her and where they had met before. He'd questioned Daniel Eldridge further that same evening as to whom the Kinsey sisters were staying with and found out it was Betram and Adelaide Cheverell, Viscount and Viscountess of Millborow.

"Lord Millborow, how are you enjoying this mild spring day?" Rylan met him at the bottom of the steps in front of the building. When Bertram saw him he slowed to a stop.

"Ah yes, I recall meeting you at the Eldridge's. I do fancy this weather. And you?"

"Yes. Do you plan to attend the soiree at the Younge's home tomorrow evening?" he nonchalantly began the questioning.

"I'm not certain, but if my wife has anything to say about it, we surely will. She wants our guests to experience just about everything during their stay for the Season," Bertram informed Rylan, who listened intently.

"Have they traveled far?"

"Not overly. The young women are from Dolbury and are our great nieces."

"I see." Although Bertram had supplied him with some valuable information, it did little to satisfy him. *At least they will be in London for the entire Season, so we'll most likely meet again,* he reassured himself.

"Well, I better be on my way. It was nice talking with you."

"And with you." The men shook hands and kindly parted ways.

The moment Rylan arrived at the home of the Younge's, he searched out the Kinsey sisters and quickly found them listening to someone singing a ballad. Because he didn't want to seem forward, he waited until later on in the evening before going over to them. The time finally came as the refreshments were served.

Rylan had just put some lobster and chicken salad on his plate when he realized that Miss Kinsey was also in line and only two people behind him. Little did he know, Brenna was equally aware of his presence from where she stood. Once he was through, he slowed his pace until she and her family were finished and past by him before he spoke.

"Lord Millborow, we meet again."

"Certainly. How are you?" Bertram stopped and shook his hand.

"Very good." Adelaide, Scarlette, and Brenna stopped and politely stood behind Bertram.

"I say, what did I tell you?' Bertram leaned closer to the young man and slightly lowered his voice. "You see that my wife did wish to attend after all."

"Indeed," Rylan chuckled and glanced at the three women behind him.

"Let me introduce my wife, Adelaide. Dear," Bertram turned as Adelaide gracefully stepped forward. "This is Rylan Lennox, Earl of Quenell."

"Pleased to meet you, Lady Millborow." Rylan bowed as Adelaide curtsied.

"As I, you."

Brenna watched the whole exchange in sheer amazement. She could only wish to someday be nearly as ladylike as her great aunt.

"Have you met my nieces?" Bertram stepped back to present Scarlette and Brenna, who nervously smiled.

There goes my face becoming warm again, Brenna thought to herself. What was it about him that caused her to feel this way? His piercing, grey eyes didn't miss a thing. She couldn't help but wonder if he noticed her uneasy thoughts.

"Yes we have met." Her bashfulness grew worse when Lord Quenell's gazed rested upon her as she curtsied and he bowed slightly.

"Are you enjoying the evening?" Rylan tried to come up with something to say to stir up a conversation in hopes of awaking some kind of recollection of where he might know Brenna from.

"Yes," was all Brenna could think of for a suitable reply.

"Very much so," Scarlette also spoke.

"Are you?" Brenna forced herself to boldly ask.

"Yes," he could have said more, but at that moment another piano selection began and everyone present began to make their way to their seats.

"It was nice talking with you again," Bertram nodded to the young man.

"And with you," Rylan watched the four walk closer to the performance.

Well into the song, Cora Eldridge drew near to Scarlette and sat down on the empty seat beside her.

"Cora, how are you? I didn't know you were here!" Scarlette spoke to her softly so not to distract from the entertainment.

"I arrived only an hour ago. I'm well, and you?"

"Good. You remember my sister, Brenna?" Scarlette leaned back to let Brenna in on the conversation and Cora politely nodded. Cora's expression, usually full of excited delight, suddenly became serious as she leaned in closer for Brenna to hear also.

"I noticed Lord Quenell talking to you."

"Yes? He was merely saying hello."

Is there something wrong with that? Brenna thought, but didn't say anything.

"That isn't the only thing. He deliberately slowed his pace and made a special point of speaking with you."

"Really?" Scarlette exchanged a quick glance with Brenna, but she was unable to tell what she was thinking.

"It is true!" Cora stated with as much enthusiasm as possible. She nearly gasped as if this single bit of information was the most consequential piece of gossip and needed to be made known right away or she might burst. "It was quite obvious that he clearly wanted to make himself known…to you!" Cora waited for their response. However, when the sisters didn't immediately say anything, she sighed heavily with disappointment. She was no doubt, frustrated that they didn't share her important observation and concern.

"How did you witness this?" Brenna couldn't remain silent any longer.

"And why such interest?" Scarlette added.

"Well!" Cora huffed, "Well, dearest…one has to know these things about eligible gentlemen, which I pride myself to know! He is an Earl after all," she finally leaned back in her chair, exasperated. She apparently didn't want to talk to them anymore and scanned the room. "Oh, I must speak to someone," Cora rose, but at least kindly said goodbye, "I'll see you later. Bye."

"Goodbye," Scarlette replied and watched her flitter away. She turned to Brenna. Although she didn't say anything just then, Scarlette could tell by the amused light in Brenna's eyes that she felt the same.

"Then spake Jesus again unto them, saying, I am the light of the world: he that followeth me shall not walk in darkness, but shall have the light of life."

John 8:12

CHAPTER THIRTY-SEVEN

*T*he next morning Brenna and Scarlette donned their new riding habits for a leisurely ride at Hyde Park. The park, reserved for high society, was only a few blocks away from the Cheverell's home.

Once they rode under the grand arched entrance to the park, they slowly made their way, sidesaddle, to Rotten Row.

"I still don't understand why this beautiful place has such a terrible name such as Rotten Row," Brenna's nose wrinkled when she said it. "There's nothing rotten about it. Do you know?" she glanced at Scarlette.

"No, I guess I don't." They led their horses onto the sandy path and rode in silence, enjoying the loveliness of the day as two more riders came upon them. Brenna figured it must have been someone very important for as they stiffly passed by them, the regally dressed man and woman said nothing to them but only stuck their noses into the air. Why, even their horse seemed to do the same. Their position remained until they were far ahead of them. Unfortunately, the pompous couple weren't the only ones in the park who acted that way. The majority of the people there were just the same. Too high-minded to acknowledge anyone who might be below them.

"Scarlette, I think I know what this path is named for," Brenna said.

"What is that?"

"Well, what would you call that snobbery? Just what it is…rotten!" They both laughed at this.

"That makes perfect sense! At least we don't have to let it ruin our day. Did you enjoy the soiree last night?"

"Yes I did. I don't think Cora did though."

"Oh Cora…." Scarlette sighed, "She's always been that way. I just hope and pray when it finally comes down to it and she marries, that she'll make a wise decision, not only based on rank or income." Brenna nodded in agreement.

"Other than all of that, did you enjoy yourself?"

"Immensely!" A smile broke out on Brenna's face, "I did something for the very first time last night."

"Such as?"

"I haven't told anyone this, but…."

"What is it? What is it?" Scarlette eagerly wanted to know.

"I ate blackberries for the first time in my entire life!" she blurted.

"Are…you quite…serious?" Scarlette stopped her horse. She was certain Brenna must be jesting.

"I'm very serious."

"What did you think of them then?" Brenna stopped as well and suddenly put on her best smug expression, lifted her nose in the air, and stated in her most lofty British accent, "Blackberries might be pleasant in appearance and taste divine, but the feeling I get when I touch one to bring it to my lips is quite ghastly!"

"And why is that?" Scarlette tried her best to play along, but wouldn't be able to contain her delight much longer.

"Instead of blackberries, the texture feels more like…cold and clammy baby toes!" Both of them burst out laughing but Brenna wasn't finished. "No…more like bulbous baby toes!" As they howled even louder, Scarlette quickly glanced back at their two servants who accompanied them. Because they were out of earshot to allow the young ladies some privacy, they were completely oblivious to the giggling girls. Although the two servants were unaware, there was someone else who was watching them from a distance.

He had been going for a brisk stroll through the park when he came upon the young ladies, having a wonderful time and almost laughing uncontrollably. Rylan couldn't help but smile at Scarlette and Brenna, who he couldn't stop thinking about. He was glad to see they weren't stiff, boring, and consumed with who might be watching to make a respectable impression on. Most women he knew were always concerned about their strategy to make a rich match.

He took a step forward to make himself known when the young ladies' attention was drawn to something ahead of them. Instead of going further, Rylan followed their gaze to find out what the commotion was.

When Scarlette and Brenna heard a horrible noise that sounded like someone was choking, they looked ahead where the snooty couple was. Sure enough, the sound came from the woman's horse. The poor animal was hacking so hard that the lady atop it was being tossed up and down.

"Horace! Make it stop, make it stop!" she shrieked. She was more worried about her appearance than her horse. "Horace!" she now shouted above the noise, "Make this dreadful beast stop this!" But the man hadn't the slightest idea of what to do other than take the reins from his wife and try to coax the horse along to hopefully make it stop coughing. This went on for some time.

Scarlette and Brenna tried their very hardest to hide their sheer amusement by the pathetic scene. Brenna covered her mouth to keep from bursting as it became more humorous all of a sudden.

"Don't just sit there…do something!" The woman started to slap her husband's arm. It wasn't until he finally dismounted and walked the horse a little ways before the commotion eventually ended and the couple went back to the way they were. Brenna didn't know how they could keep a straight face and just go on with their ride without so much as a chuckle. Even Horace remained solemn through the entire ordeal.

The minute Brenna glanced at Scarlette, holding back was all over. They roared so hard that they nearly fell off their own horses.

"Oh…my…face hurts!" Scarlette gasped as she wiped away joyful tears. Brenna did the same and sat up from her bent position to see Rylan approach.

"Lord Quenell," she blurted without thinking, "How are you?" but quickly recovered her surprise.

"I'm glad to see you're both enjoying yourselves."

"Perhaps too much," Scarlette put in.

"I rather like it." Brenna's gaze shot back to the earl. While he seemed very nice from what she'd seen so far, Brenna expected him to be like everyone else that shared his rank in society.

When Rylan saw that they were taken back by what he said, he continued to explain further.

"I find it refreshing to see young ladies such as yourselves truly at ease without pretense or poise all the time. It shows true character." Brenna and Scarlette didn't know how to respond to this. They knew Adelaide most likely wouldn't agree. She was trying to teach them how to appear ladylike and becoming, showing just enough character to attract the right husband without revealing too much intellectual or literary interests. It was known as bluestocking tendencies.

"I'm also relieved that your horses didn't catch anything such as a coughing spell." Scarlette and Brenna chuckled softly.

"You were present during the episode as well, I see."

"As I recall, I read somewhere that horses often experience coughing symptoms when they're in the presence of insolent behavior. An irritant in his throat as well as on his back most likely." If they hadn't been so astonished, the sisters would have been laughing outright as his witty remark.

Is he truly an earl? They thought, for he was far too genuine and unpretentious. Whatever he was, Scarlette and Brenna's impression of Lord Quenell completely changed at that moment and their admiration grew greatly.

"Well, I leave you two lovely ladies to your ride. Have a wonderful and eventful rest of the day."

"Thank you," Scarlette replied.

"And you as well." Brenna said.

When Rylan turned to leave, he was again tempted to just ask where Brenna and he had met before, but then decided against it, at least for the time being.

"For ye were sometimes darkness, but now are ye light in the Lord: walk as children of light."

Ephesians 5:8

CHAPTER THIRTY-EIGHT

anic stirred in her as her arms and legs were held down. She was completely constrained, as she was thrown inside and the cover came down on top of her. All was dark as pitch with only enough room to pound her fists against the lid until her hands burned. Brenna's screams were all but muffled as her mind reeled with thoughts of never escaping.

"No one will ever find you," the darkness seemed to whisper in her ear. She held her breath for she would rather do that then feel her shallow breaths slowly smothered from the lack of air as she waited. Brenna eventually moved from one horror only to face the next. The single thing that held comfort was the faint breeze she finally felt. The thick heavy air, laden with salt, in the alley was better than no air at all.

Brenna tried to calm her shaky breath and wobbling knees and slowly stepped deeper down the filthy street. As she past it, a thought came to her. *passed*

Look at it! Just look! Something she wouldn't have braved to do before crossed her mind, *Perhaps if I do what I haven't tried yet, I'll wake up…sooner…and escape this.* Brenna was about to turn to the dreaded spot when she was swiftly distracted by something strange.

The horrible event that usually took place next still happened but this time much more suddenly. The hand before her, the terrifying presence that gripped her from behind occurred all at once.

Was it because I dared to glance over and take in the deathly— Brenna didn't have time to ponder over it for her thoughts were immediately interrupted by the rumbling behind ∧ her as the wind from the shadows, filled with fear, came at her. No longer creeping over her shoulder as in previous times, but *no* poured over her in torrents. She only glanced up at the hand before the blackness encompassed her completely.

Brenna awoke with a gasp and gripped her disorderly blankets. Although her eyes were wide open, it was so dark in her room it almost seemed unnatural. For a brief moment, Brenna wasn't sure if she had awakened, but was still in danger. The daunting sensation of the shadows overtaking her wasn't dwindling like it usually did, but was slowly growing worse.

Am I truly awake? Brenna sat up and looked around the eerie room. One thing was certain, she couldn't sit there and do nothing and wait for the presence to leave. The longer she gazed all around her room, the closer the feeling got and began to suffocate her as if being locked in the trunk all over again.

She stumbled out of bed, tripping over her sheets in haste and rushed to the wash basin. She cupped her hands in the water and splashed it on her face in hopes of waking herself up. After drying her face, Brenna blinked several times and scanned the room again. This time it seemed a bit brighter, but didn't feel relieved just yet. The little light there was, coming from the window was still queer. She hesitantly turned from the dresser to peer out the window. The moon was covered by dense fog so thick she couldn't see the street from her third story window. It gave the haunting sky a yellowish glow that made her shiver.

Brenna knew something wasn't right.

"God, please make the morning come quickly," she prayed. Her voice quivered with fright. She continued to stare outside until she thought she saw something through the mist. It appeared to resemble a figure of a person. *Impossible! I'm far too high up to see anyone.* It then began to dawn on her that something was very wrong! "Lord, make me wake up from this!" a terrified cry escaped her lips as the dark figure slowly got clearer. She couldn't remain silent any longer. "Wake up, please wake up!" Brenna backed away from the window. What should she do? *Scarlette! I'll go to Scarlette.*

Brenna was in a cold sweat by the time she reached the door. Her hand shook with urgency as she pulled it opened. She no longer cared if anyone heard her. She had to escape! Scarlette's room was down the hall Brenna started to run for it. Her heart beat so loudly it rang in her ears as she ran from whatever might ~~lied~~ *lay* be lurking behind her. However, when she saw what ~~lied~~ before her, her heart leaped inside her chest and she instantly came to a halt. Brenna shrieked in horror, for a dark, black cloud crept toward her just like shadows in her dream. But this was no dream.

She spun around and retraced her steps back to her room as fast as she could. What at first sounded like a sure plan to get away now proved to be the worst of all. She was too scared to cry out for help as the darkness chased her down the hall. Until she reached her room and slammed the door, she knew all too well that a mere wooden door couldn't save her from the evil presence. Fear gripped her as she tightly shut her eyes for she didn't want to see what most likely waited for her in the room. All Brenna could do was lean against the closed door and try to catch her breath. She felt like she might faint because she couldn't slow her heart beat and hard breathing. She had no strength left.

Why should I fight the darkness if there's no hope of escaping it? Brenna slid to the floor, her back still against the door, tempted to give in to the darkness and simply give up. She kept her eyes shut as she quivered against the door and began to cry. "God, where are you?" she screamed.

"Miss…Miss Brenna?" Brenna slowly stirred at the muffled voice coming from somewhere far away. It slowly came closer and closer. "Miss…are you alright?" Whoever it was knocked several times. It seemed to draw Brenna out of her tortured sleep. She was just opening her eyes when the door opened, causing her to fall back. "Oh, Miss!" the ladies' maid gasped and jumped back when Brenna unexpect~~antly~~ *edly* sprawled out onto the floor. "I'm so

sorree. I knocked many times. I thought somesinc wass wrong."
Brenna moved her hand to her pale forehead as she slowly sat up.
Pensee had never seen Brenna like this. She looked sickly with
dark circles under her eyes and was ghostly white.

"Are you alright?" She helped her to her feet.

"I...think so," Brenna didn't know what to think. The last
thing she remembered was weeping in the midst of the hopeless
dark. *How did I fall asleep? Maybe I was asleep the whole time
and it was all a horrible dream?* She asked herself. She felt awful
with a crick in her neck from lying against the hard door for the
remaining hours of the night along with a bad headache. She still
felt very anxious and shaky. Although it was morning, it
remained gloomy from the fog that lingered outside. Not to
mention the fearful cloud that Brenna felt inside of her as well.

"I came to 'elp you dress for breakfast. I 'ad come earlier
and knocked, but when zere was no answer, I sought you were
still asleep," Pensee talked as she went to pick out a suitable
dress for the day. She didn't notice that Brenna wasn't listening
in the least. She was much too busy trying to reason through
everything she'd experienced during the never-ending night.

"'ow about ziss one?" Pensee held up a light flowered day
dress. She glanced at Brenna, whose gaze was fixed on
something out the window.

"Miss?" she called. Brenna finally turned to face her.

"I'm sorry, but I need a moment to myself. You can lay out
the dress on the bed."

"Yes, of course, Miss," Pensee quickly heeded her and
opened the door to leave.

"Thank you," Brenna didn't want to sound mean and quickly
forced a smile, "I'm fine," she reassured her ladies maid when
she caught her worried expression.

"I will let my lady know zat you will be late to zee table,"
she walked out and closed the door behind her.

Brenna sat down on the edge of her bed and peered out of the
window again. She pondered over the night long and hard,
though it was still very real and frightening. The very thought of

the darkness made her tremble all over again. She dreaded the fact that it would only be night again. She couldn't escape it.

I don't want to ever fall asleep for fear of that dream. Tears came to Brenna's eyes as she wrapped her arms around herself. All of a sudden, a thought came to mind. It was almost as if it wasn't her own because it came out of nowhere.

"What was different about the last dream than any of the others?"

"The dream quickly ended," Brenna soon recalled and spoke aloud.

"Why?"

"Because I was about to turn and look at the spot...where...." It was too painful to finish. Brenna stood to her feet at the abrupt idea. *If I go to the alley, to the same place...perhaps I will finally be free of all this.* It was the very last place she ever wanted to see again. Ever since Hephzibah's death, Brenna tried all she could to forget it. *But if it will help get rid of this torment, I have to go.* "Before I lose my mind over it," Brenna sighed and rushed over to her dress to get ready to leave. Doubtful reasoning soon rose up and she slowed. *How will I ever find that place in this city? It's impossible.* The only thing she could remember was that it was close to the harbor, but the Port of London was several miles long. *There is also no way I'll be able to get away without Scarlette or Adelaide accompanying me.* Brenna's shoulders slumped in hopelessness.

As she gazed around her room trying to come up with a way, she saw something move in the corner. Even though it was daylight some shadows lingered in places. Brenna only dared to quickly glance at it again. This time it looked bigger. The darkness was very present and loomed in the room, waiting for its time. She had to get out of there! Brenna got dressed as fast as she could and ran out of the room. She couldn't look back, for it felt as if whatever it was, was at her heels.

She ran all the way down the hall and down the stair case until she reached the dining room. Before entering, Brenna stopped to calm her racing heartbeat and to catch her breath, all the while refusing to look back.

Will anyone else be able to see this dark presence? Brenna took a deep breath and went in.

"Good morning, everyone," she greeted and put on a smile. Albeit, there was nothing good about the last few hours.

"Good morning," Adelaide replied. The minute she saw her great-niece she knew there was something amiss about her. Her usual cheerful countenance and neat attire was marred by over-tired, nervous expression, and unkempt hair horribly put up in some kind of bun. Pensee had informed them that Brenna would be late, but this was far more than merely oversleeping.

"Are you feeling alright, dear?"

I should have known she wouldn't miss a thing. Brenna thought and felt Adelaide's and Scarlette's concerned stare as she was seated. She couldn't reveal what was truly going on for they wouldn't understand. How could they? No, this gloomy oppression was hers alone to endure. It was as if Brenna was held captive within herself and no one could rescue her from it. "Yes, just a bit tired," she lied and neatly folded her napkin in her lap, all the while she felt their lingering gaze.

"We were just going over the day's schedule. Scarlette has been invited to the Eldridge's for tea. The invitation is extended to the rest of us as well, if we so wish to attend." A maid entered just as Adelaide finished, holding an envelope atop a silver tray.

"Pardon me, My Lady. This came from the dressmaker," she approached and handed the message to Adelaide.

"How delightful…most likely informing us that your debutante gowns are finished." Adelaide glanced at the young women, opened the wax seal, and began to read.

"Is everything alright?" Scarlette asked when Adelaide's smile faded.

"Well, it appears the dressmaker needs to see Brenna straight away for some sort of refitting. I don't see how we can fit it in today." Brenna's gaze shot up upon hearing it. Was this her chance? Her hopes were raised, only to have them smothered by uncertainty.

But how? How can I possibly find one alley in all of

London? Well, I've got to try, she firmly told herself, *There's nothing else I can do. I can't just sit here and wait until this goes away, for its only getting worse!*

"However, I suppose we must have the gown finished with plenty of time for portraits to be made in preparation for being presented," Adelaide went on.

"I could go," Brenna spoke up. "You and Scarlette could still go to the Eldridge's."

"Are you certain you're up to it? It won't hurt to postpone it for another day."

"I'm quite certain." Brenna tried not to sound overly insistent, but she knew this might very well be her one and only chance to steal away long enough. *All I can do is try.* She held her breath as she waited for her reply.

"You don't mind going alone? Of course, Pensee would accompany you."

"Not at all." Brenna could easily force her ladies maid to complete secrecy about her plan.

"Alright, that settles it then." Adelaide turned to her maid, "Please send word to the dressmaker that Brenna will arrive this afternoon."

CHAPTER THIRTY-NINE

"Miss, Miss!" Pensee called out after Brenna as she emerged from the dressmakers shop, but she wouldn't slow her hurried pace down the street and to the carriage. By the time she caught up to her, Brenna was just climbing into the carriage.

"Might I ask why we're in such a hurree?" Usually it wasn't customary for a mere ladies maid to question her mistress, however, from the time they had been introduced, she and Brenna had a slightly different relationship. It was more open and informal than other women she'd attended to.

"I need to stop somewhere before we return home," Brenna simply replied. She knew it wouldn't be the only question she would have to face before it was over.

Things went swiftly at the refitting.

Plenty of time to search for it and be home before we're missed.

"Home, Miss?" the driver asked before closing the door after Pensee and Brenna were seated.

"Actually, no." His eyes widened at this as he looked at the ladies maid. It had never occurred to him that the answer would be anything but agreement. Unbeknown to them that their surprise was about to worsen. "Please take me to The Port of London."

"The east side, Miss?" The poor driver nearly gasped. Because he knew the young lady wasn't from London, he felt free to quickly inform her. "The east side isn't for you, Miss. There's nothing grand or suitable in the likes of that place."

"I must go there nevertheless," Brenna calmly stated, though a bit ruffled by the waste of time.

"I don't think you realize—"

"I must. It's imperative!" she cut him off. She knew they had to heed her command. The driver grudgingly shut the door to the carriage and shuffled to his seat.

"I don't sink ziss iss wise, Miss. You 'eard wat 'e said." Pensee looked at her pleadingly.

"I have to. It will be alright…trust me," Brenna sat back in her seat as if her word was final. She refused to speak again and ignored Pensee's occasional stare, as the carriage slowly headed to The Port. Brenna intently stared out the window the entire time, hoping against hope there was a small chance she might recognize something. That day, years ago, was a day like any other. Brenna hadn't paid much attention to her surroundings other than noticing the dirt, waste, and poor state within the enormous city. The only thing she had been interested in was hurrying to the market with Hephzibah so they could restock The Hester with food for the journey home.

If I would've only known what awaited us in that horrible alley. Tears tempted to fall at the sad thought. *I could have stopped Hephzibah from taking that shortcut.* Brenna abruptly put a stop to her musings that were getting away with her. Blaming herself wouldn't help her find peace.

It wasn't long before the streets and houses noticeably changed from wealthy and grand to poor and rundown. As they passed a busy market, her thoughts were pulled back to the dreadful day.

I wonder if that was the market we were supposed to get to? If we wouldn't have taken…. The carriage rounded a few more filthy street corners when something seemed to sweep over her. It held no comfort, but at the same time, the feeling sparked a small recollection. It wasn't until they had driven further down the block that Brenna realized what it really was.

"Tell him to stop!" she exclaimed. The sudden noise caused Pensee to jump in her seat. Brenna buttoned her cloak as her ladies maid signaled the driver and they lurched to a halt. Pensee retied her bonnet to accompany her mistress when she glanced up and saw Brenna already looking at her.

"Please stay here. I have to go alone." If Pensee was taken

back before, she was completely aghast now. A young lady of society never went anywhere alone. This was unheard of!

"Sacre bleu! You can't go alone...and in such a place as ziss," Pensee shrieked and waved her hand avidly.

"Well, I have to!" Brenna stood.

"Please don't...what would My Lady sink if she knew?" Brenna was almost out the door when she swiftly spun around to face her.

"She's not going to find out. Now stay here...the both of you!" Brenna glared at Pensee sternly until she was certain she clearly understood what she meant. Pensee now knew there was nothing she could say or do to stop her. The driver felt the same as he silently held out a hand to help Brenna step out. The ladies' maid was helpless as she peered out the window and watched Brenna walk down the street on a mission, alone and completely unprotected.

Although her mind hadn't a clue as to why, she somehow knew they had passed the longed-after alley. Something deep inside her confirmed it to be true. Nothing really looked familiar. All the gloomy, hideous streets, filled with rats and homeless people both young and old, all looked the same to her. Yet the sorrowful feeling in her stomach and the way the heavy fog loomed over this one street was evidence enough that it was unquestionably the God forbidden place where Hephzibah breathed her last. As much as Brenna wished she could forget every last one of her haunting dreams, she now found herself trying to remember the details of the alley way she'd been forced to return to countless times. Because she already felt insecure and forsaken since that morning, no amount of frightening stares from the street urchins, who immediately noticed the finely dressed woman walking alone, could make her waver. No one could stop or scare her away when she was persuaded that she was so close to it.

Brenna took a few more steps toward the opening in the middle of the block and came to a halt.

"This is it!" she whispered to herself as she felt the cold, foul smelling breeze envelope her. *I found it! It's nothing less than a miracle! I actually found it.* She thought, but her emotions were mixed. It was wonderful and terrible at the same time. The last place she ever wanted to see again, held her only chance to escape from the dark presence that chased her. *What if this doesn't work to free me from it?* A fearful thought came, but she pushed it aside. There was nowhere else she could turn to other than this, so it had to work.

Brenna stepped inside the alley as if stepping into her dreams. She slowly made her way deeper in and neared the place. Memories, terrible memories flooded over her. Not from the attack from the two men, but of her last moments with Hephzibah. It was etched in her memory.

She gave her life to protect me. Brenna gazed up at the darkened sky. Tears sprang to her eyes when she recalled how Hephzibah had bravely stepped in front of her.

"Why...why did you save me?" Brenna didn't bother wiping away her tears. There it was, where she had fallen. Brenna stopped and gazed down at the ground, now covered with leaves, trash, and other loathsome things, but she didn't care. She fell to her knees and wept. "You should have let me die! Instead of leaving me here...alone."

"Everything will be alroight." When Brenna shut her eyes, she was back with Hephzibah before she was gone. The older woman even tried to comfort the girl at her own death. *"There is noffin' ta fear. God will always be wif ya."* Brenna now knew nothing was further from the truth. Albeit she had been convinced of His presence, it had all but left, along with Hephzibah. At least that's what it seemed like to Brenna. *"Death is noffin' ta be scared of...if thee serve The King."*

That's another thing she was wrong about, Brenna thought. Death, the evil dark shadow, stalking her to no end, was no doubt something to fear. She could feel the grasp of fear itself in the cold, damp alley.

"I need help! Help me," Brenna cried out, but not overly loud so no one would come running to her rescue. She was too distraught to really know ~~who~~ her desperate pleading was [to whom (handwritten correction above "who")] referred to. She was too distraught to care. "I can't do this alone...I need someone...to save me! I need you!" Brenna leaned forward and placed her hand on the dirt ridden ground, her cries momentarily growing louder. Under some rubbish and rotten leaves, she felt something under her hand. Through blurred vision, Brenna pushed aside some of the unknown waste until she saw a small book. Hope stirred in her as she carefully picked it up. She was instantly reminded of the precious book Hephzibah often read from each day.

Hephzibah's Bible! How can it be?

"Why do you read that all the time? What is it?"
"It's The Holy Bible. God's Word ta wee. An' when theur read His Word, it brings 'ope and peace. It is the light of life."

She read it to find hope. Brenna remembered Hephzibah's words as if it were yesterday and sat back up to get a better look at it.

Rylan walked down the street, minding his own business when he heard a strange noise. He briefly stopped and looked around to see where it had come from. It sounded like crying, but he didn't see anyone. He took a few more steps when he heard it again.

What is that noise? It has to be crying. He glanced around, trying to locate the soft whimpering. He then looked ahead, down the street and saw a small opening between the cramped housing. Surely that's where it was coming from. Nothing could have prepared him for what he found. Deep inside the alley, there was a young woman kneeling in the dirt and mire, sobbing. Rylan promptly had the urge to rush to her aid, but he hesitated when he saw that she was finely dressed.

Is it? No...it couldn't be. After he observed more closely, he slowly realized that the woman was none other than Brenna Kinsey! *My eyes must be playing tricks on me. It couldn't be her...in a place like this. And all alone? I wonder what happened to her to make her so upset?* Rylan thought and blinked several times just to be sure. He was in indecision if he should go to her and see if she was alright or not. undecided

Brenna stood up and wiped her dress off as best she could, still crying all the while, when it hit him. He suddenly remembered where he'd seen Brenna before. Rylan had racked his memory for days, severely trying to figure out where he knew her from, but this was the very last place he would have guessed. It wasn't until he saw her distraught, tear-streaked face when he >that instantly beheld the same terrified girl, who had just lost someone dear to her. He had saved her years ago. He'd often wondered what had become of her.

When Brenna started down the alley, toward him, Rylan backed away from the opening. He didn't know why, but he didn't want her to see him, at least not yet. He needed a moment to think.

What should I do? I can't leave her out here unattended. Neither do I want her to think I've been spying on her. Rylan stood still against the building and watched Brenna come out of the alley and wander down the street. *I have to go to her and see if she's alright,* he thought. However, when he saw that she was still wiping her eyes, he decided to at least give her a moment to compose herself before approaching. While he waited, Rylan quickly sought guidance.

Lord, should I ask her about that day? Should I say anything? He didn't have time to wait for an answer, for he didn't want to lose sight of Miss Kinsey.

As she made her way back to the carriage, Brenna held the cherished Bible close to her. It was so dear to her. It was as if she was able to get back a part of Hephzibah. Perhaps she wasn't as alone as she first thought.

Was this why I came back here? To find it? Brenna wondered. There had been no sudden change in her surroundings. The darkness still haunted her, accompanied with the fear and grief, but she felt like a small change had taken place inside her.

Along with her many tears, Brenna left part of her hopeless sorrow that weighed heavily on her in the alley. She felt a bit lighter than before.

Brenna gazed down at The Bible and sighed heavily. Instead of dreading the next few hours that led to nightfall, she found she had something to look forward to. She gingerly opened the book where a small crocheted bookmarker was.

"John…chapter fourteen," she muttered to herself. *I can't wait to get home and begin reading!* Though Brenna didn't know how or why, somehow she was confident the book she now possessed held her only rescue.

Because she was already enveloped in The Bible, she barely heard someone come up behind her.

"Miss Kinsey?" Brenna jumped and spun around to see Lord Quenell of all people!

"Oh, I'm sorry." Rylan quickly apologized when he saw that he'd startled her. He had called her twice, but she obviously hadn't heard him. His presence instantly flustered the young lady. For that, Rylan felt truly sorry. He doubted if he should've drawn near to her.

"Lord Quenell," Brenna nervously curtsied and glanced down at the front of her dirtied dress. *Now I've gone and done it. Why is he here…in the east side? Did he see me in the alley? Oh! How I must look to him! And without a chaperone. What should I do? What should I say?* Her mind raced, only she couldn't avoid his gaze. The only thing to do was to stand up straight and face him with confidence. Brenna recalled some of Adelaide's tips to becoming a fine lady.

"Are you…alright? I didn't mean to alarm you." Rylan didn't quite know what to say. All he wanted to do was ask her outright, but he couldn't just blurt out that he'd been there that night and ask if she remembered him or not. There was no doubt she was still upset, for anxiety was all over her. The way she shifted back and forth almost seemed like she was being watched or chased by someone or something. She wouldn't look him in the eye.

What is going on? Rylan asked himself. Brenna still hadn't said anything and the silence began to feel awkward. "I merely came over to make sure you were alright." He finally spoke.

"Yes....I'm very fine. It was kind of you to inquire."

That's it! I'm just going to say something about that night. What do I have to lose? Rylan got an idea. "I was actually going to ask—"

"Miss Kinsey!" He was interrupted by Pensee, who stuck her head out of the carriage door and eagerly called once she caught sight of Brenna. She remained watching, but didn't say more when she saw that Brenna was talking to someone.

"Oh, please forgive me. I must go...thank you again!" Brenna turned to leave, exasperated as she rushed to the carriage and got inside.

A pang of embarrassment hit her when she looked out of the window once they began to move, and saw Rylan watching them leave.

What he must think of me! I've made a fool of myself, besides being positively rude! Brenna didn't have much time to reprimand herself. She glanced down at The Bible in her hand and all was forgotten except to quickly get home and start reading!

"Thy word is a lamp unto my feet,
and a light unto my path."

Psalms 119:105

CHAPTER FORTY

ensee and Eleta were making their way to the third story from the servant's hall and met Scarlette and Brenna trudging up the stairs, dressed in their debutante gowns. They tried to hide their amusement, for it was a bit humorous watching the girls walking up the stairs in their full attire which included the court train, veil, and large headdress. Not to mention their already heavy white silk chiffon gown with full, several layered skirts.

"How did your portraits go?" Eleta asked.

"It went very well," Scarlette replied.

"I dare say, a bit long sitting in one position," Brenna put in. Both young women huffed and puffed once they had ascended.

"Well, let's get these off of you." Scarlette and Brenna went to their separate rooms to change, their maids following.

"At least you won't 'ave to don ziss again until your presentation to zee palace in June," Pensee chuckled. Brenna had never felt so free after ridding herself of the beautiful gown. But then again, she rather liked wearing it for it made her feel like a queen. She'd never seen such a stunning dress, much less get to wear it!

"How long until we get dressed for the ball?" Brenna asked before lying on her bed and sighing heavily.

"Right after tea." Right then there was a knock on the door. "Come in."

"Do you want to go over everything we want to wear this evening?" Scarlette asked after poking her head in the door. Fantasizing and discussing their apparel, accessories, and hair styles, were Scarlette's favorite pastime of late. She almost enjoyed the preparations more than the ball itself.

"Yes," Brenna's hesitant reply caused Scarlette's excitement to waver. "I do want to, but…perhaps in an hour or two." When Brenna saw that her answer did nothing to satisfy her, she went on to explain, though she knew it would do very little to change anything. "I want to get a little reading in if that's alright."

"I suppose," Scarlette's expression fell as she fingered some lace on the sleeve of her dress, "My, you've been taken with reading from that small book recently. It must be very intriguing to take up so much of your time and interest," she tried not to sound hurt, but she was beginning to feel neglected. For the past week all Brenna wanted to do was sit in her room and read almost the entire day. In fact, Scarlette was surprised that she planned to attend the ball at all. There hadn't been any large balls in the last few days, but she had declined to go to a couple of luncheons and dinner parties. When Scarlette had begun to grow concerned, she finally questioned Brenna about it and found out she was reading The Bible. It relieved her fears a little, along with seeing that Brenna was more at ease and a bit more relaxed.

But it is beginning to go too far. Scarlette finally looked up to meet Brenna's gaze. There was another change in her sister that accompanied the pleasant ones, and it troubled her. It seemed to Scarlette that Brenna had become more secretive about things. The first time she noticed this was when she had tried to question her further about her sudden need to read from The Bible all the time. Brenna instantly put up a defensive wall and shut her out.

It's not like her at all.

Brenna knew Scarlette was worried about her. The whole household felt the same. But she couldn't explain everything. No one could ever put themselves in her place.

No one can ever find out either. Brenna fearfully thought. *They would think I've gone mad.* She stepped over to Scarlette and took her hand. "It's just for a little while. Please stop being anxious. The Bible helps me…I can't explain, but just trust me. You must trust me." No matter what she said, it did little to ease Scarlette's mind.

"Alright," Scarlette replied with apprehension. She moved to leave nevertheless.

Upon first obtaining The Bible seven days prior, Brenna had begun reading from where Hephzibah had left off with her bookmarker. Since then Brenna grew to love every moment while she read. Not only did the words bring her comfort, it was as if it came alive to her. She had never felt so close to Hephzibah in knowing that she was reading the same words the older woman had deemed so precious. Brenna now easily understood why Hephzibah had to read from it every day. It was life to her and it was slowly becoming very crucial to Brenna as well.

After Pensee finished arranging the debutante gown and the accessories safely on a hanger, she left the room. To Brenna, it couldn't have been soon enough. She wanted to get as much reading in as possible. While she had read a vast amount already, the anticipation seemed to grow. It was like a hidden treasure, waiting to be found. Every time she opened the book, she was one step closer to finding it. Although, she hadn't the slightest idea of what that treasure was.

When she had first opened the book, the marker was at John chapter fifteen. Along the way, Brenna had come across several queer markings that Hephzibah had written by some of the verses such as arrows, stars, and sometimes small notes concerning the scripture. At first, Brenna thought it very strange, but she soon remembered that it was Hephzibah's Bible. There had been nothing ordinary about her whatsoever.

Brenna opened the book where she had left off and began reading in Philippians. She soon finished the four chapters and moved on to Colossians before she found a considerable amount of Hephzibah's writing in the very first chapter.

This must have been especially important to her. Brenna thought. She would read this part all the more carefully because of it.

10 That ye might walk worthy of the Lord unto all pleasing, being fruitful in every good work, and increasing in the knowledge of God;

11 Strengthened with all might, according to his glorious power, unto all patience and longsuffering with joyfulness;

12 Giving thanks unto the Father, which hath made us meet to be partakers of the inheritance of the saints in light:

13 Who hath delivered us from the power of darkness, and hath translated us into the kingdom of his dear Son:

14 In whom we have redemption through his blood, even the forgiveness of sins.

"He has delivered us from the power of darkness…into the kingdom of His dear Son," Brenna read that part again out loud. *Can this really be true? It's too good to be true!* Her thoughts reeled with questions. For the past few months, even years, darkness controlled her life. It haunted her every turn. Did it truly have no power over her? If so, then why did it seem so powerful? When Brenna had first become a daughter of the King, as Hephzibah had described it, she was confident that she'd come upon something life changing. To be a daughter of the King of kings? Who wouldn't be excited? However, after Hephzibah's death, Brenna had held onto that as long as she possibly could. Her stay at the dreary orphanage had stripped her of all hope…everything. Her faith had dwindled to nothing. And without anyone to turn to with her many questions, Brenna resigned herself to the sorrowful fact that her once childlike faith in God, Hephzibah's loving Father, was nothing more than that…childish. Although she would admit that God was real, Brenna was unable to attain Him like Hephzibah had. Either she wasn't good enough or just couldn't figure out how.

If I was good enough, then why have all these horrible things

? reach?

come upon me? Brenna asked herself. She was missing something Hephzibah had, and she was the only one who could show her. As Brenna read from The Bible, those feelings she'd lost, were beginning to stir. Was this verse somehow connected with what she was missing?

Brenna read the verse yet a third time.

"He has delivered us from the power of darkness…has delivered…has," she repeated over and over. *Has means it's already past. He already has done it?* "I've already been delivered from the darkness?" she asked the empty room and rubbed her head to think. *So if He has…then maybe it's not a question of why haven't I been able to get free from this shadow, but why doesn't it seem like I'm delivered?* This dismal thought hung in the air for some time before she started to read again. She moved her gaze to the next verse, but couldn't continue on. Not when she was so close to reaching it.

This is silly, Brenna replaced the marker within the pages and shut the book. *I don't even know what I'm looking for. How can I be close to finding nothing?*

CHAPTER FORTY-ONE

B renna shot out of bed with a shriek. Her hand instantly gripped her chest, her heart beating wildly. The moment Brenna realized she had awoken from another horrible dream, she pounded her clenched fists on her bed in anger.

"No! No! No! Not again!" Tears stung her eyes in rage. It had been nearly a week since she'd experienced the reoccurring nightmare and without so much as a feeling of dread or fear lurking in the shadows. Brenna was beginning to think they were gone for good.

Was it too much to hope for? Was I foolish to think that the dream had passed? Without thinking straight, Brenna reached for Hephzibah's Bible that still lay beside her from falling asleep while reading from it, and roughly picked it up. She looked up at the ceiling and held the book up.

"I thought this had helped. I thought this would bring me at least a bit of comfort! You couldn't even allow me that?" Brenna cried loudly and threw the Bible across the room as hard as she could. As soon as it hit the floor and some delicate, well-worn pages had fallen out, the fight in her completely disappeared. "I thought I had finally gained my freedom from all this," she whispered, her shoulders slumped in defeat.

Suddenly something seemed to speak to her and caused her to jump in surprise.

"You are already free. You've been delivered from the kingdom of darkness." Though it wasn't audible, it was more real than if someone was in the room with her.

Am I going mad? I was seeing things, and now I'm hearing voices? Whatever it was held authority unlike any passing thought.

Brenna rose, went over to the Bible, and gathered the pages to place back inside it.

"How can I be free? There is no way…I can't ignore this fear. It certainly doesn't seem like I'm free," she muttered to herself. *Great…now I'm even talking to myself.* Brenna didn't get up, but instead knelt on the floor. She still didn't dare to look around her room for she could feel the ever dark presence around her, pressing in. It was usually more intense following her dream.

As skeptical as she was at the thought of already being free, she wanted to believe it nonetheless. There was nothing more she yearned for, than to be free once and for all. For a small second, a glimmer of hope shined through to her.

What if there is a way? What if the verse is true? Brenna glanced up at the same spot where she had yelled at God. The verse seemed to play in her mind over and over.

"You've been delivered from the kingdom of darkness, into the kingdom of the Son."

"How? If this is true, what do I need to do?" There was no doubt in her mind that she would be answered. She continued to gaze up at the ceiling, waiting and hopefully expecting. She closed her eyes. Sure enough, the same inner voice spoke to her heart.

"You are already free. It's done. Fear not…only believe." The last few wonderful words echoed in her. They were so steadfast and sure, filled with peace and a love so great it overwhelmed her. It was as if someone had handed her a lifeline to pull her higher, out of the shadows to safety.

Brenna finally opened her eyes with a new boldness. She now knew what to do. She stood to her feet and looked directly at the darkest corner of the room.

"I am a daughter of the King! I have a part of the inheritance of the saints in the light. I…." As she spoke, the shadow rose up higher and eventually took the form of a person just like it had when it chased her in the hall. A shiver crept over Brenna as she forced herself to stay put. She would have wavered, but her thoughts were reminded of the verse she had read. *I will not be moved. Not this time!* Brenna told herself and regained her courage. "I have been delivered from the power of darkness and translated into the kingdom of His Son. Darkness, I have been delivered from you. I am free from you and I will not be afraid of you anymore!" By the time she finished, Brenna was shaking. Not with fear, but with assuredness and a strength not her own. She watched in wonder as the dark cloud moved to the window and disappeared through it. It was gone! Completely gone and with it the feeling of dread and fear. For the first time since she could remember, Brenna could breathe without any hindrance of anxiety and apprehension. She felt free at long last.

"Thank you so much, Lord," Brenna thanked and worshiped her Heavenly Father until she choked with emotion, then continued to cry with joy. "I'm free! Thank the Lord, I'm free!"

CHAPTER FORTY-TWO

"*T*heodore...Theodore." From his straw mattress on the floor, William reached over to where his son still slept on his bed beside him. "Theodore, wake up already," he nudged him and whispered. He went on nudging harder and whispering louder until his son moved.

"What?" Theodore moaned and turned away from William. Someone then shushed him. A few of the men who shared the lodging house and hadn't gotten up to attend church, were enjoying their one day to sleep in.

"Where's Edwin?" William ignored the man and asked. Theodore sighed and opened his eyes.

How many times will he ask the same questions over and over? He thought in frustration. "I've already told you. Edwin left." He hoped that was the end of it as he tried to get comfortable and fall back to sleep, but he knew better.

"Where's Benjamin?" William persisted. Theodore finally gave up and turned to his father with a huff.

"You know where he is. At the orphanage," he sat up and rubbed his face when a pang of all too familiar guilt hit him. It had been nearly two months since they were forced to leave Benjamin, and Theodore was constantly haunted by the boy's frightened face and screams. *But now with an honest job, board, and enough money to live on...we could go and get Benjamin. Our lodging isn't much, but it's more than likely better than an orphanage.* Theodore mulled over these things almost every day, but he had to wait for the right time when he could ensure that they could feed and care for Benjamin. *Perhaps now we can!* Theodore got up and quickly dressed. "Father, get ready."

"Why?"

"We're going to go for a walk, so dress warmly."

"Alright. Is it a surprise?" William gasped with excitement.

"Yes," Theodore smiled, but it soon faded. *We would have been able to get Benjamin a lot sooner if it weren't for Edwin's selfishness........*

"I'm leaving tomorrow," Edwin simply stated between bites.
"Are you completely daft?" Theodore nearly dropped his own plate.
"This kind of work doesn't suit me."
"Oh yes. You haven't done a single hard day's work in your life." Theodore regretted his words as soon as they left his mouth.
"And you have?" Edwin angrily stood.
"We've been given a job, food, and board! Mr. Morrison is a good man. Maybe we can save enough to travel back home, but you want to ruin everything."
"It's all my fault! I know, I know! Well, I won't bother you anymore. Don't worry about me, brother. I don't need your help. I'll make my own way and get home myself." Edwin was about to storm out of the room, but surprisingly stopped when Theodore spoke.
"How?"
"Just like the countless people we witnessed in the markets."
"Thievery? That's what you plan to do?"
"Like I said...you don't have to worry about it," he moved to the door.
"Edwin," Theodore called after him.
"Don't concern yourself! And stay out of my way......."

Edwin's last words echoed in Theodore's mind as he buttoned his jacket and heard William calling for him to hurry up.
Fine...do it all on your own, Edwin. I'm finally rid of you.

"This is where Benjamin is, right?" William asked once they rounded the corner and the orphanage came into view.

"Benjamin! We're here!" He suddenly took off running and shouting happily. It caused several people on the street to stare.

"Father, you must be quieter!" Theodore caught up with him and tried to calm him down.

"Are we going to get him out now?"

"Not we…you have to stay here. I'll be right back." Theodore expected him to object, but it did nothing to cause his childish grin to waver.

He left his father outside the gate and approached the front entrance. He was greeted by the maid, same as before and was led inside to Mr. Thordon's office. Theodore found him much like he had before, pouring over the papers on his deck.

"Someone to see you, sir," the maid declared then left. When Mr. Thordon saw Theodore, he frowned.

"What can I do for you?" he asked coldly as if he'd never seen the young man before.

He probably helps many people, so why should he recall me? Theodore figured. "You might not remember me, but I brought my brother here a few months ago. I've come to see him. His name is Benjamin Dorcet," he determined not to mention his plan to take his brother with him just yet.

"Yes, well I'm sorry but there are strictly no visitors on Sundays. You'll have to come another day."

"Uh….um…I've come quite a long way. Is there some way—"

"Mr. Dorcet, I've come to find that people come to me for help. They beg for it, without any objections. Then, when I enforce my rules, they don't want any part of them. Only what they want. You'll have to come another day, and if you don't leave, I'll have you escorted out. Good day. Marian," Mr. Thordon called for the maid, who stood just outside the door.

"Yes, sir?"

"Show this…fellow out." Theodore was ushered outside without another word and the door was shut behind him. The noise seemed to bring him out of his confused stupor.

What just happened? He looked back at the closed door. *Just because he owns this establishment, doesn't mean he can keep Benjamin from me!* Brotherly indignation rose up in him and he pounded on the door with a clenched fist. When no one answered, he grew louder until he began to shout as well.

"Answer this door! You have no right. Benjamin!" It was some time before he gave up. No one answered and he was angrier than ever. There was a deep fear that washed over him as he glanced toward the street, not knowing what could be done.

What if something is horribly wrong? What if Benjamin never got better…and they just don't want to tell me? Theodore rubbed his face in anxiety. "Why won't they answer the door?" he mumbled to himself and reluctantly walked down the stairs. He sauntered back to the gate, still deep in thought as to what to do now.

"He's not here." Theodore jumped nearly a foot when someone out of nowhere spoke. His gaze shot to a middle aged man, most likely a groundskeeper who had come around the side of the brick building.

"Excuse me?"

"Benjamin, the person you were hollering for…he isn't here."

"What do you mean not here…where is he then?" *He's dead! He's dead! First Brenna, now Benjamin!* Theodore's mind screamed.

"I'm sorry to say, I've seen it before. They throw you out…probably told you there were no visitors today. Thordon is only covering it up to hide the truth." Theodore was much too shaken and confused to say anything. He could only listen as the man went on, "He sells 'em to a factory. If the orphans are old enough to work, he sells 'em."

Benjamin is only five years of age! "You're sure of this?"

"Aye. I've seen it many times before. Say you come back on a day you can visit…he'll say the child is ill. Next, their on a walk. Thordon will keep covering up his actions. And if people eventually catch on that something is wrong, he just throws them out. He holds the signed papers that release the children to him."

Exactly what I did. That's why he was so eager to take Benjamin without question of payment. Theodore, you're so stupid! He scolded himself. "What factory? Where?"

"I'm sorry, lad. I don't know. I'm trying my best to find out what I can, but he is very sly."

If only I had the resources to get help...somehow. Theodore's knees buckled slightly at the thought that he and he alone was at fault. Yet again.

"Oh Benjamin! I'm so sorry," he cried, not caring who heard him. He had no dignity left anyway.

"There, there, lad. You had no way of knowing," the man pulled his hat off and solemnly held it, nervously.

"Thank you for the information," Theodore forced himself to say something and moved to the gate. *Now to face Father.*

"May God be with you."

"Yes...God indeed," Theodore grunted, *He's the last one who's with me.*

The groundskeeper watched as the young man shut the gate and hopelessly made his way with slumped shoulders, to another man, waiting for him on the street.

CHAPTER FORTY-THREE

nd they were off. The tremendous buildup of anticipation over a thrilling horse race lasting only a matter of minutes, then it was all over. At least that's what it seemed like to Brenna. Though she might not feel the same, she noticed large portions of the endless crowd in attendance were truly enthralled with it all. Men, who had placed substantial bets were either please or unimpressed with the results. Brenna had to admit it was a bit exciting and gripping, especially at the end. She marveled at the amount of people of nearly all stations present. But if what Scarlette had told her on their carriage ride was true, the horse race was only a small reason why The Epsom Derby attracted so many. In truth, this was the chosen place to be for everyone who had a part in England's high society during the Season. Every Lord, Lady, and any member of peerage were there. Even parliament was adjourned so they could go.

Brenna gazed up at the Queen's stand, a large grand building that towered over the crowd. It was where Her Majesty's royal entourage comfortably viewed the race. Although she was too far away to see clearly, Brenna hoped she could gain some kind of advantage or tips in watching them. Anything that might help her prepare or at least know what it would be like when she was to be presented at court in a few days. She would most likely be more than ready for it with Adelaide's help, but she was growing more nervous with each passing day.

"Did the horse of your liking win?" Bertram turned to Brenna and Scarlette.

"Yes," they both eagerly replied.

"I enjoy taking in the beautifully dressed people almost more than the horses though. Especially the hats! Breathtaking!" Scarlette sighed.

"I must say, you two young ladies are equally breathtaking. As do some young men, I've noticed." Bertram winked as Scarlette and Brenna blushed.

"You are too kind, Uncle. Surely you exaggerate," Scarlette replied.

"Oh no, not even a little. I speak the honest truth. I might not notice things like Adelaide has the ability to do, but there are several young men who have taken notice of you. No doubt just waiting for the moment you are officially out in society."

"Did your horse win?" Brenna asked and changed the subject to stop from growing any warmer from Bertram's all too kind remarks.

"Well, it was close, but not close enough. I was fond of one filly. Unfortunately, she didn't keep her pace until the end. And now you know why I've learned my lesson of betting. Nothing comes from me and my intuitions."

"You couldn't be more right," Adelaide spoke and readjusted her oversized scarf that surrounded her hat and was tied at her neck. "Let's make our way to the entrance, shall we? It's becoming warm and I'm beginning to tire of these crowds." The group gathered their things and rose to leave.

It wasn't long before Rylan spotted Brenna and her family among the droves of people. She was only about thirty feet from him. During the race he would glance in her direction to make sure he wouldn't lose sight of her. He wanted to be sure to speak to Brenna or at least say hello, but with the number of people, he didn't know if it would be possible. How they had parted ways the last time they spoke weighed heavily on him and he hoped to make things right ever since.

Rylan looked to the same spot again to find all four of them gone! The last time he'd seen her, she and her family were happily talking amongst themselves while waiting for the race to start.

And now they're gone. Rylan scanned the bustling crowd

headed in all sorts of directions, preparing to leave. *There!* He'd found them. *Now to get to them without being trampled!* "I'll be right back," Rylan briefly turned to the people he'd come with before rushing off. His gaze never left the departing family.

Brenna was bringing up the rear when she thought she heard someone calling out to her.

"Miss! Miss Kinsey!" Because of the commotion and trying to stay together, she didn't think anything of it.

Perhaps it only sounded like my name. Maybe it's a friend of Scarlette's, trying to get her attention.

"Excuse me…pardon me," Rylan weaved through the mass.

"Miss Kinsey!" he tried again. It wasn't until he tried once more that Brenna finally heard him and came to a stop. When Scarlette felt Brenna's hand pull away from hers, she stopped also.

Lord Quenell…calling for me? Brenna was flabbergasted to see who it was and didn't quite know what to say. Unbeknown to her, Lord Quenell didn't either. He was never at a loss for words, but it seemed like every time he was in her presence, he couldn't think of what he planned to say.

"I'm glad to see you again," he blurted.

"Hello," Brenna replied nervously. She looked up to face him and felt Scarlette at her side. However, Lord Quenell didn't look at her or acknowledge her in the least.

"I wanted to speak to you about the other day." Brenna tried to hide her horror, especially when Scarlette glanced at her in question.

"Oh?" *Please don't say it! Please don't say it!*

"I must apologize again for intruding and…well…for causing you any dismay."

By now Adelaide and Bertram had approached, conducing him to lose his train of thought. That is, until Rylan saw his family coming up behind him as well. He was relieved to have a new initiative, for the situation was growing awkward.

"Oh, I would like you…all of you," his gaze left Brenna and

moved to the others, "To meet my parents. Reid and Eibhleann Lennox, Marquess and Marchioness of Kerrich," Rylan then looked at his parents, "And this is Lord and Lady Millborrow, and their great nieces Miss Scarlette, and Miss Brenna Kinsey," he ended with Brenna and rested his gaze upon her again. His warm smile made her blush. All this time Brenna believed that Lord Quenell was undeniably interested in Scarlette. He had danced with her at the ball, but his present behavior indicated otherwise.

Bertram and Reid shook hands while the women curtsied to each other.

"Why, you are a member of The House of Lords, are you not? I don't know why I didn't realize it sooner," Reid spoke up and he and Bertram immediately started talking about parliament. Adelaide took this opportunity to approach Lady Kerrich.

"It's an honor to meet you," she graciously said.

"Thank you," Eibhleann quietly replied and exchanged a nervous glance with her husband.

"As are we," Reid seemed to be aware of her look as if some kind of signal and stopped talking business. He entered their conversation instead and responded kindly.

How strange. Brenna thought as she tried to figure out Rylan's parent's character. First impressions spoke volumes. Reid stood tall and erect, a stature much like his son. He was indeed an older version of Rylan with dark hair, greying at the temples, and warm eyes that held something more than what Brenna could tell. Was it a hint of sorrow? She recalled what Scarlette told her about Rylan and his family.

Was it all true? She asked herself and she tried to gage it by looking at them. There was something about Rylan's mother. Sure she was shy, but her reserve was almost unnatural, as was her withdrawn manner. Nevertheless, what showed forth the most was how beautiful Eibhleann was. Even with some signs of aging, she was very attractive. *How much more when she was younger? A beauty for certain.*

"Were you happy with the results of the race?" Reid asked Bertram.

"Not really, but it was a fine race all the same. How about you?"

"Well, there are several fine horses, but none of them really catch my eye. I don't attend these things often."

Rylan stood by and enjoyed watching their exchange. Needless to say, not many people cared to speak or be anywhere near his family, especially people in high society. But the Cheverell's were different. The same difference he noticed in Brenna.

Perhaps they are believers? His impression of them grew considerably when the unthinkable happened. Adelaide stepped forward and kindly took his mother's hand.

"As you might know, both of our nieces will be presented at court in only a matter of days. Would you all do us the honor of attending the debutante ball following the presentation?" Rylan couldn't help but smile at his parent's sheer amazement. An invitation was a rare occasion and at first, they didn't know what to say. Eibhleann's eyes widened as she looked at Reid, who meekly nodded his agreement.

"We wud love to come," her face lit up and her eyes seemed to glisten with her reply. Brenna hardly noticed Eibhleann's heavy Irish accent. She was much too consumed with the thought of Lord Quenell, of all people, attending to her coming out ball. Did this mean something? Something more than just the polite thing to do?

"Wonderful! I will send you the time and other information. It was so nice to meet you," Adelaide said.

"Thank you...thank you very much," the Lennox family said several times, though no one other than them would know the meaning behind their earnest gratitude. they

"They seemed quite pleased at our invitation." Bertram commented once they had said their goodbyes, made their way to

the carriage, and were on their way home.

"It's curious...I don't recall seeing them at any social functions. I've only seen Lord Quenell at a few of them also. Did they just move to England?"

"No, if I remember right, he's had a seat in The House of Lords for some time."

"And we've only just met?" Adelaide thought hard as she tried to remember if they'd met before and she'd only forgotten. Brenna and Scarlette sat opposite them, listening quietly. They shared one exchange in recalling the rumors Cora had told them.

"Perhaps they were more than grateful to come because they know it means a lot to their son...because of a certain interest." Bertram couldn't contain his thoughts any longer and looked at Brenna. She only smiled sweetly in return.

"The night is far spent, the day is at hand: let us therefore cast off the works of darkness, and let us put on the armour of light."

Romans 13:12

CHAPTER FORTY-FOUR

She was held down, unable to break free and thrown into the darkness with the lid shut over her. Brenna only struggled for a time before the eerie light came and drew her to it. The air was heavy and hovered over the alley. It was deathly still all around her as she stepped further in. Because she didn't care to see what else was in the alley, Brenna kept her gaze straight ahead and waited for the tiresome, yet fearful dream to unfold. Sure enough, though it seemingly took a while, the strong hand reached out to her. All she wanted to do was rush to it, but it was no use. Brenna was fixed on the rescuing hand until she felt it. The horrifying presence that lurked behind breathed over her neck like a haunting hand placed on her shoulder. It caused her to tremble as she shut her eyes, knowing all too well what was to come next.

Something deep inside her spoke.

"Fear not! Only believe...fear not, only believe!" Brenna's eyes shot open. She suddenly realized what was happening.

I don't have to put up with this any longer! I am free! She felt evil all around her, growing with each passing second. "I am free." she spoke out loud, "I am free at this moment! I am free!" The moment she said it, it felt like the farthest thing from the truth. But something in her, surpassing her mind, showed her otherwise. Right then, a wind picked up from nowhere and pulled at her hair and nightgown. This was it. The moment right before being overtaken by the shadows.

Not this time. Brenna swiftly turned to face whatever skulked behind, with boldness outside herself. The wind was now blowing so fiercely, she could barely keep her eyes open to see the endless, most pitch-black darkness she had even seen. At first she was tempted to waver at the enormity of it, but she was soon reminded that what was inside her was well able to overcome it.

She opened her mouth to repeat what she'd told the same darkness in her room.

"I am a daughter of the King. I have been delivered from the power of darkness and translated into the kingdom of His Son," Brenna had to shout over the blustering wind, "I have been delivered from you. I am free from you and I will fear you no longer!" The wind that almost blew her over changed all at once and now pulled into itself with significant force. If Brenna wouldn't have stood her ground with all her might, it felt like she would be consumed into it as well. All the dark shadows in the entire alley gathered into itself and quickly compressed and dwindled down to the size of the eye of a needle before Brenna awoke.

Her whole body shook and trembled along with her gasping breaths. However, she wasn't oppressed with fear this time, but overcome with joyous emotion.

I'm free...it's over! It's done!

CHAPTER FORTY-FIVE

veryone at the Cheverell's home was up especially early for the day of Scarlette and Brenna's presentation to the palace was finally upon them. The days of preparations, fittings, gathering of all the necessary accessories, and the deportment training had all led up to this day and were finally over. The girls had trained for days to learn how to walk gracefully in the Queen's presence, the proper curtsy, kissing Her Majesty's hand, and how to exit without turning her back to the royals. While they were excited beyond words, Brenna had even more to rejoice about. After finally putting a stop to the pursuing darkness, she had never felt so wonderful. A huge weight had finally lifted from her and there was no dread or anxiety of it ever returning to haunt her.

After eating a hearty breakfast, Scarlette and Brenna made ready to don their court gowns. Eleta and Pensee already had everything neatly laid out.

Hours later, they were ready. The last thing they put on was the curled ostrich plumes on each of the young women's head, atop their headdress and veil. Adelaide, because she was married, was to wear three plumes on her similar attire. Though, the color of her gown was shades darker than her great niece's white silk chiffon.

"All finished!" Eleta sighed when she'd pinned the last plume in place. Both ladies maid's stepped back to see the finished product. Once the oo's and ah's had seized, both young women reached for their ten-foot trains as they had been taught, draped it over their arms, and were on their way.

It's wasn't until the carriage neared St. James Palace that Brenna started to get nervous. There was an endless row of carriages lined up in front of the palace and many people were already gathered outside, peering inside the passing carriages in hopes of getting a glimpse of the nervous girls and their sponsors.

What have I gotten myself into? Brenna asked herself. From the moment she'd woken up that morning, she caught herself, more than once, thinking about Lord Quenell and wondering if he would be there. And perhaps, secretly hoping he would be.

This is foolishness, Brenna stopped herself. *He's an earl. He could have his pick of any young woman, much higher up in society than I.*

Brenna pulled her gaze from the window and glanced at Scarlette, who looked out of the window on the other side. Brenna could tell she was equally as nervous by how silent she'd become.

"Are you alright?" She reached over and put her hand over Scarlette's.

"Yes," Scarlette met her gaze with a reassuring grin, "I'm hoping and praying that I won't trip in the Queen's presence and completely disgrace myself."

"As are all of the other young ladies," Adelaide put in, "Both of you will do just fine. You couldn't have learned or been trained any better, for you did splendidly. Not to mention you both look divine."

"The young men will be left dumbfounded to say the least." Scarlette and Brenna chuckled at Bertram's humorous yet genuine remark. The foursome grew quiet again as they patiently waited for their turn. It wasn't long until Brenna's thoughts were preoccupied again.

Several hours of waiting only led to more waiting inside the palace. All the young ladies, nearly identical in appearance, were ushered inside and were immediately awestruck by the beauty of the busy palace. It was there in the entry that the girls and their sponsors separated from the rest of the people they might have come with and were brought to another breathtaking room called the gallery. Once everyone fit inside, hundreds of giggling girls with jittering nerves of excitement began talking at once. That is until a man dressed in regal attire, along with several gentlemen in waiting, stepped into the sea of women. He tried to speak over all the others. It took several times, but everyone eventually quieted down to hear what he had to say.

"According to the debutante's father's title, please line up in order of nobility." The middle-aged man held his arms out in front of the tall double doors that led to the drawing room. "Have each of your cards ready at this time for Her Majesty the Queen is ready to see you." With that, the man opened the doors to an even grander room. At least, that's what it looked like as far as Brenna could see as the endless line silently formed ahead of them. Brenna was learning all too quickly how important hierarchy was in England. It was almost always accompanied with snobbery. Sadly, it seemed, in the room full of women, the higher up in society some were, their noses rose higher as well.

Brenna glanced down at the pink card in her hand and fingered her name, Miss Brenna Kinsey. It was directly below that of her adopted father, Stephen Kinsey. He wasn't a member of peerage, without a title of his own, but was a military officer. Because of that, Brenna and Scarlette would end up moderately far behind the daughters of a duke or earl. Brenna truly cared little about it. Everyone there was going to personally be in the Queen's presence after all, and even kiss her hand.

Adelaide showed them where to stand in line before the waiting began yet again. While she inched closer to the door, in her place behind Scarlette, it gave her a chance to watch some of the other girls take turns entering the drawing room. She intently watched them hand her card to the Lord Chamberlin. He would announce her name while the pages spread out and arranged her train for her, before she gracefully walked in.

Brenna was nearly there when an inadvertent thought crossed her mind.

I wonder what father would think if he knew I was here...at this moment....minutes from meeting the Queen of England? What would mother have thought? Brenna had forced herself not to think of her family so many times, that now it caught her by surprise. Everything going on around her seemed to fade into the background as she pictured her family. However, thinking about them was different this time. It wasn't surrounded by regret or sorrow of never seeing them again, nor with a fear of finding herself all alone with no one to turn to. She wasn't alone with her musings anymore. Someone was with her and knew everything about her. Brenna knew all too well what it felt like to be in a room full of people and still feel lonely and isolated.

But not anymore. Lord, she couldn't help but silently converse with Him. *Am I here...right now, for a purpose? Is there a reason that I'm in London...at the palace of all places? Is this all part of Your plan?* It felt so good to be in close communion with her Heavenly Father and able to talk with Him anywhere and at any time.

Before she knew what was happening, Brenna's thoughts were cut short when she heard the Lord Chamberlin announce Scarlette's name. When she set forth inside the drawing room, Lord Chamberlin reached his hand out to Brenna. She blinked, trying to think of what he might want.

"Your card, miss?"

"Oh!" Brenna quietly flinched and swiftly handed it to him, "I'm sorry."

"Not to worry." Brenna felt a gentle tug as two pages arranged her ten foot train as Lord Chamberlin read her card loudly.

"Miss Brenna Kinsey and The Right Honourable, Lady Cheverell, Viscountess of Millborrow." Brenna slowly entered the room and was surprised at how many people were there. Lords and Ladys lined the court. The ceilings were very high with intricate moldings and life-size paintings. Brenna tried to concentrate so she wouldn't trip and moved her gaze to the throne. As she did, she thought she spotted Lord Quenell among the crowd. She didn't dare glance back at him as she neared the

Queen, who was surrounded by a group of royalties in rich gowns and uniforms. Her face was quickly growing warm from every eye watching with strict scrutiny. Brenna carefully curtsied before the Queen until she was almost kneeling. She then bowed to kiss her hand. Although, as instructed numerous times, she didn't actually touch the royal hand with her lips, but stayed two inches above it. It was well known that the Queen didn't want to be touched. It wasn't until Brenna rose, curtsied to the other royals present, that she finally made herself look at Her Majesty. She was completely endowed with jewels, but wore a pleasant smile. Brenna wondered if she was weary of so many girls being presented.

She gave one last curtsy to the Queen, reached for her train, draping it over her arm that trembled slightly from her nervousness, then very carefully backed away without turning her back on the throne. By the time she had made her way back to the door she'd come in from, several servants met her there to escort her out. Brenna tried to look back into the drawing room to see if Rylan was indeed there, but she didn't get a chance. The servants, wanting to keep things running swiftly and smoothly, rushed her out.

Upon returning home from the Palace, the whirl wind would continue. The staff was still hard at work to get ready for getting Scarlette and Brenna's coming out ball that was to be held there in only a matter of hours.

Brenna went to her room and happily let Pensee free her from some of her heavy clothing, but not her entire ensemble. She traded in her long train and headdress for long white gloves. They didn't have much time before the guests were to arrive.

It was tradition for the debutantes to stand near the entrance in the ballroom in a receiving line along with her sponsor and host. This was so that when people came, the sponsor could introduce all the guests to the newest young lady of society. The whole idea was to make the debutantes known to as many eligible young men, within the bounds of class, as possible in hopes of making a good match before the Season was over.

Bertram, Adelaide, Scarlette, and Brenna had been greeting people for a little over an hour before Rylan and his parents arrived. Brenna's heart quickened at the sight of him as she began to speak to the first person in the line. She tried to stay interested in the person she was currently speaking with, but she found it difficult to listen to both conversations at the same time.

"Congratulations on your official coming out," Brenna heard Rylan commend Scarlette. She couldn't help but glance over at them once the woman who'd been talking with her had left.

"Thank you. And thank you for coming," Scarlette gracefully gave a swift bow, as did Rylan.

"Do you have a dance still open?" For a moment, Scarlette appeared surprised, but she quickly pulled out her dance card and smiled.

"Why, yes."

How curious? He didn't so much as acknowledge her presence at The Derby and now he wants to dance? Brenna thought, but smiled when she saw Scarlette's pleasure, for there wasn't any jealousy between them whatsoever. Brenna was very grateful and relieved for that. She couldn't imagine being related to someone such as Cora Eldridge. Coincidentally, Brenna saw that very person enter the ballroom with her family next.

What are the chances? She laughed within herself. The moment Cora saw Lord Quenell in line directly in front of her, her bright smile faded.

"Congratulations on your official coming out," Rylan came to Brenna and bowed.

"Thank you. I'm glad you and your family could attend." Brenna hoped she didn't sound overly pleased even though she was.

"We were delighted to come. Do you have room on your dance card as well?"

"Um…oh, yes." Brenna glanced down at her card, although

she barely looked at it for she would have said yes no matter what.

"Splendid," his eyes seemed to brighten with his smile.

"Congradulations, my dear," Lord and Lady Kerrich came up behind Rylan and Eibhleann extended her hand.

"Thank you." With that, they made their way further into the busy room.

"Well, I couldn't help but notice who was invited." Brenna heard Cora get right to the point with Scarlette. As rude as it might be, Brenna felt it necessary to enter their conversation and defend Rylan and his parents.

What if they overheard Cora's snide remark? She asked herself. She had stepped closer to the two young ladies, just as Scarlette spoke.

"We are happy to have them come. Really, Cora...what if they had heard you?"

"And what if they did? Everyone in all of England knows of the scandal surrounding their family. Need I remind you?"

"No," Scarlette curtly replied.

"Alright...well," Cora glanced at Brenna, then to Scarlette, "You're officially out in society now...and I'm happy for you," she finished quickly so she could escape the growing tension she had caused.

"And you as well. Thank you for coming," Scarlette responded as politely as she could, although Cora was already moving away. Brenna and Scarlette exchanged looks, but didn't have time to say anything for many more guests were arriving.

"Did you like the Palace?" Rylan asked Scarlette once they began to dance much later that evening.

"Very much! The beauty of it was beyond words."

"It was kind of you to share the presentation, as well as the debutante ball, with your sister."

"I wouldn't think of having it any other way. We're very close."

"I see…I couldn't help but notice how you are both different in many ways as well."

"Oh? How so?" Scarlette asked as if she didn't know what he meant. Anyone with eyes could see they weren't true sisters. Because she was still a little uneasy in his presence, she was trying to choose her words carefully, as training had taught her. A lady must keep an even balance with her speech, keeping conversation light, without showing too much of her opinion in certain matters.

Rylan on the other hand was trying to find out more about Brenna without appearing too inquisitive.

"You two are quite different in appearance and speech…among other things." Because he wouldn't relent and wanted a direct answer, Scarlette eventually answered.

"Brenna and I aren't related by blood. Our family took her in years ago." Although Rylan had known this because of the obvious differences, it was good to hear her confirm it.

Now what do I say? Rylan, who was rarely at a loss for words, asked himself, *If she goes to Brenna which she most likely will, and tells her, what will she think?* He was beginning to panic a bit when the song ended.

"Thank you for the dance," he sighed with relief at the timing and led Scarlette off the dance floor without saying anything more.

While he waited for his turn to dance with Brenna, he scanned the room to locate his parents. Sure enough, they were standing alone, looking awkward and uncomfortable. After being treated so poorly among the social scene for so long, his parents were content to avoid people all together, instead of trying anymore. Sadly, it only added to the gossip. They weren't planning to come at all, but Rylan assured them that they wouldn't stay long.

Only long enough for me to speak with Brenna and dance with her.

The anticipated dance began and Rylan led the suddenly shy Miss Kinsey onto the dance floor. Brenna's heart sped up along the way. Although she had spoken to Lord Quenell several times before, this was the first time it would seem like they were alone. It would only be the two of them in conversation for an entire length of a song.

In watching her from time to time during the course of the evening, he noticed she seemed lighter and happier than times before. He would find her laughing while talking to people, and smiling to no end. Upon closer inspection, Rylan couldn't find the anxiety that used to linger in her eyes.

"Enjoying yourself tonight?" Rylan broke the silence.

"Yes, are you?" Brenna made herself glance up at him. She felt his gaze linger when she tried to think of something suitable to talk about.

"Yes. You looked lovely at the Palace…and not a bit nervous," Rylan spoke again, trying to engage her in conversation. His attempt had worked.

"I thought I saw you there. It all seemed like a blur, and then it was over," she replied.

"Things will no doubt begin to get busier for you now that you can participate in many more things this Season, not to mention, plenty of callers now."

"I only hope I won't be too busy to…." she stopped herself and blushed slightly. At that moment, everyone changed partners during the next part of the dance. *Oh…now what shall I say?* Brenna scolded herself, *Hopefully he'll just let it go and move on to something else.*

"Too busy for what?" Rylan's curiosity of the mysterious young lady immediately roused when they soon came together again. "What sort of things capture the attention of Miss Brenna Kinsey?" he tried to lighten the mood with a more playful tone. It only caused Brenna's face to redden all the more.

What am I ashamed to tell him? I have nothing to lose…no attachment that I'm at risk of losing. "You will certainly think me foolish."

"No, not at all. At least, I will try my hardest to hide it if I should think it." Brenna's gaze shot up and her mouth opened in surprise! He was poking fun at her, something she forgot he was capable of doing. Would he never cease to amaze her?

"I've been enthralled with reading of late," she finally confessed. Rylan's thoughts instantly returned to the east side, where he found her in the alley. She was holding a book of some sort. Was it what she spoke of?

"Oh? What kind of literature do you prefer?" he asked in a nonchalant way.

"Well…it's very old." Rylan smiled wryly at her discretion and closeness on the matter.

Why does she wish to torture me so? He thought, when in truth, he rather liked it. "Wordsworth? Chaucer? Or perhaps John Donne or Alexander Pope?"

"Much older than that. It's The Holy Bible," Brenna arduously watched for his response and was relieved to find his countenance seem to brighten with familiarity.

Lord, is that it? Is it what I saw in her that set her apart from all the others? His growing affection for Miss Kinsey rose to a new level. A longing in him knew she was someone he didn't want to lose. Now more than ever, he wanted to know everything about her. He was determined to find out and it led him to ask a more direct question."From the alley?" There, he made himself ask. Unfortunately, they temporarily parted ways again during the dance.

His bold resolve wavered slightly when he glanced at Brenna, now a few people down from him in the assembly, and saw her face blushing in embarrassment.

Can't she see I'm only asking because I'm inclined towards her? Rylan thought and caught sight of his father. He stood at the edge of the dance floor and met his gaze. Once he had his son's attention, Reid motioned that they must leave. Rylan regretted the thought of leaving, yet he felt for his parents. They had stayed as long as possible.

Now there will be no time to speak with her further. He quickly motioned back to his father, telling him he would be there momentarily. He couldn't very well leave the dance. Not when he's waited the entire evening for this moment.

What shall I do? What should I say? Brenna started to panic but tried her best to focus on the dance. *What did I expect? Of course he wants to know why I was in the alley. I would be just as curious.* She had to think of a reply, for she was nearing Rylan. At that moment, the music came to an end. Rylan thought it ended far too quickly while Brenna on the other hand, was very relieved.

"I thoroughly enjoyed talking with you. Perhaps we can speak more about the precious old book some time," Rylan offered his arm to her. He wanted to say more but could feel his father's gaze, waiting on him. Furthermore, he could tell Brenna was nervous.

"A…alright," Brenna meekly replied. While he walked her off the dance floor, Rylan fought within himself. He wanted to ask more. When would the next opportunity present itself? There was no telling when he could speak to her again. Everything would be far busier for her now that she would no longer be a debutante, but instead very eligible.

Just ask! Then you'll finally know! His mind continued to reel when he bowed and she curtsied. She left without another word. Rylan could do nothing more than make his way to his parents, feeling like a coward.

"Sorry to rush you, son. Your mother wishes to go," Reid said. They turned to leave when Rylan came to a stop.

I can't leave without asking her! "Father, I must do one more thing before we leave. You go ahead, it will only take a moment." With that, Rylan turned back. His gaze was fixed on Brenna, who hadn't gone far and started to go towards her.

It wasn't long before Brenna saw him coming. Her nerves sparked again, yet she was glad to see him. She didn't know what to do! He looked as if he was on a mission.

"Miss Kinsey, I must ask you…." Rylan began only to be unintentionally cut off by Scarlette.

"Brenna, you must come with me. Aunt Adelaide wants to see both of us. She said something about her and Bertram wanting to present us with something." Scarlette hadn't seen Rylan at all and pulled Brenna away in her haste and excitement. Brenna glanced back at Rylan and saw his forlorn expression.

Rylan was now at a loss. He watched her go and decided the best thing to do was to leave. His parents were most likely wondering what was keeping him. He would have to wait for another time. He reluctantly left the ballroom.

"I'm so excited! Aunt was very mysterious about it. What do you think it could be?" Scarlette hurriedly went on but Brenna was hardly listening. All she could do was watch Lord Quenell leave. She couldn't help but feel badly about how rude she must have looked to him. While she was relieved to be spared from his questions for the time being, Brenna also didn't want to see him go. Would she ever understand exactly what her feelings were toward Rylan?

To be continued...

"Again, a new commandment I write unto you, which thing is true in him and in you: because the darkness is past, and the true light now shineth."

1 John 2:8

Kelly Aul lives in a small, rural town in Minnesota with her parents and two younger siblings. They were homeschooled which made their family very close. Growing up, Kelly had a very vivid imagination. She was always pretending, making up games with her siblings, and finding adventure around her home on a small lake. Kelly is enthralled with European history, especially the 19th century, writing, and most importantly the things of God. She is in full time ministry, along with her family, studying to be a pastor. She also works part time as a pharmacy technician.

Some people might be thinking, "Why do you have to mention God throughout this whole book? Dedication and everything?"

"Whatsoever ye do in word or deed, do all in the name of the Lord Jesus." (Colossians 3:17)

I can't stop talking about Him because He *is* my everything. And because He's my everything, God is in everything I do.

I've read some Christian novels, and it seems almost as if they try to go as close to the edge as they can and still call it a Christian book, but the question shouldn't be how close can I get before crossing the line. It should be, how close can I get to God? How much can I talk about Him? How can I give more glory to Him?

I don't ever want my readers to have to ask themselves, "Should I be reading this? Would God read this book? Could I read this book in front of my pastor or parents without guilt?"

Thank you for reading. I hope you enjoyed yourself and were inspired. And I have to say again, I give God all the glory for every part of this book. Without Him, I can do nothing.

— God bless, Kelly

Jesus said, except a man be born again, he cannot see the kingdom of God. (John 3:3) Being born again or the New Birth is not: confirmation, church membership, water baptism, being moral, doing good deeds.

Ephesians 2:8-9 "For by grace are ye saved through faith; and that not of yourselves: it is the gift of God: not of works, lest any man should boast."

You have to simply admit you are just what the Bible says — a lost sinner. Then you come and accept what Christ has purchased for you — a gift! (Romans 10:9-10)

Please pray this prayer to receive Jesus as your Savior.

Dear Heavenly Father, I believe in my heart that Jesus Christ is the son of God, that He was crucified, died, and rose from the dead.

I ask you, Lord Jesus, to be Lord of my life. Thank you for saving me and coming into my heart, for forgiving me and redeeming me from all sin.

It's important to find a church where they teach the Word of God by studying right from the Bible, and to renew your mind by reading the Bible every day.

— Maggie Aul, Senior Pastor
Love of God Family Church
www.LoveofGodFamilyChurch.com

MY STORY IN THE MIDST OF DARKNESS

I prayed the salvation prayer and made Jesus the Lord of my life when I was very young. I didn't realize how much my life really depended on Him until I was thirteen. My parents had gone on a trip for a week and we, my younger brother, sister, and I stayed with some family friends. They were really nice but they watched the news from sun up to sun down. I wasn't used it because we didn't watch those things at home. I don't know exactly what happened, but I started to think on those things too much. Before I knew it, the darkness made its way into my heart. I started to feel scared all the time. I pictured bad things happening to us. I thought it would go away when we went home, but it didn't. I didn't even know what it was until years later. Because of that, I pretty much kept it to myself.

Months went by and it got worse. Sure, I was happy and had fun at times, but a dark cloud hung over me all the time.

The best way I could describe it to my parents, when they started to notice, was that I was worried. Thank God for my parents! They brought me to the Word of God. They had me read from the following verses everyday.

Philippians 4:6-8

[6] Be careful for nothing; but in every thing by prayer and supplication with thanksgiving let your requests be made known unto God.

[7] And the peace of God, which passeth all understanding, shall keep your hearts and minds through Christ Jesus.

[8] Finally, brethren, whatsoever things are true, whatsoever things are honest, whatsoever things are just, whatsoever things are pure, whatsoever things are lovely, whatsoever things are of good report; if there be any virtue, and if there be any praise, think on these things.

Psalm 91

91 He that dwelleth in the secret place of the most High shall abide under the shadow of the Almighty.

[2] I will say of the LORD, He is my refuge and my fortress: my God; in him will I trust.

[3] Surely he shall deliver thee from the snare of the fowler, and from the noisome pestilence.

[4] He shall cover thee with his feathers, and under his wings shalt thou trust: his truth shall be thy shield and buckler.

[5] Thou shalt not be afraid for the terror by night; nor for the arrow that flieth by day;

[6] Nor for the pestilence that walketh in darkness; nor for the destruction that wasteth at noonday.

[7] A thousand shall fall at thy side, and ten thousand at thy right hand; but it shall not come nigh thee.

[8] Only with thine eyes shalt thou behold and see the reward of the wicked.

[9] Because thou hast made the LORD, which is my refuge, even the most High, thy habitation;

[10] There shall no evil befall thee, neither shall any plague come nigh thy dwelling.

[11] For he shall give his angels charge over thee, to keep thee in all thy ways.

[12] They shall bear thee up in their hands, lest thou dash thy foot against a stone.

[13] Thou shalt tread upon the lion and adder: the young lion and the dragon shalt thou trample under feet.

[14] Because he hath set his love upon me, therefore will I deliver him: I will set him on high, because he hath known my name.

[15] He shall call upon me, and I will answer him: I will be with him in trouble; I will deliver him, and honour him.

[16] With long life will I satisfy him, and shew him my salvation.

Matthew 6:25-34

[25] Therefore I say unto you, Take no thought for your life, what ye shall eat, or what ye shall drink; nor yet for your body, what ye shall put on. Is not the life more than meat, and the body than raiment?

[26] Behold the fowls of the air: for they sow not, neither do they reap, nor gather into barns; yet your heavenly Father feedeth them. Are ye not much better than they?

[27] Which of you by taking thought can add one cubit unto his stature?

[28] And why take ye thought for raiment? Consider the lilies of the field, how they grow; they toil not, neither do they spin:

[29] And yet I say unto you, That even Solomon in all his glory was not arrayed like one of these.

30 Wherefore, if God so clothe the grass of the field, which to day is, and to morrow is cast into the oven, shall he not much more clothe you, O ye of little faith?

31 Therefore take no thought, saying, What shall we eat? or, What shall we drink? or, Wherewithal shall we be clothed?

32 (For after all these things do the Gentiles seek:) for your heavenly Father knoweth that ye have need of all these things.

33 But seek ye first the kingdom of God, and his righteousness; and all these things shall be added unto you.

34 Take therefore no thought for the morrow: for the morrow shall take thought for the things of itself. Sufficient unto the day is the evil thereof.

While it helped, the anxiety was still there. Then 9/11 happened. It didn't help things at all.

During those two years, as my family and I continued to go to every prayer meeting and church event, I kept getting closer to God and His Word.

It was then I went to a Christian teen night with friends and family. The minister invited people to the front for prayer. To be honest, I don't remember what he said. All I know is, God touched me that night and even though I didn't feel a bit different where my feelings were concerned, that night changed my life.

The minute I woke up the next morning, I noticed a change in me. The dark cloud was gone. The knot in my stomach was gone. All I could do was thank God for setting me free! I will never forget what it was like waking up that day. I've never had to deal with that darkness again.

Now I didn't say that fear and worry hasn't tried to come back to me. But this time I knew what to do.

God is no respector of persons. He's not going to do something for me that He won't do for you too. All I did was what the Bible told me to do.

"But seek ye first the kingdom of God, and his righteousness; and all these things shall be added unto you." Matthew 6:33

"And ye shall seek me, and find me, when ye shall search for me with all your heart." Jeremiah 29:13

He wants to set you free! He loves you and that's why Jesus came and died on the cross. It was so you could be free.

Spoiler Alert!

The Author recommends readers not to read beyond this point
until they finish reading this book, In the Midst of Darkness.
There's nothing worse than ruining the mystery in the pages!

❖ Pronunciation of Eibhleann ~ Avelynn

* From Audrey's Sunrise (Never Forsaken Book #1)

1772		*John McNiel born
1800		Colm Brodie born
1804		*John McNiel marries Lenora
1805		*John and Lenora McNiel have son, Dennon
1806		Kylene Brodie born
		Reid Lennox (Marques of Kerrich) marries Eibhleann O'Breen
1808		*Lenora McNiel goes to America with Dennon
		*John McNiel goes after his wife and son once he saved enough money
		*Dennon McNiel dies
1814		*John McNiel gets a job with Princeton Shipping Company and eventually becomes Captain
1818		Colm and Kylene Brodie's parents die. They Move to America
		*Captain McNiel finds Pete (Lenora's Brother) and almost kills him - instead, Pete shoots McNiel in the leg
1820		*Joseph Brounry born
	April	William Dorcet meets Kylene Brodie
	August	*Captain McNiel throws Evan and Rose Fintan off of his ship, The St. Carlin
1821		Reid and Eibhleann Lennox have son, Rylan
		*Audrey Wesley born
	August	Frederick Dorcet finds out about his son's, William's secret relations and breaks them apart.
	October	William marries Harriet Edith
1823		William and Harriet have a son, Theodore Dorcet
1826		William and Harriet have a son, Edwin Dorcet

Year	Month	Event
	May	Frederich Dorcet has heart attack
	July	Harriet Dorcet dies
1827	May	Frederick Dorcet dies
		Colm Brodie is offered job in Ireland after his uncle died. Colm and Kylene plan to return to Ireland
1828	August	William finds and marries Kylene Brodie - Colm goes to Ireland alone
1828		William and Kylene have a daughter, Brenna Rose
1834		Colm Brodie marries Laura
	August	*Joseph get job on The St. Carlin
	November	William and Kylene have a son, Benjamin Dorcet
1839		*After searching for the shell for eighteen years, Captain McNiel kidnapps Audrey Wesley
		*Joseph Briouny meets Audrey Wesley
	July	*Captain McNiel dies in storm
	August	Brenna gets to London, England
	September	*Audrey comes home
		Lanna Ryan goes to Cheverell's for The London Season
	December	Lanna meets Stephen Kinsey
1840	March	Stephen Kinsey marries Lanna Ryan
	July	Joseph Briouny marries Audrey Wesley
1841	June	Joseph and Audrey have a son, Evan Briouny
	October	Stephen and Lanna have a son, Tully Kinsey
1842		Stephen and Lanna take in Brenna Dorcet
		Stephen and Lanna have a daughter, Audrey Kinsey

 Please visit the Official Author Website

www.kellyaul.com

 Like on Facebook

facebook.com/NeverForsakenBookSeries